A GARLAND OF EMERALDS

Laverne Boulogne Van Ryk

Copyright © 2012 by Laverne Boulogne Van Ryk

A Garland of Emeralds
The struggle for possession of a green string of islands flung across the equator
by Laverne Boulogne Van Ryk

Printed in the United States of America

ISBN 9781622304912

All rights reserved solely by the author. The author guarantees all contents are original and do not infringe upon the legal rights of any other person or work. No part of this book may be reproduced in any form without the permission of the author. The views expressed in this book are not necessarily those of the publisher.

Unless otherwise indicated, Bible quotations are taken from New King James. Copyright © 1982 by Thomas Nelson, Inc.

www.xulonpress.com

Acknowledgments

I want to thank my sisters, Dina Boulogne and Ada Boulogne Roeper, and my brother Jack Boulogne for sharing their memories to add to mine and where mine had faded, and also for always encouraging me!

And of course a big thank you to my sons and daughters who showed consistent interest in my writing, offered editorial suggestions and encouraged me to keep going when I almost gave up on several occasions, telling me not to abandon my ideals.

Most of all, I want to thank God for giving me strength and creative ability, for blessing my work and for making me feel that He cares!

In Memory of my beloved parents
Bastiaan Boulogne
and
Alida Boulogne-'tHart
who always encouraged me

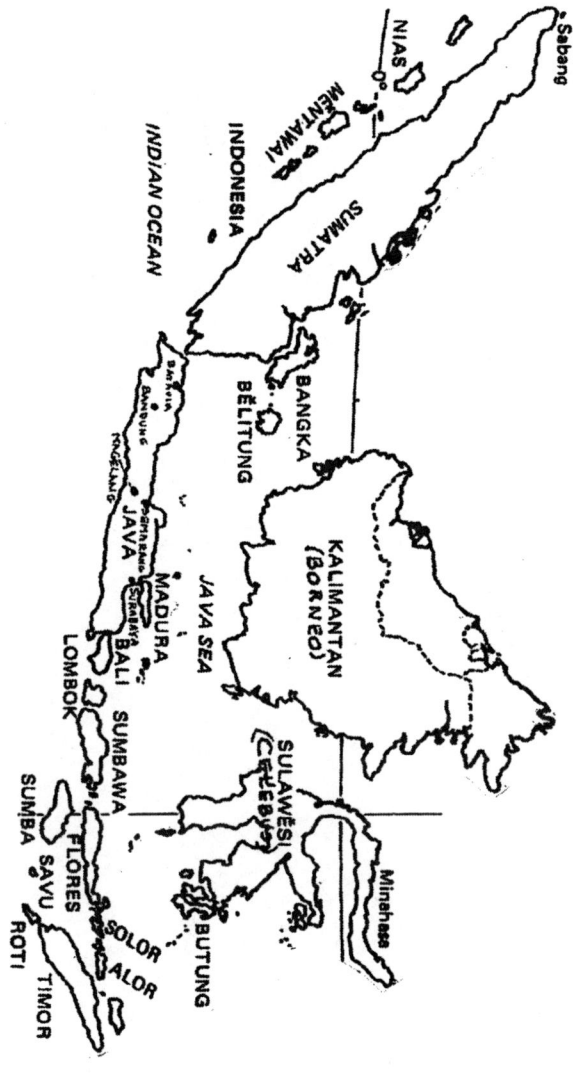

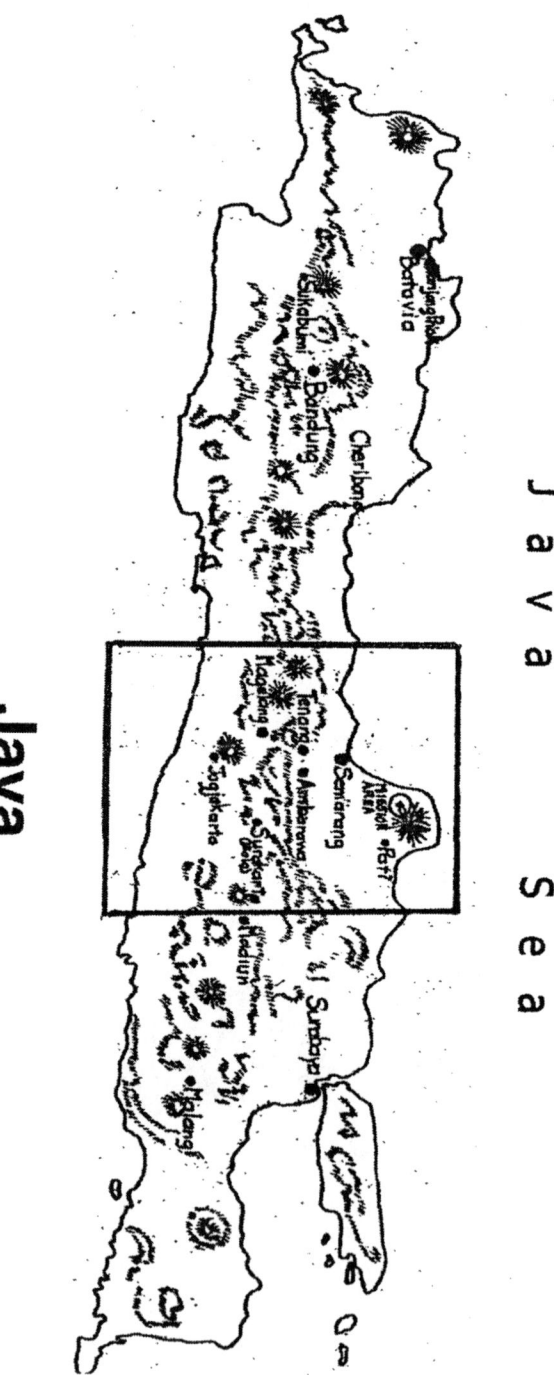

Inset

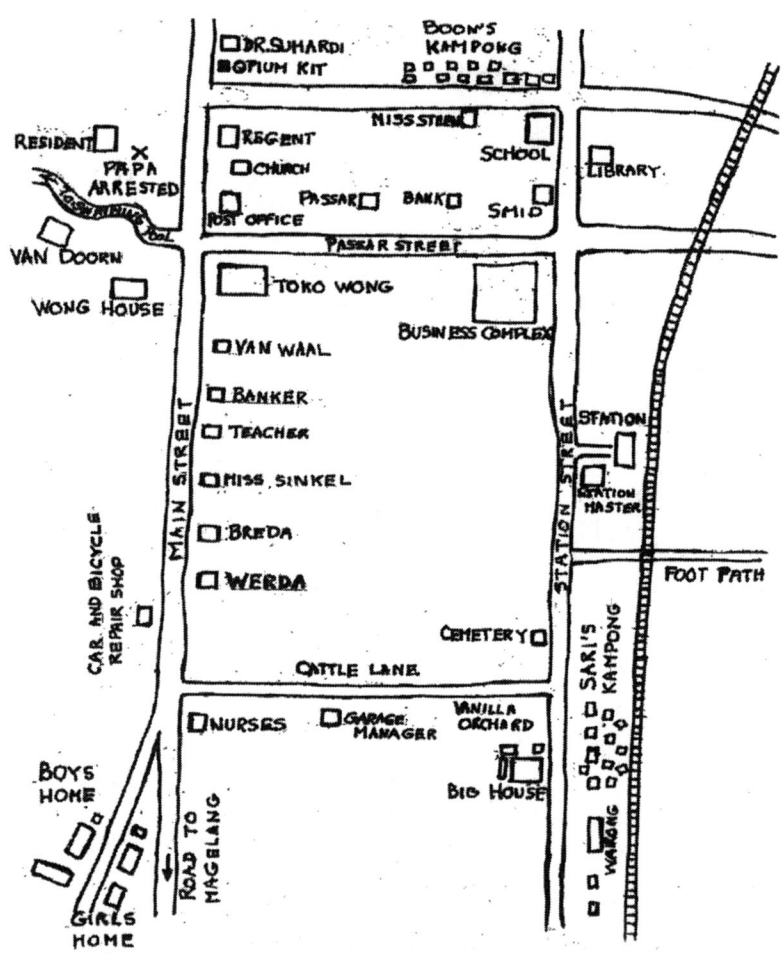

Tenang

Chapter One

Sari

October, 1941

The sun was low in the sky by the time Jasmine Carter hurried down the muddy path through a tunnel of branches. It had stopped raining, but a gust of wind shook drops from the leaves. The huddled houses of the *kampong* loomed just ahead in the fading light. She was on her way to visit Sari, her native friend.

Jasmine and Sari lived in the town of Tenang, located in the central province of Java, the most densely populated island of the Dutch East Indies. *Kampongs* were small groups of bamboo houses, owned by natives, usually on the outskirts of towns like Tenang.

It was the end of October, 1941. In two months it would be Christmas, which was of course the time Christians celebrated the birth of Jesus. But the main religion on Java was

Muslim, and a few weeks ago it had been *Lebaran*. Papa had explained that *Lebaran* was one of the greatest feast days of the Muslims. It came at the end of *Ramadan*, the Muslim month of fasting. Although Sari and her family were Christians, they had celebrated *Lebaran*. Sari said her parents did not want to offend their relatives.

At school Sari had insisted Jasmine should come to her place. "I want you to see my baby brother." They always spoke Dutch because Jasmine didn't know enough Malay, and Sari had learned to speak Dutch in school.

At teatime Jasmine had not mentioned Sari. She knew Mama did not like her to be friends with native children. Jasmine could not figure out why her mother minded so much. The native servants were always friendly. She was glad Papa didn't mind.

After she had finished her tea, Jasmine had announced, "I'm going for a walk."

Mama had nodded absentmindedly. "All right but don't be late for supper."

As she walked down the gravel road, Jasmine felt guilty about deceiving her mother, but she continued stubbornly towards the *kampong*.

Sari and Jasmine had become friends only since they started eighth grade, although they had attended the same school for years. Only the smartest native children went to Dutch schools and Sari was smart. The Dutch eighth graders were normally sent to school in Holland, but the Germans had invaded it in May 1940, so it was impossible to go there.

That's why Mr. Breda, the principal, taught grade eight as well as grade seven.

It was not hard to find Sari's house, because it was bigger than the other houses since Sari's father was the *kepala*, head of the *kampong*. The house had whitewashed walls and front steps which led to a wide front porch. When Jasmine arrived, she did not go in right away. She felt uneasy because it was the first time she had ever visited Sari.

The houses stood helter-skelter, not in a straight line like Tenang streets. Jasmine had been inside one of them once, with *Babu*, their maid. It had been dark with only two tiny windows in the main room. Two braziers for cooking made it sooty and smelly.

While Jasmine lingered, an old native woman started to sweep the dirt square in front of the house with a worn-out corn broom. She looked at Jasmine and asked in Malay, "Are you looking for Sari?"

Jasmine knew enough Malay to understand and nodded.

"She's in the house" the woman said and continued sweeping.

Jasmine nodded again and went in. Sari was sitting on a chair at a bare wooden table, her mouth full of banana. She grinned at Jasmine and motioned to a chair. An old man, probably Sari's grandfather, slept on a *baleh-baleh*, a wide bamboo cot against one wall. A baby began to cry in the next room.

Jasmine sat down.

"Are you allowed out this late?" Sari asked, shoving the rest of her banana into her mouth.

Jasmine nodded, unwilling to voice a lie. She looked around the room, wondering where Sari's brothers and sisters were.

After Sari had swallowed her banana, she said, "I'm glad your mother lets you come. Now you can see my baby brother."

A moment later Sari's mother came in, carrying a tiny brown baby with dark brown eyes. She greeted Jasmine with a smile. Sari coo-ed at her brother, and he responded with a toothless smile. After Sari's mother had shown Jasmine the baby, she took some soft cooked rice from a bowl and pushed it into the tiny mouth with her thumb.

Jasmine was watching this curiously, starting when Sari poked an elbow in her back. "Let's go outside. I'll show you something."

They went out into the dim light under the trees. Sari pulled Jasmine behind a bush, and put her finger to her lips.

"What's going on?" Jasmine whispered.

"I don't want anyone to see us, and if my father finds out where we're going, he'll be angry." Sari added, "My uncle and cousin came today, and they would be annoyed with me too."

Jasmine wanted to leave, but Sari pulled her behind another bush. They crept from bush to bush, until they finally settled behind a dense thicket. Jasmine heard men's voices not far away. As she peered through the branches, she saw a circle of men squatting around a fire. The fire made her realize how dark it had become, and she was scared. The moon shone on the banana leaves, and made a bright streak in Sari's black hair.

They were close enough to see the men's faces, but too far to hear any words. Fire light flickered over the brown faces with lips that barely moved.

Sari whispered, "Do you know who those men are?"

Jasmine was just going to answer "no", when, with a startled shock, she recognized one of the faces in the circle. A young man had just squatted down, and she remembered him from their last visit to the Mission where they used to live. He had brought the mail and she was sure then that he hated her, for he had looked at her so angrily. Aunt Beatrice, who had replaced Papa as leader of the Mission, said she suspected the man of being a nationalist, a rebel against the Dutch government. Aunt Beatrice was not really her aunt. Many close family friends were called Aunt or Uncle.

When the young man looked in her direction, Jasmine hid behind Sari, although it was already much too dark for them to be seen. She nudged Sari, and whispered, "That man there who just came, he. . .he hates me."

"Which man?"

"The one beside the old man with the sarong. I saw him at the Mission."

"Hates you? Why?"

"I just feel it." Jasmine shivered and crouched behind Sari.

"That's Sukandar," Sari said.

"You know him?"

"Yes." Sari laughed with her hand against her mouth.

"Shhhh! They'll hear us! And it's not funny. He might be dangerous."

A few more repressed giggles, then Sari whispered, "He's my cousin, Sukandar. He doesn't hate anyone."

"Why is he with them?"

"It's for the *Merdeka* cause, and it's secret. No one is supposed to talk about it."

"*Merdeka?*"

"That means freedom." Sari looked at Jasmine anxiously. "You won't tell anybody, will you?"

"Why not?"

"If the Dutch government finds out about the meetings they will exile all those men."

They were silent for a few minutes, and then Sari pulled Jasmine to the next bush from where they could hear the mumbling voices.

Jasmine did not really care about what the Dutch government would do, but she still felt suspicious about Sukandar, in spite of Sari's matter-of-fact way.

Sari boasted, "I have lots of cousins."

"So do I," Jasmine said, "in Holland."

"Bah! That's far away."

"So?"

Sari went on boasting about her many cousins. "Then there's Talitha. Her husband Alimin and Sukandar are good friends." Sari looked at Jasmine who remained silent.

Sari had not finished listing more of her relatives. "Lea is my cousin too. She's Sukandar's sister. She works at the Mission."

"I know Lea. We used to live at the Mission. I liked her, but him . . ."

Vivid memories came to her of the last time they had visited the Mission close to the North coast of Central Java, where she had been born. Papa and Mama had left Holland to come to Java. Papa was a missionary, and he had loved his work at the Mission. But Mama, who had really wanted to help Papa in his work, could not stand the heat and humidity of the coastal regions. Also, she was afraid of the natives at that time, although now that they lived in Tenang she had learned to get along with the native servants.

When they had visited the Mission last, the monsoon had just broken and Jasmine remembered splashing rain, crackling thunder and screaming wind. The whole jungle had groaned, sounding like evil spirits. Then Jasmine had understood a little about Mama's fears.

Sari broke the silence. "Lea's a Christian, and Sukandar doesn't like it."

"There's nothing wrong with Christians!"

"I know but Sukandar's family believes in Allah and the Prophet Mohammed and they don't like the Dutch, so they don't like the religion of the whites."

"You talk as if only the whites can be Christians."

"No, I told you Lea is a Christian, and so are we, and we're not white."

"My father wants everyone to become Christian."

"And believe in a different Prophet." Sari nodded wisely.

"Prophet?"

"Don't act so dumb!" Sari punched her. "You know, *Tuan Yesoes.*"

"I know! I'm not stupid." Jasmine scowled. Then, after a short silence, "What's the difference?"

"Who knows. Ask your Papa. He was a missionary."

"I will," Jasmine said, staring into the flames, trying to forget about the murmuring voices.

Sari nudged Jasmine's elbow. "You know what those men are saying?"

"What?"

"They want to be free from the Colonial rule. At these meetings they always talk about how to chase out all white people."

"Chase us out?"

"Yes. They want *Merdeka*, freedom from the *blandas*."

"Why would they want freedom from the white people?"

"Because they want to be their own boss."

"They don't like us?" That was new to Jasmine. The native *babus*, the maids, as well as their *djongos*, house boy, were always friendly. There had never been a native who had been mean, except Sukandar, and he had not really done anything. He just looked mean.

But then she remembered what Jeannie Werda, a girl in her class, had once told her. She had an uncle who was administrator on a plantation, way over in East Java. He had been very mean to the native workers, beating them for every little thing they did wrong. So they had poisoned him.

Jasmine shivered as she looked at the men. She did not really know that many natives, and maybe there were many more mean ones than nice ones. She tried to examine the faces in more detail, which was not easy in the firelight. She and Sari had moved a little closer, and she studied Sukandar's face, trying to see his expression. But even if there had been more light, he kept his eyes downcast most of the time. He didn't say much, only answered when someone asked him a question.

She turned to Sari and asked, "Do you want us to leave?"

Sari made a short motion with her hand. "No, I don't want the *blandas* to go. You're my friend." She waved the idea off as totally unimportant.

Jasmine wanted to believe Sari. "I'll stay here all my life," Jasmine said, more to encourage herself than to inform Sari. "And my father likes it here too."

"Why do you like it here so much?" Sari peered at her in the darkness.

"I was born here. It's my country. I love everything, Java, Tenang." Jasmine suddenly found how hard it was to explain her feelings, especially to Sari, who was born here too, but whose parents and grandparents had been here forever. Sari really belonged.

Sari nodded. "Good."

Jasmine was just thinking how happy she was to have Sari as a friend, when she saw Marto hovering in the doorway of the next house. Marto was another native girl in her class, but neither Sari not Jasmine liked her. Last year Sari and Jasmine had had a spat with Marto, which had made Jasmine feel much closer to Sari. Marto stood close to a woman. Her mother?

Jasmine nudged Sari. "What's Marto doing here?"

Sari whispered, "Marto's family is involved in *Merdeka*."

"So that's why she's so mean." Jasmine shrugged off her uneasy feelings, and turned her attention back to the circle of men. "What are they saying now?" she asked.

Sari whispered her reply so softly that Jasmine barely heard her. "They say they want to see all white people killed."

Jasmine suddenly felt ice cold. Her legs were strangely heavy; a rushing sound in her ears was like a far waterfall. She shivered in her thin dress. Had the air become so much cooler? She had not often been outside this late.

"I'm going home," she whispered. They crept away from the fire. Before they reached the path, they stopped. Jasmine turned to Sari and asked, "How come Sukandar is here, when he works in the Mission area?"

"He sometimes reports in sick and comes with Uncle Aminoto to Tenang to attend *Merdeka* meetings."

"How did they get involved in all this?"

"Uncle Aminoto was inspired by Sukarno's speeches at a political rally some years back. The Government stopped these rallies, and considered Sukarno the most dangerous of the leaders. Open meetings were forbidden. Aminoto told Sukandar about all that. Also, my Aunt Itjam, Sukandar's mother, told him that he would be a leader of our people, because he had been born at the crack of dawn. That means he's a Child of the Dawn."

"That's dumb," Jasmine said, even while her fear grew. "He should be smart enough not to believe that nonsense."

"He *is* smart, or else he wouldn't have gone to a Dutch school. His mother told him that in order to beat the enemy you have to learn all about him. And she also taught him to respect all who were older. So Sukandar is doing what they said he should."

"But he knows all the leaders are in exile." Jasmine had heard a little bit about the nationalist movement, but had never paid much attention to it. Now she realized it might become a horrid reality. She looked at Sari, who looked worried now too. Sari must really care about her uncle and cousin.

"A native man is not too young to support the *Merdeka* cause," Sari finally said as if to defend her cousin.

Jasmine said, "I hope he doesn't get in trouble over this. You should tell him to stop it."

Sari smiled sadly. "He wouldn't listen. He's very stubborn."

"But why does he hate the Dutch?"

"Actually he started hating white children in the school, because they teased him, and called him names. He could have gone to secondary school, because the principal had said he learned well, but Sukandar didn't want to. He knew enough, he said. He could speak, read and write the Dutch language, learned history and geography, and of course arithmetic, and a few other things like Bible stories."

"What did he do then?"

"He started his job as a mail carrier around where the Mission is. It is of course a Government job. He wanted to help his family, since his father's fields did not yield enough for the family to live.

"How does he feel about his sister being a Christian?"

"He doesn't like it, and if he resents the Mission lady, it's because she has talked to him about becoming a Christian. According to her the Muslim religion is wrong."

"Papa was a missionary too, but Aunt Beatrice is pushier about getting natives converted. She really thinks it's evil to believe in Allah and Mohammed, and also in spirits who live in trees. Sukandar doesn't believe that, does he?"

"I'm not sure. He's been very close-mouthed the last few years."

Jasmine laughed softly. "I think I'm beginning to understand how he feels."

"Why?"

"I don't like Aunt Beatrice much either! She's so serious about her work that she forgets that people have feelings. At least she never had much patience with me or my brother and sisters. My Papa likes her, but my Mama doesn't, because Aunt Beatrice thinks it's Mama's fault that Papa left the Mission."

"Why did they leave?"

"Mama had some sort of a breakdown after I was born, and the doctor told her she should live in the highlands, if they planned to stay on Java. So they moved here when Papa found a job as director of the Boys Home."

Talking about the Home reminded Jasmine that it was late and she said, "I really must go."

"Will you be back tomorrow?" Sari asked.

"I'm not really allowed."

"Why not? You came today."

Jasmine did not explain how come she was here now. She just said, "My mother doesn't like it."

"Why?"

Jasmine shrugged. She felt sure Sari would not like her answer. How could she tell her best friend that her mother hated the natives? Well, maybe she didn't hate them, but she wanted to have as little as possible to do with the ones outside her home. "Maybe I'll come after dinner, when the others are taking a nap." She paused then said, "You're my friend, after all."

"Good!" Sari said.

When they reached the path Jasmine waved good-bye to Sari and hurried into the silent evening.

Her mind twirled with wild thoughts. Sukandar, who believed he was a Child of the Dawn, was perhaps going to be a leader. What did that mean? Dawn of freedom? Someone come to deliver the natives from Dutch rule?

Fear trembled inside her. The trees stood somber and threatening in the eerie moonlight, drawing sharp leaf shadows on the ground. At the side of the path a *gladakker*, a *kampong* mongrel, caked with mud, dug in a pile of garbage. Jasmine thought about Mopsy, her Maltese dog, so much nicer with his long white hair. Well . . . not always white. Mopsy liked mud, but compared to this ugly *gladakker!* They had a cat too, called *Mata Hidju*, Green Eyes, and Ellen loved her the most. *Mata Hidju* had kittens.

A child cried, and Jasmine wished she had gone back home sooner. She walked faster as if Marto were at her heels. It was bad enough to find out that Sukandar was in the *Merdeka* group. But Marto! A girl she saw at school every day!

As soon as she left the tunnel of trees and the dirt road, the night seemed friendlier. She walked along the gravel road towards her house which was the front section of the Boys Home. Thinking of Mama, Jasmine knew for sure that she should have gone home sooner. Mama would be angry, because she was so late.

Yet, she knew there was something else troubling Mama. Perhaps it had to do with the bad time Mama had at the Mission, when she had just come from Holland.

When Jasmine arrived the family were at the dinner table, but Mama only said, "You're late, Jasmine."

Jasmine nodded, and Mama did not say more. She seemed preoccupied.

That night in bed Jasmine could not stop thinking about Sukandar, and the men around the fire. Did they mean what they said? Strange that Sukandar was Sari's cousin. If

Sukandar knew she was Sari's friend, would he still want to chase her out? Perhaps none of them cared whose friend she was. She would talk to Papa about it. Somehow they could find a way to stay on Java.

She dreamed about a circle of men in the dark, with fire light flickering over brown faces. Above them was a wide-open gate, through which golden light streamed. But the golden light suddenly changed to a fire with dark faces floating over it.

Chapter Two

Papa

October, 1941

The dining room clock struck twice, its tones trembling in the dusky light of the bedroom, where Jasmine stirred on her bed. The afternoon stood stiff with heat outside the closed shutters, and sharp slits of sunlight were drawn on the tiles of the floor.

She turned around all the way, moving the *guling* between her knees. It was a round pillow, like a big sausage, that kept her knees from sweating together.

Mama insisted that the children take a nap, and one of her strict rules was not to get out of bed till four. But usually Jasmine was too restless to sleep.

Last night before Jasmine left her, Sari had asked, "Did you ever watch a bush burning?"

"Like Moses' burning bush?"

Sari smiled. "Well, these bushes will really burn up. They're going to put fire to the bush, so they can start new gardens, and *sawahs*."

"Sounds dangerous," Jasmine had said, but she had promised to come.

When she was sure the others were asleep, she crawled out from under the *klambu*, the mosquito net, got off the bed, and tiptoed to the door.

She met Sari at the gravel road, because Jasmine did not want to go into the *kampong* anymore. She was afraid of seeing Sukandar again.

The girls started walking towards the field. When they had reached the edge, there were some men standing close to a hole in the ground. One of them put dry moss and twigs in the hole, and started a fire.

The first small flames flickered, and nearly died. Then a breeze revived them, and the fire grew as if it knew no bounds. Soon there was a mass of roaring flames.

It was scary, but Jasmine was as fascinated as Sari seemed to be. They watched for about ten minutes and then turned to go back.

As they walked up a small hill around a stand of trees, a cloud of smoke still hung over the area, its sharp smell invading their senses.

Sari stopped suddenly. She put her finger to her lips and pointed.

Marto! She stood with one foot in the brook as if she was just going to cross it. She stuck one hand inside her pocket.

"What's she doing?" Jasmine whispered, baffled.

"Who knows. She always does strange things."

The girls came closer and watched Marto sit down on a sandy spot, strewn with pebbles with her back to them. She pulled a small flag out of her pocket. Red, white and blue! A Dutch flag! What was she doing with that? She had probably kept it from a royal celebration. Teachers always handed out flags on those occasions.

Marto fingered the blue stripe, and pulled out a pair of scissors from her pocket, and held it between the white and the blue. She started cutting. Slowly the blue separated from the white, until it was just a rumpled rag on the ground. Marto stepped on it and twisted it into the sand. Then she produced some twine from her pocket and bound the leftover flag onto a sturdy stick, which she pushed into the ground.

Sari whispered, "The red-white, *merah-putih*, the flag of the *Merdeka* people."

Jasmine felt cold in the pressing heat, and wished they had not stopped.

Marto stepped back and examined the flag. Then she turned and saw the girls.

It seemed to startle her, but when Sari asked. "What do you think you're doing?" she answered, "None of your business. Why don't you go home!"

"I'd like to know what you're up to," Sari said. "Don't you know you're not allowed to fly the *merah-putih* flag?"

Marto looked at them with such disdain that Jasmine felt like hiding. "There's no one here to see." Then she added in a threatening way, "Just you."

Marto turned to Jasmine "We want to get rid of the blue, the blue Dutch." Without another word she walked away, and disappeared behind a stand of bamboo trees.

Jasmine looked at Sari who watched Marto go with disgust written on her face. As for Jasmine, watching Marto plant a *merah-putih* flag, created the first twinges of real fear. She looked at the red and white flag hanging limply around the rough stick. At least there was no wind to make the colors fly. This made Jasmine feel better as they hurried back to her yard where Sari left her.

She was so preoccupied that she did not notice the heat as she picked at the bark of a poplar beside the gravel road in front of their house. It was quiet and she was alone, because everyone was still sleeping.

She looked up at fledglings chirping in a bird nest. A blond curl clung to her forehead and she pushed it back absentmindedly, her blue eyes narrowed with frustration and worry. She had wanted to talk to Papa about what she had heard in Sari's *kampong* and Marto's flag, but she was afraid he would stop her from seeing Sari after school.

Also, she could not get out of her mind what Sari had said about Marto. Was Marto really serious about this *Merdeka* business, or was she only showing off, as usual? But why would her mother be there? Papa would not be able to do much about Marto, except perhaps talk to Principal Breda.

Jasmine shrugged impatiently. What could Marto do anyway? And besides, she had enough on her mind, like the news that they were going to move.

She looked at the house at the end of the driveway. It was the front part of what they called the Boys Home. Papa was director of this Home for mentally retarded boys, ages three to seventeen. Papa took care of the running of the Home and also taught the boys as much as they could learn. Mama looked after the household, with the help of servants.

But lately even this job had become too much for Mama. She could not relax and Doctor Suhardi had said the responsibilities for the care of the boys might cause a breakdown. Papa would still be director of the Boys Home, but someone else would take care of supervising the house work. Whoever it was would need to live in the house. That's why they were moving.

Jasmine swallowed away a lump. They had lived here for as long as she could remember, and she loved this house. Countless memories were bound up with it. Moving seemed to be the first step to the time they might have to leave Java. The idea of moving bothered her, until she had found out that the new house was right across from Sari's *kampong.*

Mopsy came up to her. She stroked his head, and he peered at her through long hair falling over his eyes. They had gotten Mopsy two years ago, after Mama had finally given in to Jasmine's pleading. The Breda's dog had a litter and they wanted to get rid of some. Jasmine smiled as she thought about her decision that the puppy would belong to her alone. When they had gotten home with the pup Mama said, "he belongs to all of you," but Jasmine had ignored this and taken over immediately by giving Mopsy his first meal. Then she had played with him until bedtime.

She had allowed the others no chance to do any of these things, so there had been quarrels with Ellen and Yvonne, her sisters. Danny, her brother, had not cared one way or the other. To him cats and dogs were things you could hold by the tail and sling around you in a circle.

Ellen and Yvonne had given up, and Mama laid down some conditions for Jasmine. "If you want to keep this dog, make sure you look after him."

Jasmine had agreed. Although her initial ardor had dimmed somewhat, she did not abandon her right of ownership. Mopsy belonged to her. Now she sat down beside him, and whispered into his floppy ear, "No one can take you away from me."

Mopsy licked her hand, and then followed her as she walked away from the tree, along the jasmine hedge. Between the hedge and the house, lawns and flowerbeds glimmered sleepily in the afternoon. The grass felt soft under her feet. A wide, concrete path led from the road to the house and at the far end of the yard *Kebon*, their gardener, pottered among the flowerbeds. He was probably looking for the best flowers to cut for Mama. Mama loved fresh flowers in the house. It made her feel like being back in Holland.

Bah! Holland! How could Mama long for Holland while it was so beautiful here on Java and in Tenang? So many different trees and bushes lined the avenues and streets, elms, eucalyptus trees, and hibiscus or bougainvillea bushes. And there were millions of flowers. Of course there were flowers in Holland too, but not all year round. Here it was sunny most of the time. She wrinkled her nose, as always when she thought of the strange aunts, uncles and cousins who lived in Holland. But Mama was bewitched by Holland, and forever showed snapshots and taught the names of all the relatives like a school lesson.

Jasmine went over to *Kebon* and pointed to the yellow gerberas. "*Bagoes*," she said. Beautiful.

Kebon smiled and nodded, then picked one of them and gave it to her, and pointed at her hair. "*Mas. Bagoes.*" Gold. Beautiful.

Jasmine grimaced as her hand went to her mop of blond curls. But she accepted the flower, and said, "*Trima kassi*," thank you, and walked towards the house.

When she entered the dining room she was surprised to see Mama awake and packing some boxes. She looked hot and irritated. Rubbing her forehead, she said, "You'd better start packing your own things. You know we'll be moving soon. There are boxes in your room."

Jasmine lingered. The last thing she felt like doing was packing. She looked at the familiar dining room, the chairs stiffly arranged around a large oak table, the buffet against the back wall. And above it hung a large poster of Queen Wilhelmina of Holland. Mama was a true royalist, and Jasmine liked the royal family too.

When Mama looked at her, Jasmine scowled and went to the room she shared with Ellen and Yvonne. She had just begun to pack when Danny came in.

"What are you doing, curly-top?" he asked.

"Packing," Jasmine said, directing a scowl at him.

"Working hard for a change?" he jeered.

She clenched her teeth and hissed, "Get out of here. I don't need you."

He grinned, standing in the doorway, as she stuffed one of her Sunday dresses into a box.

"Aren't you going to play with me?" he said in the same tone of voice. He came closer and peeked into the box, as she grabbed her pajamas and pushed them beside the dress.

"Looks like you enjoy doing this," he remarked.

"I'm glad we're moving," she said.

"I thought you hated it."

"I did but I found out the new house is closer to Sari." She stuffed a handful of underwear into the box. "Get lost. Finish your own packing."

Danny shrugged. "I'll tell Mama you're going to the *kampong*." With a mean grin on his face he walked to the door.

Jasmine grabbed her pillow and threw it at him, but it hit the door. She sagged down on the bed. *I hate him!*

Don't hate, Jasmine. Papa. She heard his voice as if he were there. But Danny had become such a pest lately, often teasing her about her blond curly hair. She wished her hair was smooth and black like Sari's. She sighed, and left the packing. It was teatime.

Ellen and Yvonne were already in the living room. Ellen was two years older than Jasmine and Yvonne one. Yvonne's hair was as blond as Jasmine's but not as curly. Ellen's hair was darker and curled only slightly.

Jasmine sat down on her hassock by the window, and Danny lounged on the sofa. Papa and Mama sat in the armchairs around the low table in the center of the room.

Jasmine would miss this room. She would miss everything in this house. The house they were going to belonged to Miss Steen. They called it the Big House, because Miss Steen did. She herself lived with a friend, because she did not like to live alone any more.

Miss Steen, who was Danny's teacher, was not very popular. Ellen and Yvonne were discussing her. "She slapped me once." Ellen said, rubbing her cheek as if she could still feel it.

"What for?" Jasmine asked.

"I talked back at school."

Danny clicked his tongue. "Bad girl!"

Repressing her irritation, Jasmine said, "We'll be closer to Sari's *kampong*.

"You know you're not allowed there," Ellen warned, with a glance at Mama, who drank tea with a gloomy face. The move was hard on Mama. She said she didn't like Miss Steen much either, and she was sure to run into trouble with her.

While Jasmine was talking about Sari, Mama asked, "Is Sari that native girl at school?"

"Yes."

"I hope you won't go to her place."

"Why? Sari is the best friend I ever had. Dorothea's mean, Jeannie's boring, and Marto's both."

"What about Ruth Boon?"

Jasmine wrinkled her nose, and shrugged. Ruth Boon was an Indo, like her parents, half native, half Dutch. Jasmine didn't like Ruth's dad, and couldn't quite figure out why. He had made remarks about her hair, but there was something else. She often sensed that he hated the Dutch because they made Indos feel inferior. Jasmine wondered if he sympathized with the *Merdeka* movement. Papa and Mama respected the Indos, and there were some who were teachers.

"There's always Yvonne or Ellen," Mama said.

Jasmine looked at her sisters. Ellen had her nose in a book as usual, and Yvonne was nibbling on a cookie.

Jasmine shrugged. "They're gone most of the time." That was true since the school bus from Magelang came in late each afternoon. Magelang was a city thirty kilometers south of Tenang.

"Just remember what I said." Mama said, and walked away.

By Sunday Jasmine was so worried about Sukandar and *Merdeka*, that she decided to talk to Papa after all. He was the only one who would understand. But after church they had visitors. Aunt Helga Van Doorn and her husband Ben were there. Aunt Helga had been Jasmine's grade one teacher, and Uncle Ben had a Government job, Jasmine wasn't sure what. Miss Sinkel, as always with her poodle at her heels, was a single lady, a nurse.

It rained hard and Jasmine could not even see the far side of the lawn, although she sat by the window on a hassock. Behind her the grownups talked about war coming here too. Not the Germans but the Japanese. Didn't she have enough worries already? Talking to Papa was impossible now. She wished the visitors would disappear.

Ellen and Yvonne left the room, but Jasmine still hoped to have a few minutes with Papa. She noticed that Mama's hands shook, so that some tea spilled into the saucer. Mama put her cup down and pressed her handkerchief, soaked with Boldoot Cologne, under her nose. Her chin bulged up and was dotted with little dimples. All this war talk seemed to upset her.

Jasmine decided to join Ellen and Yvonne in the wide hall, one step lower than the living room. But their company was no better. With great vigor Ellen was talking about the Japanese, the "Yellow Danger" as everyone called them.

Jasmine protested. "I'm trying not to think about war, and now you two expect trouble with the Japs. Talk about war enough and we'll get one."

"I don't believe we'll get war here," Yvonne said.

Ellen moved her head, as if to shake off glum thoughts.

Jasmine felt a sensation of suffocating. She wished she could be sure war would not break out here, and that it was just a stupid idea for people to talk about.

Ellen said, "Did you hear about that incident in Bandung with the Japanese who's running a barber shop?"

"What about it?" Jasmine asked.

"They think he's a spy."

"A Japanese spy? I never heard anything so silly." Jasmine tried to laugh her uneasiness away.

"There are lots of rumors," Yvonne said, "but they could be true."

"So what?" Jasmine asked, but she *was* worried. As her sisters talked about the rumors, they gained a sinister significance.

She went back into the living room, where the visitors were finally getting ready to leave. It had stopped raining. Once in a while the sun broke through the clouds, throwing eerie yellow-orange light over the floor and furniture. Yvonne, who had come in too, was creating grotesque monsters with the shadow of her hands. Jasmine stared out the window.

Papa left for the work house after the visitors had gone, and there was no chance to talk to him.

When Jasmine came home from school the next day, she saw Mama leaning on the buffet with a letter. It was the last letter from *Oma* Van Noren. It had arrived a year ago, but had been sent before the Germans invaded Holland. *Oma* wrote about everyone being afraid of them and about Aunt Hanna coming to the Indies.

Mama was so besotted with Holland that she'd read and re-read the letter which had taken a long time to get here. It was a lifeline to her. Once in a while she would read it aloud to the family and ask questions about what might have happened. Was Uncle Jacob, who had been mobilized and taken prisoner, still alive? Would any of the family survive the war? They would not find out until the war was over. Mama's brow puckered with worry.

Jasmine had never liked to hear about Holland and the relatives. In the first place they were strangers to her, and, secondly, they seemed to work like magnets to draw Mama away from Java. Jasmine sighed because she knew they would have to listen to the whole letter again at teatime. She managed to slip outside without being seen.

But moments later Mama's voice boomed through the wide hall, calling her name. When Mama called like that it hardly ever meant a pleasant surprise, only that she wanted something done which Jasmine did not feel like doing.

"Jasmine!" Mama's voice became louder, more insistent,

Jasmine hesitated. "What?" she called loudly, as she opened the side door into the hall.

When Mama came into view she asked crossly, "Is that a way to answer?"

Jasmine muttered sullenly, for now there was no escape. She waited.

"Go to the workhouse and tell Papa tea is almost ready."

"Okay." Jasmine's spirits rose. It was a pleasant surprise after all, for the workhouse offered many interesting things. Also, she might be able to talk to Papa. She had tried to forget about Sukandar and the *Merdeka* men, but the grownup talk about war and the Japanese made everything more threatening.

She went out through the side door, and turned left onto a concrete walk.

The Boys Home had long dormitories for the boys, a huge kitchen and other back buildings. The workhouse where Papa taught stood apart.

Jasmine had always loved to watch the boys transform an ordinary piece of wood into doll furniture which was sold. Papa also taught boys to weave cloth on big looms, like the ones in the Mission school.

She saw Walter near the door. Of all the boys in the Home, she liked him best. He was handicapped like all the other boys. He was seventeen, but mentally like an eight-year-old.

"Hey, Walter, what are you making today?"

Walter smiled. "A dog house."

"A dog house?"

"Yes. Our dog had puppies in the hole where we found the snakes."

"Are there more snakes?" Jasmine shuddered.

"No." Walter kept on sanding a plank, and Jasmine watched him silently.

A little later Papa came out through the door.

"Hello, Jasmine. What are you doing here?"

"Mama says you have to come for tea."

"All right. I'll be ready soon." He went back into the dimness of the workhouse.

Jasmine walked to the door and looked in. There were other boys at work, mostly native ones as well as Indos and Chinese, all with sleek, dark hair. Suddenly she felt alone. It was true, she was not like them. She would never be like them. She had blond, curly hair, and she was jealous of all those dark-haired boys because they belonged.

She felt a strange sadness about the way she was, and that nothing could change it. But this was still the land she loved. It was always hers. She turned and stepped back from the door and looked at the field, where the *alang-alang* grass stood very tall. When she turned again Papa stood framed by the door, seeming so much part of this place.

Papa came toward her. "Let's go, Jasmine. We must not keep Mama waiting."

Together they walked toward the house. Papa's white tropical hat looked like a helmet, stiff and round. It shaded his bushy eyebrows, and his lower lip protruded slightly. Papa was not tall, but he looked dignified. His white shirt fitted him perfectly. He had gained weight the past few years. His high forehead with the receding hairline made him look scholarly. He had inherited his black hair from a French ancestor, and his large blue eyes from a Scandinavian one. Because of his short nose his face had the innocent and honest expression of a child.

"Papa. . . ." Jasmine was thinking of the best way to bring up the frightening subject of *Merdeka*, while walking past the place where the boys had once put a dead snake. Jasmine couldn't stop herself from looking over her shoulder.

The snake was gone, but the thought of it made her shiver, and she forgot what she was going to say. She often dreamed about snakes, slithering in bushes, flicking tongues, and staring at her with little black eyes. When she wanted to run in her dream, she could not move her legs.

"What is it, Jasmine?" Papa asked, looking down at her.

In spite of her worries, she said, "Nothing." She did not really want to talk about what bothered her. Papa looked so happy, that finding out she had been at Sari's and seen the meeting would worry him. And it wouldn't help much either if he said, 'don't worry about it'.

Papa went on talking, but Jasmine barely listened. All that mattered was that she loved her father.

That evening, at bedtime, she finally had another chance to talk to him, but the first thing she asked had nothing to do with Sukandar.

"What do you think about the Japs, Papa?"

"Japanese," he corrected absentmindedly. After a few moments he said, "They're no worse or better than any other people, I suppose."

"Why are you afraid of them?"

"Afraid? What makes you think I'm afraid?"

"The way you all talk about them."

Again that hesitation. Then Papa said slowly, "Well, some people believe that the Japanese might start a war here."

"Really?" It seemed so unlikely, but Papa looked serious. "What will happen to us, if the Japanese come?"

"We'll fight back and hopefully win," Papa said, and sounded again as if he did not really want to talk about it.

"What happens if we don't win?"

"Then we would probably have to leave here, or be taken prisoner."

That was an awful thought and she tried to change the subject. She thought of something else she and Sari had been talking about. "Papa, what's the difference between Jesus and Mohammed?"

"What makes you think about Mohammed?"

"Sari and I talked about it at school. Sari and her family are Christians, but some of her relatives are Muslims, and believe that Mohammed is their prophet."

Papa thought for a moment as if he was thinking of a good way to answer. "Jesus is the Son of God who rose from the dead, and Mohammed was the founder of the Muslim religion long after Jesus lived on earth."

Jasmine wanted to ask if all Muslim were *Merdeka* people who wanted to chase the Dutch out. She was not sure if Papa even knew what *Merdeka* was, so she hesitated to bring this up. But the new fear about Japanese had changed everything and she told Papa about the *kampong* and Sari, as well as the men and Sukandar.

"Sari said they are going to chase us all out, Papa."

"Who are 'they'?"

"The men around the fire."

Papa looked worried. "You should not go into the *kampong* anymore," he said.

"But Sari's my friend." She could not explain that Sari represented security and a sense of identity, even though some of her relatives wanted her out.

"I know, but a *kampong* may not be a good place to visit now." He hesitated, and then added, "These days there is a lot of unrest everywhere because of the war, but also because there are natives who want independence from the Dutch. And what you told me about this Sukandar, it sounds like some of these people are also involved."

Jasmine thought again about the meeting and the fear she had felt. She blurted out, "Can they really chase us out, Papa?"

"We don't know what will happen. In any case, I don't think you should go to Sari's house anymore. Why don't you ask Sari to come here?"

"I did, but she said her uncle told her not to, because he doesn't like the Dutch."

Jasmine wished she had not mentioned Sukandar and *Merdeka*, for Papa's last words rang threateningly. Besides, the less said about this whole thing, the faster she would forget.

More and more uncertainties had entered her life, ever since the *Merdeka* meeting and the news that they had to move. She had always thought the Boys Home was the best home to live in, and that Java was the best and safest place in the world. She had always been so sure she never would leave.

The clock struck nine as she lay with heavy eyes in her bed. A *dokar* crunched over the gravel road, accompanied by the clop, clop of the horse's hooves. Far away a *tong-tong* drummed faintly in the night. It made her think of the men around the fire, and especially of Sukandar. *Tong-tongs* were hollowed out tree trunks on which the natives beat with a stick to send certain messages. It could mean telling time or calling people to a *Merdeka* meeting.

Could they really do it? Chase out all the Dutch? That would be worse than a war, and she couldn't even imagine what a war was like. But to leave Java was the worst thing she could think of.

In her dream snakes crawled over her, and Jasmine woke up with a scream, damp with sweat. She sat straight up in bed, staring into the darkness. Then Mama's arms were around her. "I'm here," she said.

Jasmine stared at her, the fear still present.

Chapter Three

Four Ships

October, 1941

Instead of waiting for Sari the following morning, Jasmine left the house with Ellen and Yvonne who always left earlier for the bus stop to catch the bus to Magelang.

Jasmine and Sari usually walked to school. Sari did not have a bike so Jasmine did not use hers. Danny rode ahead on his bike, and Ellen and Yvonne boarded the bus. As Jasmine walked slowly down the road, a short time later Sari came running up to her, breathing hard. "Why didn't you wait for me?" She sounded frustrated, and Jasmine could not blame her. She wished she could tell Sari what bothered her, but Sari would not understand.

Jasmine herself didn't know what to make of Papa's explanation about the Japanese and his order that she should not go to *kampongs*. He loved all the people here, but now he did not seem very sure of himself. Sari had always been a com-

A Garland of Emeralds

fort, but now she reminded Jasmine of Sukandar. Anyway, since the evening of the sinister meeting by the fire, Jasmine had decided to do what Papa had advised and not go to the *kampong* anymore. A few times she had tried to avoid Sari after school, but Sari had looked so hurt that Jasmine did not have the heart to do it again.

They walked on and when they passed the cemetery, on Station Street, Sari rushed past, leaving Jasmine behind. The first time she had done that Jasmine had asked what was wrong.

Sari had looked kind of embarrassed and said, "I'm afraid of cemeteries."

"What for?" Jasmine had looked at the cemetery, as Sari urged her to hurry up.

"Spirits of our ancestors still live there. They get angry if you invade their privacy."

"You really believe that?" Jasmine was astounded.

Sari shrugged, her face pale.

"But you're a Christian—you don't believe that, do you?"

"I know I shouldn't, but lots of people still believe that, and are scared of cemeteries."

Jasmine had not mentioned it again, but she remembered thinking that it was hard to figure out natives sometimes. She had thought she knew Sari pretty well, but after the cemetery incident she was not so sure. She shrugged, caught up with her friend, and they continued on to school.

In the school yard many pounding feet made the coarse gravel fly left and right. Jasmine and Sari walked under four huge rain trees in the middle of the yard. These were trees with widely spread branches. Around them many black, brown and blond heads were bent together, whispering or talking loudly in Malay, Dutch or Chinese.

The bell rang, and the groups broke up to form neat lines along the white walls of the two long buildings that made up the school. Jasmine and Sari joined the line-up in front of one of the buildings, where grades four through eight had their classrooms. In the building across from them were the kindergarten classes and grades one to three.

Marto came to stand right behind Jasmine and Sari. She held her head high, defying everyone with bold black eyes.

Without saying a word Marto pushed herself ahead of them.

"Hey, what are you doing?" Sari looked annoyed.

"I'm standing in front of you."

"Wait your turn, Marto!" Jasmine said angrily.

Sari raised her voice, "That's right, what do you think you're doing?"

"I'm waiting my turn."

It was just like Marto to pretend there was nothing wrong, but Jasmine did not think anything they could say would remove Marto from her spot. They would only get the worst of her sharp tongue.

Jasmine saw Dorothea Breda's smirking face ahead of them. Dorothea was a lot like Marto and Jasmine could not understand how nice people like the Bredas could have a daughter like Dorothea. Even her name was atrocious!

Jasmine remembered the celebration for newborn Princess Irene two years ago. Both Dorothea and Marto had been obnoxious. The celebration on the *alun-alun*, Tenang's grassy square, was in honor of the newborn princess, granddaughter of Queen Wilhelmina of Holland. It had been crowded and Jasmine had climbed up to the lowest branches of the *waringin*, the huge banyan tree, in the center of the field, to get a better view of the raised platform, where the Regent of Tenang gave a speech.

She still remembered some of the speech. *"Dear fellow citizens, we all know the reason for this happy celebration. It is to rejoice with our dearly beloved House of Orange, and our much revered Queen Wilhelmina and her children Juliana and Bernard. . . ."*

On and on he went. His thin high words had bounded up the field like kittens. Jasmine saw several ladies nod solemnly, tears in their eyes. His last words were, *"Let us all work together towards a more enduring friendship."*

Marto and Dorothea had been standing under the *waringin*, and Marto had jeered, "Huh, he's lying."

Dorothea nodded. "He's nothing but a rebel."

They looked startled when Jasmine climbed down the tree and stood next to them.

Marto looked angry. "What were you doing, climbing the *waringin*? Don't you know that guardian spirits live in *waringins*?"

Jasmine knew that in the *dessas* near the Mission people brought daily offerings of fruits and nuts in bamboo baskets at the foot of the *waringin* to keep the spirits happy. Offerings could appease an angered spirit. In the *sawahs* were holy places too, where the twisted trees stood clustered on a hump of dirt. She had not responded and left them.

In the evening of that day there had been a parade with a band solemnly playing a song about Holland's Lion, forever on his guard, bearing his sword and his crown, so that Holland would always be free. The Lion was the symbol for Holland. Jasmine still remembered how the field had looked like a sea of colored ripples with flashes of red, white, blue and orange. The Dutch flag and orange banner.

Afterwards she had joined Ellen and Yvonne and they had bought satay at one of the *warongs*. Marto had stood in front of them, saying maliciously, "The Lion will *not* bear his sword and his crown!" Then she had punched Ellen in the stomach. Ellen had seemed more concerned about her stomach than about the insult to the song and patriotism.

Now, waiting in line, it seemed that Marto had not changed one bit. She stayed ahead.

Jasmine clenched her teeth, and Sari stuck out her tongue at Marto's back.

The second bell rang and the classrooms swallowed up the lines. It was seven thirty.

They filed into their classroom, where Principal Breda was writing a math problem on the blackboard. He greeted them then hurried to the grade seven class. He always seemed in a hurry lately, because he had to teach both grades seven and eight. In every classroom there was a large poster of

Queen Wilhelmina on the wall above the blackboard. It was the same picture they had at home, but Mama also had pictures of Princess Juliana, Prince Bernard and the little princesses, Beatrix and Irene. The Queen and the Prince were in England and the Princesses in Canada because of the war.

Sari and Jasmine fell into their desk. They shared a double one. After the roll and prayer they joined the grade seven students and listened as Mr. Breda began the Bible lesson. He always told his stories with great flourish, and this morning the story was about the Great Flood. Jasmine remembered vividly the time when she was in grade one, and Aunt Helga Van Doorn, the teacher, had told them the same story. It had been at the time of heavy rains, and there had been *bandjirs*, which were floods when there was too much water coming down from the mountains, and the rivers could not take it. Often *dessas*, native villages, were destroyed.

Mr. Breda poked with a stick at Noah's ark in the large picture hanging against the chalkboard. "Noah was a good man, but most people were wicked. So when the whole world was covered with water, only Noah and his family were in the Ark." He nodded gravely. "It was a great calamity, but God said there wouldn't be any more water calamities, although others may come."

Jasmine hoped they wouldn't have calamities of any kind, but there was always this talk about the German war, and the Japanese. Mama had said the other day, "The Japanese coming here would be a calamity," and she had looked frightened. The *Merdeka* cause was a calamity too.

Four Ships

With some words of warning about not being wicked, Mr. Breda finished the story.

When Jasmine looked up, Marto was looking at her and sticking out her tongue. Although Jasmine had to quell an urge to smack her face, she ignored her, because Mr. Breda was looking her way.

After recess Mr. Breda was in the grade seven class room. The grade eight students in the next room were supposed to be at their desks, working on assignments, but when Marto said in a loud whisper, "*Blanda*, go home," Jasmine could not let that go. She got up, walked over to Marto's desk, and said in a low voice, "If you don't leave me alone, I'm going to tell Mr. Breda that I saw you at a *Merdeka* meeting and put up a *merah-putih* flag!" With her hands on her hips Jasmine stared daggers at the insufferable girl who merely snickered. Jasmine was just turning to go back to her desk, when Sari sprang out of it, and joined her. "If you don't stop saying nasty things to Jasmine, I'll . . ., I'll. . . .!

"What are you going to do? Tell on me?"

"You know very well that if the Dutch had not been here, you would not have what you've got now."

By now more students had jumped into the fray and the class was getting noisy. Jasmine and Sari had just returned to their desk, when Mr. Breda came in. He bellowed angrily, "What is this here? Can't you be quiet while I'm gone? I ought to keep you here all afternoon! I do have grade seven to think about you know!" He raved for a while as they all bent their heads.

When he finally began the history lesson, the class was quiet. Jasmine liked history, but she was upset about what Marto had said, and was not paying attention. She knew that she would not dare say anything about *Merdeka* to Mr. Breda.

They had begun a unit about Holland, which had irritated her at first because it reminded her of Mama's attachment to that country. What was it about Holland that made people so happy and proud? She didn't understand a bit of it. It was like a threatening danger to her happiness about living here.

Last year Ellen drilled history lessons about Holland and how courageous the Dutch had been. Phooey! One thing Holland had done right, though, more than three hundred years ago, was getting hold of the Indies, and last week Mr. Breda had started the part about Dutch Colonial History. So Jasmine began to listen more carefully to find out how the Dutch came to be here. Also she hoped that it would irritate Marto.

The deep voice of Mr. Breda resounded through the silent classroom. "The 16th and 17th centuries are called the Age of Exploration. Many European countries were interested in expanding their trade. Britain and Portugal for example, but also a small country like Holland was eager to find products that the world wanted: spices. Holland had been doing well in trade in other places, but they wanted more. Spices meant gold in the treasury."

"So, in 1595 four ships sailed from Holland to the Indies with Cornelis de Houtman as commander. This expedition was successful."

Jan, the Smid's eldest son, raised his hand. "They couldn't do much trade with four ships."

"No, that's why a year later they had a fleet of 65 ships, and in 1602 the Dutch founded the VOC, the *Verenigde Oostindische Companie,* the United East Indies Company. That's why the natives still call the Government the *Kompenie,* because the VOC had ruled for so long. At one point Jan Pieterzoon Coen of the Company landed on Java, at a fortress called Jacatra. He renamed it Batavia in 1619. He became the first Governor over the entire trading area, and established a monopoly over all the islands of the Indies. Of course there was opposition, but after relentless stubborn fighting the Dutch built an empire of thousands of islands."

Jan asked, "Do you think what Holland did then is the same as what the Nazis are doing in Europe?" Jan must have read newspapers and listened to radios. Jasmine did not want to be reminded about Europe or Holland so she ignored newspapers and radios.

"Imperialism means grabbing another country and trying to keep it," Mr. Breda said. He shrugged then continued, "Of course I love Holland, but I also realize that Holland has been guilty of practicing imperialism since the four ships in 1595."

"They did that to trade," Ruth Boon observed.

Jasmine looked at Ruth, surprised, because Ruth never had much to say.

Mr. Breda turned to Ruth. "True, but the Dutch East India Company couldn't tolerate interference and began to drive out the English and the Portuguese."

Jasmine said, "It still doesn't prove we were imperialistic."

"Trade!" Dorothea scoffed. "More like theft."

Mr. Breda ignored his daughter, and faced Jasmine. Thoughtfully, as if he had to solve a difficult math problem, he said, "Fighting for a monopoly is imperialistic, and besides, Jan Pieterszoon Coen used weapons to achieve this purpose. Remember, many people in the twentieth century think imperialism is bad, but in the seventeenth century, Holland's Golden Age, imperialism was called, 'the spirit of exploration'. To possess this spirit was always considered admirable."

Jan said, "We've been here for more than three hundred years, and we're doing a lot of good, like the missionaries and doctors."

"And good teachers like me." Mr. Breda grinned. "Yes, of course we've done many excellent things, especially for the poor and ill. Many people in Holland were concerned about the conditions of the people here, and there was an article in 1899 called 'An Honor Debt'. It was about Holland paying back in services what they had taken out of the Indies in products. Some books too were published about injustices against the peasants, often through native chiefs. But the changes for good did not start until after Queen Wilhelmina announced the Ethical Policy in 1901."

"You said that native chiefs did injustices to their own people," Jan pointed out, "so native chiefs were just as much to blame as the Dutch. The good we did should get us some gratitude."

"Of course, but you're not going to convince the nationalists of that. They've forgiven their native chiefs because they are part of their heritage, but they won't forgive us, the foreign intruders. I'm sure many realize the Dutch have done a lot, but to most *Merdeka* people it is, 'Too little, too late'."

Dorothea said, "The Dutch have stuck like a burr in the Indies. Even the *Merdeka* people are going to have a big job getting rid of us. All they can do is call us the Infidel Dogs."

Mr. Breda looked at Dorothea, and nodded. "Yes, that's where religion comes in. Many fanatic Muslims are behind the nationalist movement. They want *Merdeka* now. Freedom, their own national anthem, flag, and language."

Jasmine was shocked that Mr. Breda seemed to know about *Merdeka*. "Are you saying we really don't belong here?" she asked.

"I do, and since we have taken the Indies by force, it will be taken from us by force."

It sounded ominous, something like, 'What you don't look after you'll lose.' "Our servants like us," Jasmine said lamely.

"Of course."

"It's sad," Jasmine said. "I always think of the natives as our people. I love our country."

"Our country?" Dorothea asked with a fine smile.

Jasmine looked at Dorothea, and could not keep the anger out of her voice. "Oh sorry, I forgot that we have no business here! I was *born* in this country and it's as much mine as theirs!"

A Garland of Emeralds

Dorothea just grimaced, and Jasmine turned to face Mr. Breda. Dorothea sure knew how to get under her skin! To Jasmine's surprise, Mr. Breda nodded. "Yes, our country."

Jasmine looked at him. "I thought you said we don't belong here."

Mr. Breda looked sheepish. "I know I did. My reason tells me that we don't belong here, but my feelings . . . ."

Jasmine saw Jan smile and nod. She felt good herself, but the mention of *Merdeka* scared her, and she didn't want to hear anymore.

As if Mr. Breda had guessed her thoughts, he finished the lesson, arms spread wide. "So, from the four ships grew a fleet, and after the East Indies Company had ruled for about two hundred years, the Netherlands Indies became a colony, property of the Dutch king. The native princes actually sold their independence to the Dutch, enabling them to take possession of an empire, the East Indian archipelago which include the main islands Java, Sumatra, Borneo, Celebes and the western part of Timor. It was the Dutch who unified the Netherlands Indies, our Garland of Emeralds." His hands came down like the wings of a tired bird.

Jasmine slid down in her desk beside Sari, who had not said anything. Maybe Sari did not feel comfortable discussing the Dutch and *Merdeka*. Jasmine had never thought she'd appreciate Mr. Breda. She knew he had come to love the people here as much as the country, and really thought the Dutch belonged here. She wondered for the umpteenth time what he did with a daughter like Dorothea.

Four Ships

Jasmine wished it was time to go home, but they had one more class. The little ones had gone home at twelve o'clock, but the higher grades would not be finished till one. The *kentering* heat pressed on the class, and even with both doors and all windows open, there was no breeze. The *kentering* was the time of the doldrums, between the dry and the wet monsoons. When the rains did not yet come regularly, it could be terribly hot, and the *kentering* was the most dangerous part of the rainy season, a time of *bandjirs*, dangerous floods.

Most students hung listlessly in their desks. Mr. Breda wrote another math problem on the chalkboard with his right hand; with his left he wiped sweat off his face. He searched for a victim to come and figure out the problem. Sari bent her head low over her scribbler, and Jasmine ducked. He picked on Jeannie Werda to come to the blackboard.

"Phew!" Jasmine whispered.

When finally the bell rang, and Mr. Breda let them go, the weather had changed. It was wild and windy. Jasmine walked outside with Sari. For a while they heard the shouts of children, but soon the drumming of feet and the shouting were lost in the distance. The girls leaned into the wind, which broke their sentences into pieces.

Jasmine hopped on one foot, yelling her pleasure into the wind. She loved the wind, and did not even mind when the heat almost choked her. She loved everything about Java.

Sari hopped and cheered too, until they reached her *kampong*.

As Jasmine walked away, a mangy *gladakker* looked up from a pile of garbage. A native woman yelled and threw stones at the dog, so he ran away, looking longingly at the garbage from a distance. Jasmine kicked a pebble, and then another, until a steady jet of pebbles preceded her on the road.

As soon as she got home it started to rain.

When she stepped into the hall, she could smell the *rysttafel*, a traditional celebration meal in the Indies. They did not have *rysttafel* every day, but it was Mama's birthday.

"Delicious!" Jasmine said, as she took off her shoes.

Djaidin their *djongos* had set the table neatly and stood against the wall, waiting for orders to serve. He was proud of being a house servant, and not a yard servant like *Kebon*. *Djongos* wore a white jacket over a sarong, which many native men wore. *Kokkie* Noenoeng, their cook, and *Babu* Roes, who did most of the other housework, wore sarongs and *kabayas*. Then there were the *mantries*, male attendants, to look after the boys.

Hungrily Jasmine prowled around the table. There was rice steaming in a big bowl, a dish with hard-boiled eggs in peanut sauce, another with string beans in a hot sauce, a third with little fish in a red sauce. There were also lots of vegetables and bean sprouts, sliced cucumbers and tomatoes. There was chicken in a white sauce and some pieces of meat in curry sauce. The curry smelled good.

They sat down, and Papa prayed. Jasmine heaped her plate with steaming rice.

Four Ships

"Are you sure you can eat all that?" Mama asked.

"I'm hungry."

"I hate to waste food."

"I'll eat it." Jasmine put a scoop from each dish on her plate until it became a colorful mountain. Not too much *sambal*, for even a little of the hot pepper paste was so hot that by the time the meal was over you had to hiss through your teeth. For dessert there were bananas, but Jasmine only ate half.

"I'm glad we don't have *rysttafel* every day," Mama said as she covered the bowls, which were still half-filled. I have enough problems inspecting *kokkie's* job with regular meals. Who knows what she puts in the food if I didn't watch her all the time. I sometimes wonder. . . ."

"Wonder what?" Papa asked. "Why we have servants at all?"

"Yes, it seems to me that checking up on all they do takes more time than doing it myself."

Papa smiled. "I don't think you would like to light the charcoal *anglos* and clean the fish, and . . ."

"Never mind. I get the picture." Mama made an irritated gesture.

"Anyway, you always have her cook too much," Papa said and pointed at the bowls with his neatly folded serviette. He dipped his fingers in the finger bowl half-filled with water, and wiped them on his serviette. Then he turned on the radio.

A man's voice announced something about some battle somewhere. Mama's face turned somber. "What do you think that means?"

Papa shook his head. "Who knows. . . ."

Jasmine thought back to the history lesson. She didn't want to admit it, but this time Principal Breda had gotten through to her. She thought about Holland and the Indies, and their relationship. Mr. Breda had said the Indies were a unified nation, but natives and Dutch could never be close. The Dutch would always be master over the native people. Most natives accepted this, and their *djongos* Djaidin, *Babu* Roes, as well as *Kokkie* Noenoeng and *Kebon* were faithful servants. The natives had basic respect for any kind of masters, whoever those masters happened to be, like the native princes on Java in their *Kratons*, palaces, who ruled even before the Dutch came. It was the ones who were more like Western people who demanded *Merdeka*. But the Dutch had ruled for many centuries now. It was amazing! Only four ships and now an empire!

Chapter Four

The Meeting

November, 1941

The silver moon gleamed in silence as Sukandar entered the tunnel formed by the trees over the path leading to the *dessa* where the meeting was going to be. Silvery darts of moonlight attempted to penetrate even the darkest sections of the forest. He adjusted the empty mailbag over his shoulder. He feared the potent force of the moon a little. There were also the spirits. One had to be cautious not to attract their attention, for these unseen beings of the lower world inhabited ravines and caves. They could drag you down into their joyless eternity.

The Prophet Mohammed had advocated prayer. Five times a day. Sukandar was not sure if prayer was sufficient protection against evil spirits. He found more reassurance in his exuberant youth which resisted their power by playing flute, and vigorous work on the *sawahs*, or briskly walking with the mail.

Was there not this solid land? Java, the land he loved. No spirits, evil or good, could extinguish this love. Sukandar's great grandfather was *pangerang*, prince of the blood, who was a child of this land and had loved it. The Netherlands Indies government allowed the title *pangerang* to Regents who helped them rule the people, but those who rebelled openly against the government were exiled. The Regent of Tenang was one of those who rebelled, but not openly, and the government trusted him to be a Regent in Tenang, and believed he was on their side. Informed nationalists knew that he was one of them.

Sukandar thought again about his so-called destiny. Because he was born under the sign of the Twin at the crack of dawn, he was destined to be a leader. That's what his parents had always told him. "You're a Child of the Dawn, Sukandar. One day you will be a leader of our people." Since his earliest memories he had accepted this, and had been proud of being such an important person. Now he realized that this dream had never truly become his own. He had known for some time that his heart had not been in the *Merdeka* activities, and he had begun to resent being forced to go to meetings. It was the same at every meeting, endless talk about what the nationalists would do once the opportunity arose.

His bare foot slid on a muddy stretch left by the last rain. He came onto a path and approached the *dessa* with its

The Meeting

small houses of wood and bamboo. Tiny yards were circled by banana trees and coconut palms. There were children's voices, a barking dog. This *dessa* was almost the same as his, which lay to the north.

The *waringin,* the holy banyan tree, stood right in the center of the square. Near the *pondok* to the right a few scabious dogs sniffed in a pile of garbage. Further on, beneath the roof of two large rain trees, a *warong* was still doing business, selling syrupy drinks and satay. On the threshold of one of the first houses sat a young woman.

"*Malem baik,*" she mumbled her shy evening greeting.

"*Malem baik,*" Sukandar answered, then hastened to the meeting which had already begun.

"You're late, Sukandar."

With a nod he acknowledged *Pak* Suyono's rebuke. *Pak* Suyono was one of the older men, and the leader. The oldest man was *Pak* Kromo. He was to be respected, for he was *dalang*, puppeteer of the *Wayang Kulit* shows.

Sukandar joined the young men in the second circle. The men in the inner circle, all on their haunches, sarongs tight about their legs, sat absorbed in their thoughts. In the second circle the younger men all sat on their haunches too, but most wore pants and loose shirts. They preferred that and agreed that the old men were going too far in thinking one could not be a good nationalist without the batik sarong and the black velvet *pitjih* cap. In spite of that they all listened respectfully to the wise old men. They knew so much more, had lived many moons, seen many things.

Except for the murmuring voices all was quiet until suddenly there was a noise in the branches of one of the rain trees. Preceded by a vibrating sound the almost human voice of the *tokeh* called its own name, "*Tokeh, tokeh. . .* five times. Then the sonorous voice died away. Only five times. Seven times meant good luck and happiness.

An old woman swept the tiny yard in front of her house in the light of a kerosene lamp. Many women were listening. They formed a straggly third circle around the two circles of men. Some sat against the nearest bamboo huts. Some carried a sleeping infant in a *slendang* on their backs.

The men talked of ordinary things. When would the rice be ripe for harvest, and who would serve the next *selametan*, a ceremonial meal, and for what reason, and what auspicious date had the priest set? The last *selametan* in Sukandar's *dessa* had been for his old grandfather, the fortieth day after his death.

Ordinary talk never lasted long. Soon they were in a serious discussion about the *Merdeka* cause. Sukandar thought about the many years he had believed that the land he and his people loved was tainted, like a leprous wound. Sukandar, like his friends at that time, could not understand why Allah had allowed this injustice for more than three hundred years. The invaders of the West had come. First the Portuguese and English, then the Dutch, after setting up factories, and establishing a trade monopoly, settled themselves confidently after booting out the Portuguese and the English. They knitted together the islands, calling it the

The Meeting

Dutch East Indies then ruled supreme, successfully strangling most native commercial activities.

At first they were supported and encouraged by local kings and princes who offered no resistance because they thought the Dutch were allies against the Portuguese. The Colonial government followed a course of politics which had been called good business by some, greediness by others, and loving possessiveness by the sentimental ones. Whatever anyone called it, Holland stuck like a flea in a head of hair.

It was true that all the islands were in the beginning only loosely connected. The Dutch welded them together and had made the Indies productive, but all the profits went overseas. *Learn everything you can about them, Sukandar.* He had read Aminoto's books and listened to his stories. Sukandar remembered being proud to learn so much.

He had learned Dutch only because he had been one of the privileged natives who could attend a Dutch school. There should perhaps have been many more, but the people were too numerous. Of course many of the native children did go to native elementary schools. Also, many young native men were sent to Holland to study.

The only school with room available for Sukandar had been a Christian one. His mother knew the risks and often questioned him suspiciously about his beliefs. He had stood the test and he had remained faithful to the precepts of the Prophet Mohammed, even though it had not been easy to pretend he believed the white way. Yet he had found stories from the Bible interesting. At school he had also learned about the exploits of the imperialists, but history had a way of changing circumstances, and now the time for change had come. It was his uncle Aminoto who always egged him on since he was young, assuring him that a native man was never too young to support the *Merdeka* cause.

It troubled Sukandar that his old certainty was no longer there. He feared rejection if he told anyone openly. It was his sister Lea who often spoke to him about this. She was maid to the *'nDoro*, leader of the Mission, which paid its workers well. "I hope you don't get in trouble over this *Merdeka* stuff, Lea had said. " You should stop it before you get hurt."

He hadn't wanted to listen then, and she had said with a smile that he was stubborn. Lea was always gentle and kind and he talked to her whenever he could. She once had asked, "Why do you hate the Dutch?"

He had told her that he started hating white children in the school, because they teased him, and called him names. Many were spoiled, getting what they wanted. He thought it was unfair that they should have more than he ever had, and that his family had to scrape a living with thirteen of them jammed into a bamboo house with only two rooms.

The voices in the inner circle rumbled on quietly. There was no fire needed as the moon was full and they could see each other clearly. *Pak* Kromo, with dark brown wrinkled-apple skin, spoke in a low monotone, all the time chewing a blood red *sirih* quid, tobacco mixed with betel nuts and lime. His toothless mouth was red from *sirih* chewing. A few tufts

The Meeting

of grey hair around his mouth and near his temples was all the hair he had. But his coal black eyes were bright with life. *Pak* Kromo looked like the poorest of them all, yet Sukandar knew he had the nicest house in the *dessa*, even bigger than the *lurah*'s.

"A revolution is what we need," *Pak* Kromo said.

"A revolution," said the younger men, a little louder.

A revolution, Sukandar thought, would cause blood to flow, but he refrained from saying so.

Aminoto said, "When I was young, I came in contact with many of the nationalist leaders in Surabaya. Every evening they met in one of the homes of our group."

Aminoto, who always smoked *strootjes,* read a lot. Sutan, one of Sukandar's best friends, asked, "Why has there been so little progress if the leaders came together so long ago?"

Aminoto thought a moment. "I believe it was because our leaders always had to struggle alone, each with his own group of followers in scattered districts later to be united in a cause."

Pak Suyono started talking about Sukarno, their most inspired leader, who was popularly called *Bung* Karno, Brother Karno. "It was *Bung* Karno who managed to create a sense of unity by working on the emotions of the masses. He wanted to make them feel important, and made the *pitjih* cap, a mere peasant cap, into a national symbol. It was also *Bung* Karno who wanted to get rid of the sarong, because he thought this piece of clothing had a humiliating effect on men. He wanted all men to wear slacks, for only then could they walk proudly."

Pak Suyono disagreed. "I believe it is just as important for our sense of national unity to wear the traditional sarong, as it is to wear a *pitjih*."

Aminoto objected. "It is important that we become more like modern people, if we want some day to become an independent nation. I believe we should get accustomed to wearing slacks."

Pak Suyono and *Pak* Kromo sat in mute disapproval for a few moments, and then *Pak* Kromo said on a note of triumph, "*Bung* Karno was the only one who thought the sarong should be discarded. The other leaders saw value in keeping the traditional ways."

Sukandar looked at his white cotton slacks, cleaned at the river that afternoon, and he wondered why the elders scoffed at this western wear. His friends Sutan and Alimin wore pants and shirt too. He did not object to the *pitjih*, but with a sarong he could not walk as fast.

Night surrounded the *dessa*, and farther out the jungle whispered a secret life of its own in private darkness. In the *dessa* were the human noises. Laughter, the shrill voice of a mother calling a child to order. The moon weaved its rays around the squatting figures as the talk circled aimlessly around the struggle for *Merdeka*. A war had been declared, secret, somewhat uncertain. It was like a fire glowing beneath still black charcoal. Now and then a tongue of flame would reach up, soon to be quenched by the whites.

"The *blandas* have to go," murmured Aminoto.

Soft voices rose in chorus.

"Long live *Merdeka*!

"Long live the *merah-putih* flag!"

"Long live Indonesia!"

Pak Kromo nodded in rhythm with the words. His *pitjih* stood crooked on his head.

Sukandar, mesmerized by the intensity of the voices in spite of himself, was jerked to attention when *Pak* Suyono asked, "What have you learned these past weeks, Sukandar? Anything important about the *'nDoro* of the Mission?"

"No, *Pak*. The *'nDoro* seems concerned only with matters of her religion and is totally obsessed by them."

"Pah! The white religion!" Sutan scoffed.

"Do not underestimate the white man's religion." *Pak* Suyono corrected, and Sutan bent his head in silence.

Pak Suyono was toothless also, but his eyes were intelligent and piercing, black as the night, but with flames of strong fire. He kept looking at Sukandar who said rather lamely, "I have not been able to discover anything useful for our cause."

"Hmm."

As mail carrier Sukandar came often to the Mission, for the Mission got most of the mail. Only a few people in the *dessas* got mail, only the *lurah*s, and in town the *wedonos*. The *Merdeka* people thought he could get useful information because of the letters he handled. How he was supposed to do that and how it would help the cause he did not know. Of course there was always a chance he could intercept important letters. None of those had come as far as he could determine. The elders had given him as main assignment the job of spying on the *'nDoro* of the Mission, and report anything that might be significant.

The Mission was ruled efficiently by the *'nDoro* with the sad lips. She seemed to mourn continually, yet he did not feel pity for her. She was devout about her religion, but had not been particularly kind to him. Yet he had to admit that the Colonials had done a lot of good especially since the beginning of this century.

"Our own flag," *Pak* Kromo murmured, as his *sirih* quid moved to the left, leaving a brilliant red streak on his shriveled lips. "Some day soon, our own flag will wave proudly in the sky."

Sukandar used to think too that the Dutch flag had to go, the blue lopped off, leaving only the red and white, the red for the rising sun of freedom, the white for the pure, fragile as morning mist. The Dutch had wrung the spirit out of them Aminoto always said and that it was time to purify their country from the plague of the Infidel Dogs. That way of thinking had been ingrained in Sukandar for so many years that he was still having many doubts about what course his life should take.

Aminoto said. "We must be free! It's the only way to stop the Colonials from sucking all spirit out of us and our beloved green land, green as a garland of emeralds."

The Meeting

The men were silent after this outburst. Then Aminoto repeated in quieter, but no less emphatic words, "We must be free! This thought must be uppermost in our minds at all times, on our sleeping mats and at work!"

They mumbled agreement.

"Allah *akbar*! Allah is great," *Pak* Suyono said, as his eyes rolled up so the white showed brilliantly in the light of the shimmering moon.

"*Insh* Allah!" As Allah wills it, one young man said.

"Of course Allah wills it," Aminoto said irritably. "Allah is just!"

"*Saudara, saudara*, my brothers, "*Pak* Suyono said solemnly, "We shall return here as soon as we know the most auspicious day, as the priest will determine."

The circles began to disintegrate and the voices grew louder.

The next day, after Sukandar finished delivering the mail, he went to the Mission. Except for carrying mail he worked in the kapok now and then, which was a Mission project to raise extra money. He had not done so recently, because they had a different Dutch overseer whom he had despised at first acquaintance. When Sukandar had asked if there was work to be done, this tall Dutchman with a freckled face, bulbous nose and cat eyes, had looked down his nose as if he were an insect. Sukandar had walked away without saying anything, and the Dutchman had called after him, "Hey, stupid *inlander*, come back here!"

When Sukandar had ignored this, the man had shouted, "You need never come and ask for work again!" Yet here he was back with bowed head, asking, "Has the *Tuan* some work to do for me today?"

As before, the tall man looked down on him. "You! How dare you come back again! Out of my sight!"

Sukandar felt hot blood rise to his face and tears of wild anger sting his eyeballs. He clenched his fists and turned around. He did not want this man to see his tears.

He walked home, angry and humiliated, and worried about his mother. Where would she get the money he had promised her? She did not know he had gone to this obnoxious Dutchman. She would not have wanted him humiliated like that. But where else could he get extra work?

Totally confused and exhausted he sank down on his sleeping mat that night. He wanted to cry, but he did not want his brothers, who lay on their mats spread over the room, to hear.

"Freedom," he whispered. Aminoto and the old men must be right. The only way to escape any further humiliation was to get rid of all the whites.

Chapter Five

The Kites

November, 1941

One afternoon, in the middle of November, Mama read the last letter from Holland aloud again at teatime. It seemed that Mama always did this when there was news about the war.

"Dear Beth, Paul and children. How are you? We are well, and very busy with Hanna's things. There is so much to get ready, and of course Hanna is excited about going to Java...."

It really had been nice that Aunt Hanna had come to Java, Jasmine thought. They would probably visit her on the plantation soon.

"... about preserving peace...," Mama droned on. "...don't want another war...."

War, war, Jasmine thought, always war! She hated people talking about war, because it frightened her.

"... Well, I must end this letter. Hope to get one from you soon. Love, Mother."

Mama folded the letter neatly, and put it in a buffet drawer. When she left the room, Jasmine wondered what to do next. She thought of Walter. Of all the boys who lived in the Boys Home, Jasmine talked to Walter most. Walter could always be counted on to do something interesting, like building a beetle house, in which he raced beetles.

Jasmine walked to the workhouse, and peered inside to make sure Papa was there. He was supervising a group of boys in the back and did not see her. She liked to watch the boys at work when Papa was there teaching them how to make things. She went straight to Walter's workbench, where he stood bent over a mass of orange and black paper and thin sticks.

"Now what are you making, Walter?"

"A kite." He smiled at her, and proudly lifted the delicate looking construction.

"A kite? It looks more like a lion mask."

"Yes," he said proudly. "A lion kite. You can tell it's a lion?"

"Of course." The kite was made of orange paper shaped roughly like the face of a lion. It had a long tail.

"Are you going to fly it?"

"As soon as it's done."

"Do you like lions?" Jasmine asked.

"Yes," he said with enthusiasm. "Lions are big and strong. They always win in fights."

Jasmine nodded, impressed. "Are you going to put glue and ground glass on the string?"

"Lots of it. I'm going to the field tomorrow. Fight with other kites. I'll win." He beamed, then sobered. "I don't like those native boys. They always make fun of me. I'm a *blanda*, they say and I must go away."

Jasmine said, "I know some natives don't like us." She was going to tell Walter about *Merdeka*, but he would not know what she was talking about. She changed the subject. "Can I come to see the kite fight?"

"Yes, tomorrow after dinner."

"Wait for me."

"All right," he said, and started on the lion's mane using black crepe paper. She handed things to him, and silently they worked till the kite was finished. Jasmine decided to get Sari to come see the kite fight.

The next day, after Jasmine sneaked out of the bedroom, careful not to wake the others from their naps, she found Sari in the yard. They walked to the field, where they found Walter already rigging up the kite.

"It sure is big," Sari admired.

Jasmine nodded. It had to be the best kite flying that day. There were other kites already up in the sky, belonging to native boys. One of the kites was impressive, Jasmine had to admit. It was a dragon, yellow and brown, lurking threateningly overhead.

Soon Walter's kite was up too. It swayed proudly high up in the sky, its long tail swishing fiercely, challenging all other kites, even the dragon one, which came ominously close.

"Look out!" Sari shouted, startling Jasmine.

Sari was obviously not as confident as Walter about the lion's invincibility, but he brazenly approached the challenging kite.

Then the unbelievable happened. The string of the dragon kite touched the lion's string. There was a brief, cutting struggle in which Walter vigorously pulled his string up and down, and before their incredulous eyes their own string snapped.

They could hear shouts of glee, then a clear voice, "*Blandas*, go home!"

Walter said an ugly word, which made Jasmine wince. The native boys had more glue and glass on their kite string, and had won the war. The lion kite came down, and the native boys celebrated with shouting and jeering. Then there was a single loud yell, "*Merdeka!*"

"Sounds like Marto." Jasmine forgot the kite for a moment, as she looked at Sari.

Sari nodded, but Walter just shook his head sadly, and looked about to cry.

Suddenly Jasmine thought of the men around the fire, planning to go to war against the Dutch, and hoping to get rid of them. She shivered, and remembered what Marto had said about the Lion, Holland's symbol.

The Kites

All three stared up to where the kite descended mournfully, zigzagging in its last chance to imitate the first proud movements. The tail dragged limply, and then it disappeared behind the trees.

Jasmine looked at Walter, who had tears in his eyes. Without a word he walked away.

"Aren't you going to look for it?" Jasmine called after him. "We can fix the string."

"Maybe later," he said and left.

"I'm going to look for it," Jasmine said. She clenched her teeth. She would not give up without a fight!

She started walking, not waiting to see if Sari followed. Then she remembered that it had to be almost time for the others to get up from their naps. She hesitated. She did not want to upset Mama. "We'll look later," she informed Sari, and turned to walk back to the house.

"Come and get me," Sari said.

"All right."

"When?"

"I'll let you know."

Just then Mama called and she hurried to the house.

It was not until a few days later that Jasmine and Sari had a chance to look for the kite. They crossed the yard to the field, which used to be a large garden, but was now wild and neglected. In the yard the grass was smooth and short, the flowerbeds were circles, with plants neatly within their borders. There were a few respectable trees. In the field were pits, and rough stubble grass, while tough vines twined about the trees as if to strangle them. In this place every plant and tree grew crisscross over one another. Lianas, ferns, bananas, papayas fought for a place in the sunshine.

They walked far into the riot of trees and shrubs, but the kite seemed to have disappeared. But Jasmine was determined not to give up. She wanted to find it and bring it to Walter, to cheer him up. He loved the kite with the long lion's tail as much as she did.

She thought again of the kite fight. It really *had* been a war. *Merdeka* and *Blanda*? The sun burned as they walked and searched, but still there was no kite.

"Let's just forget about it," Sari said, but Jasmine was not ready to give up yet. She looked left and right, as they penetrated further into the wilderness, scratching themselves on thorny bushes. Jasmine's feet hurt from the stubble and sharp grass. She regretted not having put on her shoes.

Then she saw it. "There!" she shouted and ran to it.

"That can't be yours," Sari said.

It *was* theirs, but broken, ripped up. In many places it was pierced through, by a pointy branch, a knife?

"Native boys," Jasmine said. Her throat closed up.

"Why would they do that?" Sari asked.

Jasmine swallowed the bitterness "They wanted to show us we're beaten." She picked up the crushed kite. "I wonder if we could fix it."

"I doubt it."

Jasmine had to agree. "It's quite dead," she said trying to make a joke of it.

The Kites

"Yes, quite," Sari said and giggled.

Jasmine did not feel like giggling. "Let's bury it here."

She was just telling Sari to stay with it while she went for a spade, when she was startled by a raucous laugh. Marto stepped from behind some bushes. It seemed almost as if Marto had been following Sari. Jasmine was furious. "Did you wreck our kite? You did, didn't you?"

All Marto said was, "*Blanda*, go home!" She stepped closer to Sari, and poked her finger into Sari's chest. "And you! You'd better decide where your loyalties are!"

Sari looked at Marto with dislike. "And you . . . you'd better be careful about what you *Merdeka* people are doing! When the Government finds out. . . ."

Marto snorted. "The Government will be ousted, you wait and see."

"Get lost, Marto," Sari said, and Marto disappeared into the bushes again, snickering.

"Come on, let's get out of here," Sari said impatiently.

"You go."

Sari shrugged. "I'll see you later," she said and walked to the road.

Jasmine walked away to get a spade from *Kebon*.

After she had dug a hole in the ground and covered the kite with dirt, she stood leaning on the spade, looking at the lumps of clay that hid the broken kite, which would never fly again.

Jasmine did not know how long she had been leaning on the spade, deep in thought, when Yvonne called her to come in for tea. Jasmine walked away from the kite grave, dragging the spade behind her.

Chapter Six

Two Visits

November, 1941

A few days after the kite incident, Sari came to the Boys Home. She said she wanted to see the place where Jasmine had "buried" the kite. They were just coming from the bushes when Mama called. Jasmine told Sari, "Wait here," then she walked to the house.

Mama stood in the hall with the others, and she told them, "Get into your Sunday clothes."

Yvonne who hated dressing up asked, "What for?"

"We're going to visit Grocer Wong."

Yvonne pulled her fingers through her sleek blond hair as she got up to go to the bedroom. "Finally! Every time I go to *Toko* Wong he asks me when we're going to visit him." Ellen had already left obediently. She always wanted to do the right thing, although she hated knitting, and often balked at Mama's insistence that the girls learn this useful skill.

Jasmine liked dressing up for special occasions, and she liked Grocer Wong, who had always treated her kindly. When they were little, he used to give them lollipops. She looked at Mama, hesitated, then asked, "Can Sari come?"

Mama nodded. "I'm sure the Wongs won't mind."

While Sari waited in the yard, Jasmine looked for her Sunday dress and put it on as fast as she could. Yvonne and Ellen were still in front of the mirror. They looked pretty in their frilly blue and white dresses.

Since Mama did not like *dokars,* she decided to walk, and she said she needed the exercise. It was just as well, because with Sari the *dokar* would be too crowded.

Mama had accepted Grocer Wong's invitation because she wanted to make friends with people of other races. But she found it hard to do that with the natives. There was Doctor Suhardi, of course, who came to see them when someone was sick, but they never went to the Suhardi home. Dutch people did not associate with the native population much, only in the government and with servants.

It was different with the Chinese. They had come from overseas like the Carters. Wong's grandfather, along with numerous Chinese, was brought to the Indies as an immigrant coolie, but over the decades the status of the Chinese improved, mostly because of shrewd dealings and hard work. Many of the Chinese were store keepers. When natives ran a business it was mostly as hawkers or stall keepers.

Mama felt more at ease with the Wongs because they acted more like Western people. The Wongs had adopted many of

Two Visits

the Dutch ways mostly because Mrs. Wong was brought up in the Calvinistic-Dutch tradition, and spoke Dutch fluently. Wong himself was more comfortable with Chinese. But he was eager to please the Dutch so his *toko* was filled to overflowing with rice, sugar, flour, sweets, and all kinds of things he thought Dutch families wanted.

"He's probably the richest man in Tenang," Jasmine said to Sari, as they walked along Main Street.

"I know, but you sure can't tell by looking at his *toko*."

Ellen and Yvonne had joined them. Ellen said, "All the Chinese are richer than everyone else, and the natives don't like it."

"I don't think natives hate Chinese, do they?" Jasmine looked at Sari.

Yvonne grinned. "Sari doesn't hate the Chinese. Grocer Wong has given her lots of lollipops."

Sari looked up and smiled a little. "The *Merdeka* people hate the Chinese because they make much more money than *dessa* and *kampong* people. They can hardly wait for the Japanese to come. They think the Japanese will get rid of everyone but the native people."

"Do you think they will?"

"I don't think the Japanese really care about the natives. All they're interested in is expanding their Empire, something like 'Asia for the Asian' with the Japanese as leaders. But they can't ignore them, so they try to get them to support their ambition."

"How do you know all that?"

"Sukandar's family talk about it a lot."

Jasmine knew she was right. There were many stories in the newspapers these days about the Japanese. And sometimes Papa and Mama discussed this.

Ellen who went to high school, nodded thoughtfully. "Sari's right about that. We discussed it in school. As for the Chinese, the teacher said that they're afraid of the Japanese."

"Why?" Jasmine asked.

"Because Japan is at war with China, and the *Merdeka* people hate them. When the Japanese come they may free all the *Merdeka* leaders."

"Do you think the Japanese expect Sukarno and his people to work with them?" Jasmine asked.

"I'm sure they hope for it."

"They probably think three hundred and fifty years of Dutch rule is long enough," Yvonne said.

The sky had cleared when they arrived in front of the walled courtyard of the huge Wong house. They walked through the gate, and Papa rang the bell beside the massive front door, which soon opened, showing a smiling Mrs. Wong.

"Good afternoon! Come in!" She led them all into the living room, and seated Papa and Mama on a velvet sofa. Mrs. Wong had ordered refreshments and when the *djongos* brought them in there was tea, *stroop*, which was a cool drink, and cake. But there was also something that looked like slippery flattened balls of matted glass, which Mrs. Wong assured them was a Chinese delicacy.

Two Visits

The children had their refreshments at a table in the corner, and when Yvonne held up her slippery ball, she whispered to Jasmine, "I don't like it, do you?"

"I don't either," Jasmine said softly, holding her oval, translucent delicacy of which she had taken a bite.

"What are you going to do with it?" Sari asked.

Yvonne grinned. "Take it home, or sell it. I want to get rich."

All three giggled, and they were still giggling when Papa made a comment about the war. Jasmine stopped giggling, her slippery ball still in her hand. There they go again, she thought, and asked if they could go in the yard.

Mrs. Wong suggested they all sit outside. She rose to lead them under an arbor covered with bougainvillea on one side and *kembang sepatoe,* hibiscus, on the other. Jasmine sat beside Sari on a bench. They had taken off their shoes, drowning their feet in the thick grass. Jasmine sniffed the fragrance of *melatti,* frangipani flowers.

The adults sat in comfortable chairs around a table, and continued the discussion. Grocer Wong pursed his lips and looked worried, but had not said much. Mama was silent too, but Jasmine could see she was annoyed.

Mrs. Wong, who was more talkative because she knew Dutch so well, said, "I pray that the Japanese will never come."

Papa agreed and they got into a discussion about what the Japanese had done in China.

Mrs. Wong, who had relatives in China, said, "It was a shock to us when they started the war in China. Of course you must have heard about the incident at the Marco Polo Bridge in 1937. By the end of that year the Japanese had conquered Nanking."

Papa nodded. "Of course they didn't stop there, and Japan had already taken over Korea and Manchuria and other territories." He shook his head. "And it seems clear that they won't stop until they have all of Southeast Asia."

Mr. Wong nodded, and looked grim. "*Japanee* bad for *Chinee*. Many troubles."

Jasmine and Sari walked to the other side of the yard. Yvonne followed. They walked to a passageway, and sat down on its raised edge. Not far from them was a culvert. Jasmine pointed at it then squatted beside it. Yvonne and Sari did the same.

"What are you doing?" Sari asked.

Jasmine opened her hand and held the ball above a slit in the culvert. "There goes a penny in my piggybank," she said, and dropped Mrs. Wong's delicacy. "I want to get rich."

Sari and Yvonne, who had put their treat in a pocket, started laughing. "There goes mine." Sari's ball disappeared as well, but Yvonne, who always wanted to do something different, said that she had better plans for it.

"What?" Jasmine asked.

Yvonne took her ball out of her pocket, stuffed it in her mouth and started chewing.

"Yuck!" Jasmine said. "I thought you didn't like it."

Two Visits

"Can't I change my mind?"

All three laughed.

Soon after that they went home, and Jasmine was glad. In spite of the fun they had with the ball snack, the talk of war stayed in the back of her mind. Every time she heard the word 'war' it was a threat glimmering at the rim of her thoughts.

The visit to the Wongs made Jasmine realize how many different kinds of races, and nationalities there were on Java. It occurred to her that there were two people in her life who were neither Dutch nor native, and who had an effect on her—Grocer Wong and Mr. Boon. She recalled Wong's kindness, so opposed to Mr. Boon's snide remarks about her hair, making her feel different, while she so much wanted to be like Sari.

She appreciated Grocer Wong, a Chinese, while she intensely disliked Mr. Boon, Ruth and Louisa's father. This was strange, because Mr. Boon was part Dutch. His father had been Dutch and his mother native, and even though he had not claimed Dutch citizenship he should be more similar. She concluded that it was people's behavior which made them likable or hateful.

One afternoon, a few days after the Wong visit, Ellen, Yvonne and Jasmine were bent over the cat basket. *Mata Hidju's* kittens had grown big. Mama came in and looked at them thoughtfully.

"You should bring one to the Boon's. Mrs. Boon wants one."

The Boons lived in one of the *kampongs* on the other side of Tenang from where the Boys Home was.

"I'll go." Ellen got up off her knees.

"Me too." Jasmine and Yvonne said in unison.

"All right," Mama said, but only if you have finished your knitting." She peered suspiciously at them, because she knew that her girls did not like knitting. Yet she kept to the strict rule that as soon as the girls turned ten they had to do five rows of knitting every day. A girl is not properly educated until she knows how to knit, she always said.

Yvonne and Jasmine nodded, but Ellen wrinkled her nose, and grumpily admitted that she had not done it.

"Do it now. Yvonne and Jasmine, you go to the Boon's." Mama walked to the dining room.

Yvonne and Jasmine left the house with a bamboo basket between them, the kitten mewing under the lid. Mopsy wagged his tail as he trotted along beside them.

They had just reached the intersection where the *passar* was, when they met Sari. She was carrying a basket with some fruit.

"Been to the *passar*?" Jasmine asked.

Sari nodded. "Where are you going?"

"To the Boon's to bring a kitten."

"I'll come too," Sari said, and they continued to the Boon house, which was bigger than the others. Thinking of Mr. Boon, Jasmine wondered why she had wanted to come. He was sure to say something about her hair. 'White and kinky', he'd called it once. Of course she should be used to that by now. Native and Chinese children often chanted mean jingles, "White hair, blue eyes, eh, eh." But the worst was when they singled you out. "Eh, eh, curly hair!" Having blond, curly hair was a disaster. But with Mr. Boon, it was the way he said it that made the difference. He was the only person who made her feel unsure of herself, as if she did not belong here. She hoped he was not home. Mrs. Boon was all right.

When they walked through the door, Ruth and Louisa shouted happily. Ruth took off the lid and picked up the shivering kitten.

Sari put her *passer* basket down and stroked the little animal.

"Give him some milk," Mrs. Boon ordered.

When Ruth and Louisa left the room, Mr. Boon came in and sat down on the *baleh-baleh*, with a loud yawn.

"Well, well, the Carter girls." The bamboo lounging cot creaked under his weight. He looked at Sari, and then at Jasmine and Yvonne. "Good friends are you?"

Sari nodded. Jasmine just shrugged, but Mr. Boon was not finished yet. Facing Jasmine he said. "How come you have a native friend? Aren't your Dutch friends good enough? Oh, I understand! You want to stay on the winning side!"

Jasmine stared at him. "Winning side?"

"Yes, the Japs are on their way here, and the Dutch will be defeated." He continued, as if he enjoyed harassing her. "Didn't you know that Japan has been expanding their territory for years? They're all over the Pacific, and even the United States is getting scared." He sniffed. "The Dutch have become arrogant. They really believe they can keep their Colony forever, but they haven't got much to defend it."

Jasmine turned away from him, wondering why Mama and Papa wanted anything to do with the Boons. Of course Mrs. Boon was nice, and both Papa and Mama did their best to get along with everyone. Jasmine shrugged again and joined the other girls.

While Mr. Boon had been talking, Yvonne had been busy helping Ruth and Louisa, who had brought a basket and a saucer of milk. They were watching the kitten lap up the milk.

Mr. Boon got off the *baleh-baleh* and left the room. Jasmine sighed with relief. Soon after they left for home.

As they walked through the front yard, and reached the road Jasmine said, "I don't like Mr. Boon.".

"He's all right," Yvonne said. "Maybe he's not a happy man. Papa said Mr. Boon feels out of place, because he's an Indo."

"He doesn't look unhappy. He laughs and says mean things."

"Maybe he's sad when no one's looking."

Jasmine, irritated about Yvonne's attitude, did not answer. As they walked on silently, Jasmine thought about what Yvonne had said. Was it really true that he felt sad because he did not belong? She knew Papa always spoke kindly of him, as he did about all the natives and Indos.

Two Visits

Sari left them when she reached her *kampong*, and Jasmine and Yvonne continued on home.

When they entered the house they found Mama in the living room reading a letter. Jasmine thought it was the same old letter from Holland, but Mama lifted the letter, and said with a happy smile, "From Aunt Hanna. She wants us to visit."

"I know she does, but when?" Jasmine asked.

"I'm not sure yet. I'll have to talk to Papa. He may not be able to get away just yet."

Jasmine was glad the letter had cheered Mama. Her mother's depression seemed to come more often lately. She sighed and went out again with Yvonne.

Chapter Seven

Mama

November, 1941

The *kentering* had passed and it rained every day. One gloomy afternoon at tea time, Jasmine sat on her hassock near the living room window. The window was wide and low, with flower boxes on the outside, in which *Kebon* had planted some bright orange *afrikaantjes* and purple pansies. She was glad *Kebon* was still working for them. He was always nice and chatted with her. She had learned most of the Malay language from him, because he did not know Dutch. Of course she still didn't know all that much Malay. He gave her flowers every time she saw him. She usually put those in a vase on a side table in the hall. *Kebon* worked for other families of course, because taking care of a yard did not take every day of the week.

Sipping her tea Jasmine listened to the wind and watched raindrops splash against the window. She could not see the other side of the yard. She held the warm cup between her hands, and turned away from the dreariness outside. The living room was somber too, yet it was a nice room. In the middle of the floor was a soft red rug, on which stood a low round coffee table, a blue vase in the center with white daisies in it. Smaller rugs were in front of the doors. Around the table were four low upholstered chairs. The floor around the red rug was shiny and dark. In one corner stood Papa's desk.

Mama had covered the walls with light beige wallpaper. There were several paintings; one a green meadow with some cows; another was a sea scene. All paintings were scenes from Holland.

Ellen, Yvonne and Danny had finished their tea and cookies and were leaving. Jasmine always tried to stay as long as possible, mostly because she enjoyed afternoon teatime, but also because sometimes she liked to listen to her parents. Today especially she sensed something important, but did not understand the uneasiness she felt. As her parents started talking, she watched her mother.

Jasmine remembered that when she was little she used to tremble in awe, when Mama was angry and glared at her with her green eyes. Her mother looked like a lady, with her hair done up in a knot at the nape of her neck. But today some hairs had come loose from the smooth knot, and she stroked them from her face with nervous movements. Her nose was slightly curved, her cheekbones high, her mouth a little too wide but well shaped.

Today Mama's voice was as dark as the clouds. "I was hurt because you seemed to care so much about your work. I used to be jealous of you for adjusting so well." Mama smiled faintly. "I know that's unfair."

Papa smiled too and Mama continued, "I remember that one time you made a mistake in your sermon. When you wanted them to stand up, you said, "Congregation, please wake up!"

Papa laughed. "I know! They were too polite to laugh."

Jasmine remembered her parents telling the children that Papa had to learn *Javaans* before he came to Java. At the Mission, the people did not speak much Malay.

Mama continued with a slight smile. "Remember our beautiful furniture in that bamboo house? I really got homesick then, and cried my eyes out, while you were patiently trying to understand."

"Oh, I did understand, but I think it was because you were expecting a baby, and we were in the middle of the *kentering*."

It seemed as if talking about these memories made Mama feel better, for she began to laugh. "I remember rearranging the furniture, but everything still seemed out of place. Most of all I resented having the legs of my fancy oak buffet and dining table in tin cans filled with water to prevent ants from crawling up. I often wondered what Mother would say, had she seen that bamboo house."

Papa observed, "Of course the houses of the native residents were no better."

Mama said, "Beatrice never complained, even though she lived in a similar house."

Mama

Papa nodded. "I think you felt inferior to her because she seemed so suited to her surroundings."

"And I was annoyed with her, because both of you were taken up by your work." Mama sighed "I wish I could have adapted to the tropics as well as you have." She shook her head. "Not only that, but I sensed something I couldn't put a finger on. The danger of war I can understand, but what I felt at the Mission was different."

"You should become more philosophical, like the natives."

"I don't want to become like them!" Mama grimaced. "It took me a long time to distinguish between them."

Papa moved forward in his chair, swallowing the last of his tea. He brushed cookie crumbs off his pants. "Pastor De Waard is coming soon. Maybe you can have a good talk with him again."

Mama nodded while putting some more Boldoot cologne on her handkerchief to wipe her face.

Papa got up, patted Mama's hand and went into the hall to go back to the work house.

Mama sat quietly a few minutes longer, sighing deeply. She still did not seem to have noticed Jasmine crouching by the window. She got up too, went to the doorway and called Djaidin to clear the tea things, then left the room. Jasmine followed.

For the next few days Jasmine thought about her parents' conversation. She was annoyed with Mama one minute, and the next sorry for her. Mama's stories about the Mission were always peopled with evil spirits and unconverted natives.

Jasmine had liked everything at the Mission, except Sukandar. She could still remember the dark eyes staring at her. She forced herself to think about something else.

The day after her parents' conversation, Jasmine found Mama sewing dresses on the dining room table. Dresses faded in no time here, and Mama liked lively colors, especially polka dots and flowers. The new dresses were of white material with light blue flowers. They needed new clothes for their visit to the plantation.

"Are the dresses almost finished?"

"I'd like to get this one done before Pastor De Waard comes for tea."

Jasmine went out into the hall. Yvonne came out of the bedroom, and joined her on the top step of the back stairway that led down to the lawn. Across from them was the dining hall for the boys and on the left and right the long dormitories. Silently they watched the rain fall from the gray sky. Jasmine always found comfort in rain. There was soothing mystery in it. She loved to hear it droning on the roofs, rustling in the trees.

Yvonne made a sucking sound.

"What've you got?" Jasmine asked suspiciously.

"A candy." Yvonne had one hand in her dress pocket.

"You've got more?"

"Uh-Huh."

"Give me one."

Yvonne rummaged in her pocket and handed Jasmine a candy.

"Where did you get them?"

"Took them from the dish"

"Mama will find out."

"She won't. She's too busy worrying about other things."

"Holland?"

"Yes, mostly."

Jasmine really did not want to talk about Holland, but she asked, "Do you think we'll go back to Holland when the war is over?"

"I don't know." Yvonne didn't seem to be her usual confident self.

"I like it here," Jasmine said, as tightness pinched her throat.

"Me too." Yvonne's sad voice made Jasmine feel worse.

"And Papa," Jasmine said, trying to cheer herself.

"Anyway, we can't go back to Holland now."

Jasmine almost said, "Good," but stopped herself.

They were silent for a while, watching the rain, but Jasmine was no longer enjoying it. She got up and Yvonne followed.

When Pastor De Waard came at teatime it was still raining, but the pastor's face was friendly and rosy. He was tall and had a lot of thick white hair. His hair was arranged as neatly as the papers on Papa's desk, and his pants were creased as sharply as the pleats in Mama's lampshades. Jasmine found him impressive, like one of the apostles in the picture on the hall wall.

Mama guided the pastor to her best chair, the upholstered beige one, and sent Djaidin for tea, *stroop* and the best cookies and cake.

Papa had come in too. "I'm glad you came," he said.

The pastor smiled broadly.

After Djaidin had left, Mama poured the tea, and Jasmine sat down on her hassock. She nibbled slowly on her piece of cake. When visitors came they always got cake. She pushed back the hassock a little so that she was half hidden by the drapes, hoping Mama would forget her presence. She was sure to send her out of the room today, because of Pastor De Waard. Yvonne, Ellen and Danny had left already. They found adult talk boring. Of course mostly it was, but sometimes you could learn things.

At first the talking was no different from what it usually was; about the Home, people they knew, the church, the war and the weather.

Papa helped himself to another cup of tea, and took a cookie.

The pastor stirred sugar in his second cup of tea, and then he said, "I understand that you've not been feeling well lately."

Mama nodded, and told him about everything that bothered her, the heat, her headaches, her worries about the war, and the relatives in Holland.

The pastor had listened attentively, then he asked, "Did it take you long to adjust to Java when you first came?"

Mama

Mama said, "Yes, a long time. I was homesick, and felt uncomfortable with the native people although they were all very kind. Yet there was a lot on the spiritual level that I sensed as being evil, and I think that was because of the animistic beliefs of so many of the people."

The pastor nodded gravely. "You're quite right. Even though they profess to be Muslims and even Christians, they still hang on to the old beliefs."

Papa said, "I enjoyed my work on the Mission and felt needed there. So of course I preferred to stay because I liked not only the work but the country as well."

Jasmine was happy he had said that, and it gave her hope that they would not leave even after the war.

Mama smiled sadly. "I should have been over that by now after so many years."

Pastor De Waard nodded. "What you should do is go to the mountains, stay for a few weeks in a holiday cottage. That will give you a break."

"At this time of year?" Mama asked. "It would be much too damp."

Papa's face lit up. "An excellent idea! The *pondoks* all have a stove, and we can burn wood."

The pastor nodded, satisfied. "Mrs. Carter, I'll keep you in my prayers, and perhaps we could pray together."

But Mama had apparently not finished explaining how she felt. She said that what actually bothered her most was that she had no news of her family in Holland, and that she was afraid of a Japanese invasion here in the Indies while they had thought to have escaped the 'Teutonic barbarians', as some newspapers had labeled the Germans.

At this the pastor raised himself up and forward in his chair with slow, solemn movements, and began to speak in the same slow, lofty way he did when he preached. "*Mevrouw* Carter." He paused. Jasmine held her breath. His head stretched up as if he was trying to touch the ceiling. He looked straight at Mama. Each word came out with emphasis. "If God wants you to go back to Holland, it will come to pass, even if he has to unleash another war for it." He looked at Mama, his head moving in a friendly nod, and then he brought it closer to his shoulders again.

Jasmine's body sagged too. She could not arrange her thoughts in proper order. It seemed incredible. She didn't believe God would unleash another war. It was bad enough there was war in Holland. But here? Also, God would have a problem, for which prayer would he answer? Jasmine was praying to stay on Java, and Mama prayed to go to Holland.

Mama had straightened her body and took the handkerchief from her mouth, and Jasmine was surprised to see her smile.

"I know I don't have much faith," Mama said.

"We all lack faith, but I'm sure everything will turn out well, you'll see."

They exchanged a few more words until the Pastor said he had to leave. He prayed earnestly for recovery for Mama, and also for protection against all enemies.

Jasmine could tell that the pastor's statements about God, war and Holland had comforted Mama perhaps just as much as the prayer, for when he got up to leave, Mama shook his hand firmly, smiled and thanked him.

It was strange that the prospect of a war could cheer Mama. The very idea of war here on Java became more frightening. Papa had a few big books about wars, with gruesome pictures of cannon, guns, blood and broken bodies. They were about the Big War in Europe from 1914 to 1918.

After the pastor had left, Mama went back to her sewing. Jasmine emerged from behind the curtain. Papa poured another cup of tea.

"You still here?"

Jasmine nodded, nibbling on her third cookie. Holland. She had to get it out of her, and quickly, "Papa, will we ever leave Java?"

After a moment Papa said, "I hope not, dear. Why do you ask?"

"Mama would like to go wouldn't she?"

Papa nodded.

A heavy rock lay in her stomach. "Do you think we would go back to Holland if there had not been a war there?"

Papa smiled. "I don't know. Don't you think we can leave it up to God? You must not worry too much about Mama."

They were quiet for a few moments.

Papa finally said, "It's stopped raining. Why don't you go out and forget about all this."

A Garland of Emeralds

Jasmine looked out the window. The sun was shining, and a rainbow touched the earth, then curved up to the sky. Talking to Papa had relieved her anxiety. Papa was right. It was more fun to enjoy life here and now than to worry about distant Holland and, she hoped, an even more distant war. Relieved, she got up, and at the door she called, "Bye!" and slammed it behind her.

A few days later they moved to the new house. While they were settling in Jasmine often looked longingly at the *kampong*, and wished she could go and see Sari any time she wanted. But Sari was usually busy with chores, so she did not have much time. Besides, Papa had said again the other day that it was not a good idea to go into any of the native districts because of those *Merdeka* meetings. And now Sari was sick, so they could not even talk at school.

Jasmine sighed. She really missed her friend, and hoped she would get better soon. Now Sari lived closer and she was seeing less of her than before. She romped in the yard with Mopsy. The front yard of the Big House was smaller than the one of the Boys Home, but there was a large arbor of bougainvillea. In the flower beds were *afrikaantjes,* gerberas and sunflowers.

She walked down the road with Mopsy. After a while she could see the *sawahs*, resting in a basket of mountains formed by three volcanoes, Sumbing, Sindoro and Merapi. The Merapi was the only active volcano. *Gunung Api*, Fire Mountain, the natives called it, and they were afraid because it sometimes would spit out lava, killing people. Often in the morning, the mountain tops were lost in the mist.

For the millionth time Jasmine wondered why Mama wanted to go back to Holland. *You should not be selfish, Jasmine.* She stubbornly fought the voice inside her. This was her land, and she never wanted to leave. She pushed the plans of the *Merdeka* people to the back of her mind. For now they could not go back to Holland because of the war. That was a relief.

Chapter Eight

Child of the Dawn

November, 1941

The rains came and filled *sawahs* to overflowing. This was a blessing which should have made Sukandar happy, but as he walked slowly along the path, his thoughts were troubled. His mind had been pulling back from the goal his parents had chosen for him, to become a leader in the *Merdeka* movement. When he was younger, and remembered so vividly the teasing at the Dutch school he had attended, he had wholeheartedly agreed with that idea. He had wanted the Dutch to leave.

He had come from the Mission after delivering the mail. The jungle around him, tumid with life, held its breath in a frightened stillness, broken by a roar far away. A lion? As far as he knew there were no lions on Java. It had to be a tiger. Whenever Sukandar heard a roar he thought of a large picture in school, where the first Christians were given to the lions.

The night mist surrounded him. Dreaming pines allowed a view of the lights in his parents' *dessa*. He decided to go to the meeting, for he dreaded facing his parents if he did not do so, especially his mother, because she would be annoyed if she found out that he hadn't attended. Both his father and his mother would be disappointed if he told them of his doubts. So he had avoided the issue.

Darkness deepened. A star twinkled one moment, soon to hide again behind a cloud. The evening wind brought coolness to his glowing face. As he passed the last house of his *dessa* Sukandar still hesitated. Not going to the meeting tonight, would be a significant action, for it would mean that one period of his life was over.

A sickly odor of dried fish, spices and rancid coconut oil came from the hut he just passed. On the threshold a woman sat behind her daughter, picking fleas from her hair. Children played with old tin cans and a rope. They stopped to stare at him. His steps slowed, as he watched this familiar scene. No, he was not ready to make such a drastic decision. Another reason for his hesitations about the meetings was that he wanted to pretend nothing had changed. He sighed, feeling like a coward.

When he came to the *dessa* square the elders had squatted down around the fire already; the young men stood near the *waringin*. Sukandar was happy to see Alimin and joined him.

Pak Suyono called them to order and soon the talking began again. Sukandar vaguely registered the same phrases and sentences he had heard numerous times. With difficulty he strung their meaning together, while he looked at each man in turn wondering why they were here, why he was here.

A voice predicted darkly, "We might all be exiled."

Many heads nodded.

A bolder voice in the dimness asserted confidently, "But we shall one day be free. Let the *blandas* go back to where they came from!"

To be in exile, Sukandar thought what would it be like? The Dutch exiled those native leaders who did not say yes and amen to all they said and ordered. It was amazing that they had even allowed organizations like the *Budi Utomo*, Sublime Endeavor, and the *Sarekat Islam,* Islamic Union. Aminoto said that it was all child's play. Aminoto's comment now came to him so vividly that he asked, "What was the purpose of the *Budi Utomo*?"

Pak Suyono scratched his scalp beneath his *pitjih*. "It was all for *Merdeka,* for Indonesia. As was the *Sarekat Islam.*"

"Why did the Dutch allow it?" Sukandar asked, now genuinely puzzled. It had never occurred to him before how incongruous this behavior of the Dutch was.

Aminoto, who knew a lot and had been involved in youth movements, said, "A short time after the Atjeh War, in May 1908, the *Budi Utomo* was organized, Sublime Endeavor. It was mainly a youth organization run by students. Its purpose was educational and social improvement, The Dutch did not object you know, for they have their Ethical Policy which aims at the same thing." He cleared his throat.

"Yes," *Pak* Suyono said, "but for us it was all for *Merdeka*. What our fathers began we shall complete."

"Certainly," Aminoto agreed. "But the worst struggle is still to come."

"We need more men like *Bung* Karno to fire the people," *Pak* Suyono said, his black eyes intense.

Sukandar was drawn into the conversation against his will. How he used to dream of becoming a leader like *Bung* Karno, who had ability to move the masses. Sukarno had hopes and many natives shared his hopes. His spirited speeches of nationalism and *Merdeka* had excited the people out of their indifference, only because rebellion had always been suppressed. *Bung* Karno the hero. *Bung* Karno who would lead them. *Bung* Karno was about Sukandar's age when he started to rebel against the Colonial regime. He was of princely descent, and his family had strongly felt the humiliation of having to endure the overlordship of a foreign people. He was now in exile somewhere in South Sumatra, because he spoke up. The nationalists could hardly wait for *Bung* Karno to be set free, for with him in exile everything seemed hopeless.

Pak Kromo's tired voice lilted its litany. "The dawn of our deliverance is drawing near."

Being a Child of the Dawn, did that mean dawn of freedom? Sukandar had pondered about the significance of dawn lately. It had never occurred to him to question his mother about being born at the crack of dawn.

A chill had come down from the mountains, and the old men snuggled closer into their shawls. The fire crackled crisply, and as Sukandar concentrated on the flames he felt again, as he used to, the throb of revolution in his blood. There in the flames he saw the former visions of his future, although these visions had become confused. *Remember, Sukandar, you're destined to be a leader.* His mother's words so often repeated. For a long time he too had thought he had wanted to learn the way of revolution. Now he had to admit that he had never really made his mother's ambition his own. It was like constantly trying to decipher the mystery of life, never quite succeeding.

All he knew was that he dreaded to disappoint his parents who had such high hopes for him. He would have to tell them though, for that was the proper way. But when?

He tried to find an answer in the familiar sight of the *waringin,* staring at the drooping roots which faintly reflected the fire. The voices intruded into his thoughts.

"A revolution may be the only way." a young man hissed, "but where will we get weapons?"

"We have our knives," *Pak* Suyono said. "Even the holy *krisses* and sticks could be used." He scraped his throat and settled more comfortably on his legs, then began one of the many stories of heroism he had heard of and experienced. It was as if he wanted to inspire the group with the same confidence *Bung* Karno had instilled in them.

"The Atjehnese of Sumatra were brave warriors. They did not surrender to Colonial rule until the beginning of this century, and they had no more weapons than we have. The Dutch lost thousands of men, hundreds of thousands of guilders. The Koran promises that the Faithful would rise straight to Paradise, and Allah had made known his intention that they were to get rid of the Infidel who had stationed themselves on the islands. But the Infidel remained the stronger, their *Kompenie* seemed invincible, but Allah was still with the people and told them to persevere."

There was a long silence. Sukandar thought that being full of an ideal was all right, but he could not believe Allah willed there to be violence.

One of the younger men interrupted his thought.

"*Pak* Suyono, how long do you think we'll have to wait for victory? And who is going to lead us into battle?" Sukandar looked at Sutan who often asked the same question.

Pak Suyono said, "Sooner or later *Bung* Karno and the others will be freed. He predicted a great battle in the Pacific Ocean, which would overthrow the Dutch. It is not Allah's will that we be forever ruled by white people. Why should a tiny nation, thousands of kilometers away, rule our people, who are counted in the millions?"

Pak Kromo nodded. "Our people were once so powerful that we beat the great Kubla Kahn."

"Now, of course," Aminoto said mockingly, "the Dutch are always much more clever, much more energetic than we are."

Pak Suyono nodded thoughtfully. "It's logical for them to try to perpetrate such an idea. That's what the Colonial system is all about. It could never work, unless the supremacy of whites over natives is promoted; unless it is proven that whites are superior to colored."

Alimin said, "Even if such an event in the Pacific should not take place, and our existing leaders will not be freed, I'm convinced that Allah has meant for some of our young men to develop into leaders."

"Indeed," *Pak* Suyono looked searchingly at the circle of young men.

Sukandar listened to the talk, pretending an interest he no longer shared. Being here had been useful because it had strengthened his conviction that he had no desire or intention to revolt.

From the woods came the call of an animal. Overhead domed a brilliant roof of stars. But the men kept talking, as if trying to cover up their powerlessness. Sukandar almost felt sorry for them, as the evening went by in tedious repetitions. His thoughts which had refused to fit in a pattern, now sorted themselves.

As a dog barked nearby and a few near-naked children ran screaming into a hut, Sukandar drew a circle in the dirt.

He looked up when Pak Suyono said, "Next time, Sukandar, I hope you'll have something positive to report. I expect it." The old man's black eyes looked straight into his with the authority of age.

"I'll try to bring a positive report at our next meeting," Sukandar said. He had thought to do this one thing: look for a letter to the *'nDoro* of the Mission, and find something in it that would satisfy the elders.

"Now I recognize again your spirit, Sukandar. May Allah go with you." *Pak* Suyono stretched his legs to signal the end of the meeting.

Sukandar barely heeded the instruction for the coming weeks issuing from the mouths of *Pak* Suyono and Aminoto, with the usual additions of wisdom from *Pak* Kromo.

Soon the square lay empty with only the *waringin* as a loyal, watchful sentinel.

The moon was high, full and silvery. The dancing rays, feathery light, played their games.

Could the power of the empire be broken? Four ships had sailed the seas to victory.

In spite of his certainty at the last meeting, his doubts returned during the following days. He again struggled with indecision, and still had not made up his mind about totally giving up attending meetings. It almost felt like treason if he did so. Yet he knew he was not going to do what *Pak* Suyono expected of him, that was to check the *'nDoro's* mail. In fact he hated the thought of doing that, especially because he loved his sister Lea, who loved the lady of the Mission.

Trying to forget about Lea, yet not ready to face the disapproval of the elders, he headed for the next meeting. Evening approached, and down in the valley the ripening rice fields sank down in grey. Twilight took over with a hush in which earth could only dream of a lost ambition, his fading ambition.

It was the hour of the *salat magrib*, the evening prayer, and Sukandar bent his head, wondering if he could find a prayer in his heart, and if the anger of the Prophet was against him for not being dedicated to *Merdeka*.

After the usual discussion about the present situation, Pak Suyono asked, "Anything to report, Sukandar?"

"No. . . No, *Pak*, nothing. The *'nDoro* is not a good source of information."

"Are you saying you will no longer try?" *Pak* Suyono shook his wise old head as he pushed his *pitjih* in place. "Has the spirit of the cause died in you before it has fully established itself?"

Pak Kromo mumbled, "There will be more like him."

Sukandar did not respond and soon the voices faded. His heart pulled away from the circles of wise old men and eager young men, to escape from the magnet of *Merdeka*.

Thoughts about the meaning of *Merdeka* persisted. Had there been freedom for the people before the whites came? He liked to think so, but honesty forced him to concede that even before the whites came there was oppression because native princes were ruling selfishly. Why a revolution when the Dutch Government had shown that they were willing to give them more responsibilities in ruling? Why fight if the price was so high?

It was true that the people needed leaders who would lead them to victory. But was he the right choice for this task? Every time his doubts came to plague him he heard his mother's voice. *Remember, Sukandar, you were destined to be a leader of the people. A Child of the Dawn.* Yes, that was it, a *child*. When you were a child, you thought like a child. Where had he heard those words before? But as soon as you were a man, you put away childish things. You went on to wiser things.

Flowers scattered smells through the air; the forest floor rustled with small life. But none of them not even the *tong-tong* beats in a distant *dessa* could tell him what to do. The evening wind played with the flame of the oil lamps that twisted in all directions. The fire in the center of the circle spread an orange glow over the people and up to the nearest trees.

Pak Suyono spoke again. "The Regent of Tenang will be in our *dessa* next week."

"A good opportunity to ask questions," said Aminoto.

Tenang? That was where Sari and her Dutch friend lived.

"Sukandar, what is the matter? You seem far away." *Pak* Suyono looked suspiciously at him from under his *pitjih*, his forehead wrinkled.

"I heard what was spoken."

As Sukandar peered into the darkness, listening to the mumbling of the men, there seemed a hidden threat that crept up then slunk away. From one of the houses came tones of a bamboo flute, a slow and melancholy song. Voices mingled with the singing. An owl, hooting from his perch in the *waringin,* looked down on the circles below, where Sukandar sat listening to the flute. He longed to go, but respect for his elders stopped him.

"My mother," Aminoto said, slowly, as if talking to himself. "My mother did batik work deep into the night till the candle burned low and her eyes failed, so that she could get money together for the school, where I could learn." Although I was glad I had a chance to learn, I had to endure verbal abuse from some of the Dutch students." He paused, as a sympathetic chorus rose up.

Sukandar did not join in. Although he had not liked the Dutch children, he had to admit that he should not consider them all the same. He suddenly knew that he had to come to a firm decision. Either he involved himself wholeheartedly into the *Merdeka* cause, or he should firmly withdraw and tell everyone his decision.

Aminoto looked at him searchingly, but kept silent. Then the flames shrank down into a faint glow, which barely reached the brown faces around it. Sukandar examined those faces in more detail, trying to discover what it was that gave them their passion for freedom.

The bamboo flute had been silent for some time. And still the voices rumbled on.

Sukandar looked up at Aminoto, when the other asked softly," Sukandar, where is the fire in you tonight?"

Sukandar bent his head, scratching figures in the sand. The fire had almost gone out.

Chapter Nine

The Pondok

December, 1941

*I*n spite of the Pastor's talk, Mama's depression soon returned. Like Pastor De Waard Doctor Suhardi said she should go to the mountains for a change of scene. They always rented a cottage, a *pondok*, for their yearly vacation during the long holidays.

Now it was December and it would be wet and rainy. The children would miss school, but Papa had written notes, explaining the situation. Miss Steen had scowled her disapproval. "None of us should go on vacation at a time like this." Danny had reported that with glee. Mr. Breda was more understanding, and so were Ellen's and Yvonne's teachers.

Papa arranged for someone to take over the care of the Home and Mama started packing. After school on Wednesday Jasmine found her mother bent over a large suitcase. Mama plopped down on the chair. "Jasmine, don't just stand there. Pack you clothes." She pointed at some empty suitcases.

Jasmine made a face then rummaged through the pile of clothes on the table. She frowned at Danny when he punched the pile. He seemed forever to be fighting something. She opened her blue suitcase with the pink faded lining, and began to pack. For a while there was silence, until Mama straightened up and stroked her forehead. She walked to the door and called the servants. Standing in the doorway she shouted, "*Lekas*, hurry up!"

Babu Roes moved languidly at Mama's demands for sheets and pillowslips. Jasmine looked at *Babu* and saw a glimpse of resentment in her eyes. Djaidin, on the other hand, went right away to get the picnic gear. Jasmine had noticed a few times before that some of the servants resented being bossed around. It was true that Mama was bossy and demanding, and occasionally shouted at them.

Papa came in, and shook his head. "How are we going to get all this in the car?" They had rented a car as usual and a native driver to go with it.

"It'll be chilly in the mountains and we need more clothing."

The morning they were to leave Ellen was sick.

"Probably malaria," Papa said.

Mama took Ellen's temperature and looked worried. "She has a fever. Are you sure we should go?"

Papa said. "I think it will be all right. We'll get in touch with the doctor there."

The Pondok

The chauffeur was waiting patiently in the driveway. He helped load things in the car, while Papa settled Ellen on the back seat. He covered her with three blankets. Even then Ellen shivered.

Jasmine sat between Papa and the chauffeur. The car rolled over the gravel towards the smooth asphalt road. They drove through a forest where huge spathodea trees flamed high above them. These tall trees were called flame trees, and had large red flowers.

When the road curved out of the forest they could see the volcanoes, rising from the plateaus. After an hour they pulled up one steeper slope, and reached the *pondok*.

Ellen still shivered. It spoiled the fun Jasmine had expected to have and she hoped Ellen would get better in a hurry. Going on hikes and riding ponies was always part of their holiday.

The *pondok* was one of a group of holiday cottages, which formed a square. There was a main building where you could use a telephone and borrow things. The *pondok* was a long bamboo and wood building, with verandas running along the front and back, with the bedrooms opening out onto the front and the living and dining rooms onto the back. The bedrooms were small, with bunk beds.

The car stopped at the front veranda, and Papa took Ellen in first. She was shivering more than ever, and he laid her on one of the lower bunks, covering her with blankets. They didn't need *klambus* in the mountains. Mama came in the bedroom with a glass of water. Ellen's teeth chattered against the edge of the glass Mama held against her mouth.

"Go and help with the rest of the luggage, Jasmine."

Jasmine went outside where Yvonne was unloading suitcases and bundles. When everything was in the house, they sat down in the living room, which had a fireplace. *Kokkie Noenoeng* came in with tea things. This was her task now that Djaidin had stayed home to look after things there.

They sat in rattan chairs around a low table in front of the fireplace, which Papa inspected carefully. "I think it's safe enough to light a fire."

Mama went into the bedroom to check on Ellen again, and when she came out some time later she said, "Her temperature has gone up."

"I'll call the doctor," Papa said and he left to use the telephone in the main building.

Mama sat down in a chair, her handkerchief against her nose. "There goes our peaceful vacation."

When Papa came back he said, "The doctor will come as soon as he can."

After supper the doctor came. He said it was malaria and gave Ellen an injection.

The following morning the alarm clock rattled on Mama's nightstand. It was early, but Jasmine got dressed quietly, not to wake the others. It seemed that she was the only one besides Mama who ever heard the alarm. She could hear Mama sigh deeply in the other room. She watched the sun flooding in, drawing a window with frilly curtains on the

The Pondok

wooden floor. Birds quarreled under the window, and a *grobak* rattled past with squeaky wheels. Although she was prickly with longing to go for a walk, she decided to wait and find out how Ellen was.

When the others were awake, Mama came into the bedroom. She went to Ellen first, who just woke up asking for a drink with a croaking voice.

Yvonne climbed down from the upper bunk.

Mama was stroking Ellen's forehead. Papa came in. It looked as if he had not slept very well. Jasmine's hope that they would have a good vacation dwindled. She spent the morning inside with Yvonne, who did not seem her usual cheerful self. Jasmine tried to suppress her worry. Was Yvonne going to be sick too? What kind of holiday would they have? She looked at the flowering plants climbing up against a trellis as if they could answer her question.

At teatime clouds came down and it became much cooler. Jasmine felt chilly and went to get a sweater.

When it grew dark Papa pumped up the kerosene lamps and lit them. He put pieces of wood in the fireplace, and as soon the flames blazed up, he held his hands over it. "Brr", I'm glad we don't live here all the time. It's as chilly as Holland."

Jasmine observed, "If Holland is this cold, I wouldn't want to live there."

Mama started to talk about warm summers in Holland, while Papa walked to the table to check the radio. A few moments later he said, "It's not working. It may be the battery or a loose wire. I'll take it to the caretaker." He picked up the radio and left.

While he was gone, Jasmine sat on one of the rattan chairs watching the flames coil around the blocks of wood. The sizzling resin between the fibers came out in tiny bubbles. Smoke swirled up the chimney, and the room was warm.

Yvonne had slumped in the chair. There were goose bumps on her arms. Jasmine looked at her anxiously. "You look awful."

Yvonne shrugged. "I'm all right."

Jasmine knew Yvonne was lying and Mama didn't believe her either for she pushed Yvonne's chair closer to the fire.

Papa came back with the radio. Jasmine put two more logs on the fire then sat down again to stare into the flames which threw an orange glow on their faces. Above them the hissing white flame of the kerosene lamp cast a white light throughout the room.

"Will Ellen be all right?" Jasmine asked.

"Of course," Mama said. "We'll pray for her."

That evening in bed Jasmine folded her hands and tried to pray, but all she could come up with was a confused mumble of words.

When she woke up the following morning, she heard Ellen breathe heavily, while Yvonne moaned, her face flushed. So Yvonne *was* sick.

Jasmine dressed quickly and went into the yard, where the fresh mountain air embraced her. The flowers nodded hello in the breeze, and high above her a bird chattered in a

The Pondok

tree. Dew on the grass pearled in the sun which slowly crept higher. From a *dessa* higher up the mountain smoke blew over the trees. In spite of her anxiety Jasmine sighed her contentment as she entered a path between the trees that led up to the *dessa*. She did not want to go too far from the house, and after standing for a while she walked back. Papa sat on a bench on the back veranda with a cup of coffee.

She sat down beside him.

Mama came out, looking worried. "Yvonne has a high fever too."

Papa got up and set his cup on the table. "I'll phone the doctor again." He left with quick steps.

Jasmine and Danny had breakfast, and the rest of the morning they spent in the woods. Danny waded in the brook, and got some stones for his collection. Jasmine picked wild flowers, until she had an armful.

"What do you want with all those? Build a fire?" Danny asked, a smirk on his face. This broke the fragile peace between them.

"None of your business. What are you collecting all those stupid rocks for?"

Danny grinned. "I like getting you to lose your temper."

Jasmine shouted, "You brat! Why don't you . . ."

Before she could finish her sentence the water carrier came by with his yoke and two pails of water. He looked at them, mumbled something in Malay, and made some gesture with one hand. All Jasmine could catch was *Merdeka*.

One of the reasons Jasmine had been happy to go to the *pondok* was that Marto wasn't here to remind her of *Merdeka*, and now this water carrier brought it all back again. She turned around with a jerk and marched back to the house.

The doctor was there and gave both Ellen and Yvonne an injection. Jasmine wasn't sure what it was, probably Sulfa for Yvonne who had pneumonia, and quinine for Ellen's malaria. He would come back in the evening.

The doctor came and went, giving injections. Every morning mist hung low over the trees, and Jasmine tried to revive her happy feelings by sniffing the fresh air, but fear stood beside her, walked with her. Mist clung in transparent veils between the trees, its long cold fingers holding branches in a deathly grip.

Every evening as she sat near the fireplace, Jasmine tried to pray. She often went to the bedroom, hoping to find the sickness only a dream, but found Ellen and Yvonne still turning and moaning. Mama said they were delirious.

Was it evening, was it morning? You lay down on the sofa while it was light, and when you woke up it was dark and time to eat supper. You weren't surprised, you didn't care. How long had it been? You crawled behind a rhododendron bush, trying to pray again. You had always been told to pray when bad things happened. Yet Jasmine could not believe that her mumbling "Please God make them better" were really an effective prayer.

Sinterklaas passed unnoticed. It was not until Ellen and Yvonne were better that Jasmine remembered. On the fifth

The Pondok

of December they always celebrated *Sinterklaas*, when some men dressed as Saint Nicholas and his servant Black Peter. When *Sinterklaas* came to visit, he always rode a white horse, with Black Peter walking beside him. Black Peter gave presents to good children, and put bad ones in a sack. Jasmine smiled, remembering how scared she used to be. It was silly that she always looked forward to *Sinterklaas*. She was too old for that! But it was fun giving each other silly gifts. Last year she had given Danny a clothespin to put on his lips, and she had written a long poem about talking too much. Danny had been annoyed.

For the next two days Jasmine kept her sisters company. They listened to music or to the news on the radio. The girls went for short walks, and when they returned one afternoon, they found Mama next to the radio with a pale face. Papa stood beside her, looking worried.

"It can't be," Mama said.

Suddenly Jasmine remembered the day the news came last year that the Germans had attacked Holland in the middle of the night. There had been hard fighting. Rotterdam had been bombed, and Mama had sat on her chair, pale and mumbling, "War in Holland! Impossible! The family!" Jasmine remembered the announcer saying that Queen Wilhelmina had gone to London from where she gave a speech: "Don't give up the fight," followed by the national anthem. Mama had burst into tears and her skin had stretched over her knuckles.

Now Mama looked just as pale and her strangled voice sounded just as bewildered. "The Japanese have attacked Pearl Harbor!"

"It can't be!" Papa sounded astonished.

Mama looked up and whispered, "War with the United States!"

Papa went out and Jasmine followed him. "I need to call the Boys Home," he said. When the connection was made, even Jasmine could hear the excited voice on the other side.

"Yes," Papa said, "we heard it on the radio. We'll come back as soon as we can."

In the living room they found Mama still beside the radio. She got up when they came in and said, "We're going back home!"

Papa nodded, but Jasmine protested, "What about our hike and picnic?"

"We'll have to forget about it," Papa said. "I should be at the Home now."

Jasmine started to say something, but suddenly she thought of Marto, could imagine a satisfied smirk on her nasty face, saying, "You are next!" Even with Marto far away *Merdeka* intruded. Jasmine forgot about the picnic. She wanted to go home too. To Sari.

When Mama groaned, putting her hands over her face, Jasmine sat down on a chair, and stayed as if glued to it.

Chapter Ten

The Yellow Danger

December, 1941

A few days after they got back from the *pondok*, the Van Doorns invited them over for tea. Miss Steen and the Van Waals were there too, but they never called Miss Steen Aunt Clara, or Mrs. Van Waal Aunt Alie. They were not close friends, and although Jasmine liked Mr. Van Waal, she didn't even know his first name.

Jasmine sat next to Yvonne who was still not quite over her illness. It was lucky for her that school was canceled because most men had been drafted into the army. This visit was a farewell for Uncle Ben and Mr. Van Waal. Jasmine felt sad, and she was happy that Papa did not have to go. He had a special job, and was exempted.

Danny listened open-mouthed. Yvonne was silent, and Ellen looked as if she didn't care. As for Jasmine, this visit focused all her vague anxieties into one sharp fear. People she knew were going to fight in a war. Yet through the palms across the road from the Van Doorn house, the river was quiet and peaceful, even while the radio poured out bad reports about the Pearl Harbor attack.

Jasmine was relieved when they left for home. Miss Steen joined them in the *dokar*. She said, "I can't believe the Japanese dared attack America."

Jasmine's throat felt tight, but Danny put up his fists. "If the Japs come here, I'll beat them."

"I'm sure you'll beat them with your fists." Ellen laughed, but Miss Steen pursed her lips.

Papa smiled faintly. "You'll need guns, tanks and bombs."

"So I'll join the army," Danny said, and this was so ridiculous that everyone laughed. Even Miss Steen smiled.

"The Japanese have lots of guns and bombs," Jasmine said, but she did not feel like laughing anymore.

"Who could have imagined it," Miss Steen said, as she crossed her legs. She shook her head. "I didn't think they *could* wage a proper war."

"Right," Ellen said, "We thought their planes were old-fashioned, their pilots bad, and their war ships so top-heavy, they would capsize." She sounded bitter, and Jasmine looked at her sister closely. Ellen was not as indifferent as she often looked.

More and more often the pictures in Papa's war books occupied Jasmine's mind. War was gruesome. And now they might soon be in the middle of it.

Miss Steen said bleakly, "I wonder who they'll attack next."

"Us," Papa said.

"They wouldn't dare," Miss Steen said. "We've been here for more than three hundred years."

As if anyone cared, Jasmine thought. Miss Steen was just trying to put on a brave face. After all, she had come back from Holland because she had been afraid that the Germans would attack that country. Although most people in Holland thought their country would stay neutral, some had believed that this time Hitler wanted all neighboring countries.

The *dokar* reached their front drive shortly after dropping Miss Steen off at her house. They continued the discussion in the living room. It seemed war was stuck in everyone's mind.

"The Allies will come and help us, won't they?" Mama asked.

"They might," Papa sounded doubtful.

Ellen observed, "The Allies want Java because of our resources."

Japan's declaration of war had been in the newspaper. It was elegantly stated:

'We, by the grace of the heavenly Emperor of Japan,. . .make known to our loyal and courageous subjects that we herewith declare war on the United States of America and the British Empire. . . .'

Just as elegantly, Holland had declared war on Japan:

'By order of the Royal Government I have the honor to inform Your Excellency that, whereas Japan has opened hostilities towards two powers with whom the Netherlands is closely related, the Netherlands considers itself at war with Japan.'

The Governor-General of the Indies, Tjarda van Starkenborgh-Stachouwer, had made a speech too:

"Fellow citizens, by its sudden attack on American and British territories. . . the Japanese Empire has consciously chosen a policy of violence. . . . Men and women, of whatever race or creed, I call upon you to fulfill a difficult, but exalted duty towards Queen and Kingdom, the Indies society and yourself, the duty of subject in time of war. . . ." He further pointed out that they should take part in the defense of all that made life meaningful.

They had an early supper, which Djaidin served in his usual dignified way.

Jasmine sometimes wondered what the natives really thought about the war. The servants still seemed as friendly as always, although it was hard to tell sometimes. She believed Djaidin was sincere when he said he wanted to protect them. A few evenings ago he had politely asked permission to enter the living room. When Papa said, "*Boleh*, you may," Djaidin came in, and squatted beside Papa's chair, asking for permission to speak to the *Tuan*.

"Yes, Djaidin, of course," Papa said.

"Djaidin wants to know if it is true that the *Kompenie* is at war with Japan."

"That's true, Djaidin. The Government has declared war on Japan, just like England and the United States."

"Is the *Tuan* going to fight in the war?"

"Not yet, Djaidin. Some men have to stay home."

"I will stay to help protect the *Tuan* and *Nonya* and the children, if this should become necessary."

"Well, thank you, Djaidin," Papa said. He seemed touched by Djaidin's loyalty.

"*Tida apa, Tuan.* It's nothing."

With his usual restrained dignity, Djaidin had risen and with a slight bow gone back to the kitchen.

Now Jasmine peeked at their *djongos* again, while he was serving with a calm face.

At twilight the horizon sombered to a purplish brown. Evening fell like a dark pall. They were sitting on the veranda, listening to the radio, which seemed to be on all the time, with warnings, and announcements interrupting music and other programs.

Everything was ominous and hopeless, yet the unreality of the situation gave Jasmine a slight touch of euphoria. It seemed as if it was only a story, something that happened in another world, for the evening seemed peaceful, with the moon just rising as an enormous yellow melon in the sky. A golden stripe slipped into the dark veranda, and the furniture stood ghostly. In the back buildings Jasmine could hear splashing of water, and the voices of Djaidin and *Kokkie* Noenoeng.

After Papa turned the radio off, Jasmine closed her eyes so she could hear the silence. She walked down the steps into the front yard then to the road. Far above the rustling palms the sky stretched, sown with brilliant stars, the other worlds. Perhaps this stupid war raged on those worlds. When she went back in, and Mama wished the children a hushed goodnight, Jasmine was close to tears.

During the following days Tenang was frantic with wild rumors about the Japanese who were most likely on their way to the Indies. Mama was restless, and often sat by the radio again the way she did when Rotterdam had been attacked. When they were told that the Dutch fleet was taking up a strategic position in the South China Sea, and getting ready to attack, Mama said, "Good."

"Don't be too hopeful," Papa said.

"Why not?"

"We just aren't strong enough to resist them."

"How do you know?"

"Bobby's father is in the Marines," Papa said quietly, and Mama's shoulders sagged. Bobby was one of the boys in the Home and his parents often came to visit.

The children were delighted about the schools being closed, but Mama was near to tears with disappointment. To her, education was almost as important as going to church.

Papa said, "It will only be for a while, and I can give them lessons."

As it turned out, Papa was too busy, and Mama too upset, but Miss Steen and Aunt Helga were willing to help. All the Dutch children, whose parents wanted them to have lessons, could come to the Boys Home.

A few days after the home classes had started they had tea on the veranda. Mama sat comfortably in a rattan chair, hemming a white dress with red polka dots.

The Yellow Danger

"You like red and white," Jasmine observed.

"Yes, I do."

"The Jap flag is red and white."

Papa laughed. "The flag of the nationalists is red and white too. Those must be everyone's favorite colors."

Perhaps because she did not want to be associated with the Japanese nor the nationalists, Mama said, "Actually I like red, white *and* blue, like our own flag. And orange. In Holland, when it was the Queen's birthday, everyone wore an orange pin or bow, and all houses raised flags."

Djaidin came to tell them they had a visitor. Just then Mr. Boon appeared on the veranda. Jasmine snorted and walked away, wondering why he had come. She had the feeling that Mama did not like Mr. Boon either; at least Jasmine had once heard her say to Papa that she didn't trust him. When Papa had asked why, Mama said that she had always suspected Mr. Boon of betraying Mr. Schumbauer to the authorities when all the Germans on Java had been interned after the attack on Holland. Mr. Schumbauer was a German who always kept to himself, living in Mr. Boon's *kampong*. Yet in spite of her feelings about Mr. Boon, Mama was always polite to him.

News kept filling the air like the rushing of far away battles. Propaganda films in cinemas showed fleet and air maneuvers, and fortifications. It all looked very impressive: Brewster fighters circling in above a squadron of war ships, then being shot down like ducks by the Zeros. This went on in many battle areas. In Tandjong Priok, the harbor of Batavia, machine guns were set up, trenches dug, barbed wire and pointy bamboos put in place. There were American warships in the harbors, submarines active in the South China Sea. There was talk about setting up a Red Cross center, and drills were organized in case of an attack. Most people now were sure that the Japanese would attack all the countries south of Japan, since they had already gotten hold of Korea as well as large parts of China.

Jasmine had not seen Sari and wondered what her friend thought of all this. All she knew was that she needed Sari's friendship more than ever. She met her one morning when Sari returned from the *passar.*

Her friend seemed preoccupied, and Jasmine asked, "Are you worried about the war?"

Sari nodded, then burst out, "Marto is really getting to me! Every time I see her she calls me a traitor. A traitor to what? It's not my fault that the Japs are at war!"

Jasmine felt sorry for her, and changed the subject. "Are you getting lessons?"

Sari shook her head. "No, there's no one to teach me."

Jasmine found nothing more to say, and after she had left Sari at the *kampong,* she went home.

Chapter Eleven

The Mission

December, 1941

Mama hated the market, so *Kokkie* Noenoeng usually went to the *passar*. But *Kokkie* often came home with wilted vegetables, no matter how often Mama told her to buy fresh, even if it cost more. So Mama sometimes went herself. Jasmine loved the *passar* with its pungent smells and familiar noises. When they arrived, Mama wrinkled her nose, but Jasmine looked around eagerly.

There was a feeling of togetherness. The vendors, mostly women, had spread their wares out in front of them, either on tables or on the ground: bananas, *lombok,* which were Spanish peppers, citrus fruit, and all kinds of vegetables. To Jasmine's chagrin Mrs. Van Waal was there. The lady's endless talk about war always set Jasmine's teeth on edge. Mama was fingering a bunch of small bananas, when Mrs. Van Waal walked around the stand.

As Jasmine turned she saw Sari with her mother a few aisles away. She hurried to join them.

"What are you doing these days?" Sari asked. "Still getting lessons?"

"Yes, but we're going to the Mission soon. There's no school, so we can all go. Aunt Beatrice wrote about trouble with the natives."

Sari did not respond for a moment, then she said, "We got the same news from my cousin Lea. You know, the one who works for your Aunt Beatrice."

Jasmine asked, "Did Sukandar go back there?"

"Yes. Don't forget that he still lives with his parents, although he's staying more and more often with Uncle Aminoto, you know, the one who's with the *Merdeka* group." The girls walked silently between two long stands of fruit. Jasmine stopped to finger a papaya.

Looking thoughtful, Sari glanced at her mother who was buying some lemons. Hesitantly she began, "My Aunt Sugi, Uncle Aminoto's wife, is in the leprosarium near the Mission. The leprosy has ruined her face."

Jasmine was shocked. But before she could utter a word, Sari continued hastily, "But she's getting better."

"Sukandar's mother?" Jasmine asked.

"No, a sister of his mother's. Whenever we visit Aunt Sugi we stay with Uncle Aminoto. His house is away from the *dessa*, close to the mountains. My mother says the leprosy is a curse because Uncle Aminoto is doing *Merdeka* work.

The Mission

Some of my other relatives say the leprosy is a curse because Aunt Sugi became a Christian."

"Nonsense!" Jasmine said angrily. "You really believe that?"

"No. Yes. I'm not sure. We may visit our relatives soon. They all live close to the Mission."

"Maybe you and I will be there at the same time," Jasmine said.

Sari's mother came up to them and smiled at Jasmine. "I'm ready to go," she said.

Jasmine said goodbye and hurried back to Mama who was still with Mrs. Van Waal. Jasmine heard the latter say, "What you don't look after you'll lose."

Jasmine wondered what she meant. Mrs. Van Waal was suddenly in a hurry. "I'd better get on with my shopping. It's almost noon. Bye now." With a quick wave she left. Mama looked harassed. "Good heavens, almost twelve o'clock," she said, quickly grabbing a bunch of radishes off a stand, and paying without bargaining.

When they got home, Ellen and Yvonne were in the hall and started yelling at Jasmine. "We found Mopsy dirty and whining in one of the back buildings."

Ellen shouted, "If you think he's your dog, you have to look after him too."

"Don't shout, Ellen. What's the fuss?" Mama asked tiredly.

Yvonne said, "We should give Mopsy to someone who will look after him."

"Nobody said Mopsy was my dog," Jasmine said.

"But you always act like you own him," Ellen said scathingly. "You won't let anyone near."

With a stern voice Mama interfered. "If you want Mopsy to be your dog, Jasmine, you must look after him. What you don't look after you'll lose."

Jasmine remembered what Mrs. Van Waal had said earlier, and she was sure it had to do with war.

Mama ended the quarrel. "Everyone go wash up, it's dinner time. Papa's coming."

Mama spent dinnertime complaining about Mrs. Van Waal. "She always talks about war, as if there's nothing else in life of any importance."

"Many of Alie Van Waal's relatives are army career people."

"Yes, I know, but she kept saying, 'What you don't look after you will lose', as if something or other was my fault."

Papa said thoughtfully, "Perhaps she meant that it's irresponsible to ignore what's going on."

Mama shrugged. "*Ach ja*, you're probably right." She changed the subject. "When does Beatrice want you to come?"

"As soon as possible. I got a letter this morning. Beatrice wants me to do a church service and also, she's worried about her mail carrier, what's his name?"

"Sukarno or something," Mama said.

"Sukandar," Jasmine corrected, and felt the same fear she had felt the last time she had seen him.

"Yes, Sukandar," Papa said, then continued to talk about Aunt Beatrice. "She's also worried about fanatic Muslims riling up the people, and Lea told her that *rampokkers* may

The Mission

start plundering stores." *Rampokkers* were natives who broke into houses and stores to steal everything they could find. They often destroyed things and they always worked in groups.

"Is it safe for us to go?"

"The Mission residents are loyal people."

Mama still seemed worried, which was no wonder with all the upsetting news. But when Mama started packing, she perked up. She always liked going on trips, and when she did not feel depressed she liked organizing things.

Two days later a stinking, smoke blowing steam train released them on a minuscule platform. A bell clanged, shattering the silence. The stationmaster yelled something to the engineer and after a piercing whistle the train moved away in short jerks, slowly picking up speed.

Jasmine examined the lonely station, which stood like a forsaken thing in the middle of a treeless patch. They got into the *dokar* which was waiting to take them to the Mission.

After some prodding by the native, the small horse started pulling them into the jungle along a road of red dirt. Jasmine loved the sights and sounds of this forest. Monkeys chattered, birds chirped. A lizard slithered into a pile of dead leaves, away from the creaking wheels of the *dokar*. Half-naked native children stared at them, and native men trotted by with swinging yokes across their shoulders, supporting heavy baskets on each end.

After they arrived at the entrance to the Mission compound, Papa paid the driver and they went through the gate.

The lane was rutted and narrow with tall eucalyptus trees joining branches over it. Boys with bristly brush cuts and girls with black pigtails played in the dancing light, then stopped to stare. Jasmine smiled at them.

One of the larger bamboo buildings had half walls, a thatched roof, and a dirt floor. The smaller houses huddled together like frightened children. In the shade of the roofs a few men sat chewing on their *sirih* quids. With a high arch they spat out blood-red saliva. Some women pounded rice in a big stone bowl.

From a long low building a woman emerged. Aunt Beatrice. She had not changed. She still held her body erect and moved stiffly as if she was afraid to break in two. She looked flat in her straight dress with a starched apron over it. Her mouth drooped in a downward curve, and her forehead was puckered into wrinkles. It was as if her whole face was in danger of falling to the ground.

"I'm glad you could come," Aunt Beatrice said. "There has been unrest in these parts lately. I'm sure it has to do with renewed fanaticism."

"Are you in danger?" Papa asked.

"I'm not sure, but I know that the residents won't do me any harm."

"What about this Sukandar?" Mama asked.

"I don't trust him." Aunt Beatrice took some measured steps, looking at her feet. "Lea is his sister, and she is a good child. Quite young, but a sincere Christian."

The Mission

They walked to a large bamboo house that stood separate from the others. It had a front and back veranda. Inside the house it was cooler. A young native loomed up out of the dimness of the hall. He was dressed like their *djongos*.

"*'nDoro?*" He waited politely near the door. He was speaking *Javaans*, the language of the region.

"Amin, please bring in the tea and *stroop*."

"*Inggih, 'nDoro,*" Amin said and pulled a rolling table from the hall into the room. He left it beside Aunt Beatrice. She lifted the tea cozy and poured tea in three cups, then *stroop* from a pitcher into four glasses.

Yvonne sat on the red rug, her forefinger following the patterns. Jasmine turned her glass in her hands and looked around. They had lived in this house when she was little. Almost everything was made of bamboo, but there was a low wooden table and a large buffet shimmering faintly against the back wall. Sharp points of light formed a design on the floor from the light filtering through the bamboo wall. The rest of the room was dim.

A young woman came in, and Aunt Beatrice said. "You remember Lea?"

Lea said, "I'm pleased to see you again." She smiled and nodded, then left the room again with Aunt Beatrice who gave her and Amin instructions about supper.

Jasmine found it hard to believe that Sukandar was Lea's brother.

It was getting dark when Amin announced that supper was ready. They went to the back veranda where he had set the table. Kerosene lamps, hanging from hooks in the beams, hissed white light. There were screens, but lots of insects had already come in. *Larongs,* flying ants, drew circles around the light, and some of them fell on the table, after they lost their wings.

Midway through supper, there was a knock on the screen door.

"Come in," Aunt Beatrice said. A native man came in on bare feet, carrying a bag and a box. Sukandar!

"Good evening," Aunt Beatrice said, not looking very friendly. "Have you brought the mail?"

"Yes, *'nDoro*," he said, and gave Aunt Beatrice a bundle of letters and the box, which was used for special magazines.

"You're late, Sukandar."

"Yes, *'nDoro*." Jasmine noticed that he used the *Javaans* word for lady. Having been born in this area, he must have learned *Javaans*, for here many people spoke both Malay and *Javaans*.

Sukandar stood close to the door, his bare feet flat on the wooden boards. Jasmine kept staring at him, until he suddenly looked right at her and their eyes held for a tense moment. Then they both looked away, Sukandar at the floor and Jasmine at her almost empty plate.

Her heart pounded. She looked furtively at Aunt Beatrice, who was still frowning, while she sorted out the letters and magazines. Jasmine looked up to see if Sukandar had left yet.

The Mission

Aunt Beatrice could find nothing wrong with the delivery, and seemed to regret having no further cause for criticism. Jasmine knew that mail for the Mission sometimes arrived torn and dirty.

"It's all in order, Sukandar. You may go, but please try to be on time in future."

"I will try, *'nDoro*," he said. "*Malam baik.*" Good evening.

Jasmine was sure that he had not meant a single word of his polite phrases and wished them all every evil. Yet Sari always kept assuring her that Sukandar was a good man.

Aunt Beatrice said, equally politely, "*Malam baik.*"

"*Malam baik*," Mama and Papa echoed together.

Jasmine said nothing, and watched him disappear through the screen door, down the steps.

It seemed as if Sukandar had left his threatening mark on the veranda. Jasmine felt a chill even though her hands were sweating. She reached clumsily for her serviette and dipped it in her finger bowl, almost tipping it over. She wiped her hands, carefully rubbing each finger.

Papa said, "This man seems young and innocent."

"Young, yes, he's only about seventeen, I think. But I have grave doubts about his innocence."

"What makes you think so?"

"Nusomo, the *guru* of the school, told me Sukandar had dealings with a nationalist group, and is still greatly influenced by one of his relatives, perhaps even his parents. They're so secretive, you never know for sure. Anyway, Lea said something about some relatives of theirs, who went to meetings where Sukarno spoke some years back, before that agitator was exiled. Perhaps they still have these meetings, who knows."

"Such meetings are forbidden by the Government, aren't they?" Papa had finished his dessert and sat back in his chair.

"I suppose so, but I'm sure they keep meeting in secret, in their homes."

Jasmine almost blurted out that Aunt Beatrice was right, but she stopped herself just in time. Mama would want to know how she knew about that.

They were all silent for a while, then Aunt Beatrice said, "How it's possible Sukandar is Lea's brother, I don't know. Lea is the exact opposite!" Aunt Beatrice licked dessert off her spoon. "I'm glad her parents are not such fanatics that they cut her off, but I'm sure they're putting pressure on her. That's why she prefers to live at the Mission. She has a small house to herself."

Papa shook his head, then said hopefully, "Perhaps she and you together can bring Sukandar to the knowledge of the Gospel."

Aunt Beatrice looked doubtful. "I felt uneasy with him right from the beginning, although I could not tell why. It's in his eyes, something. . . as if he's always watching me, waiting for something. Lately he's been coming late so often that I'm beginning to wonder what he's doing with his time. Sometimes he doesn't show up at all, and they have to get a replacement." She looked grim. "When I asked Lea about her brother, she said that he's a fine person. She's very loyal."

"I would be so scared!" Mama said, and looked at the door as if Sukandar would return any minute, transformed into an evil spirit.

Aunt Beatrice squared her shoulders. "I am *not* scared!" She seemed ready to attack twenty Sukandars. "They're no more than a gang of troublemakers, those nationalists. How dare they defy the Colonial Government, whose sacred duty it is to keep law and order." She paused a few seconds. "I'm certainly most happy that they crushed the rebellion, arrested and exiled Sukarno and his cohorts!" Aunt Beatrice attacked her dessert as if it were a despised nationalist, and continued, "Freedom they want! Freedom from what? Aren't all people free and happy here?"

Papa said, "Of course they have in mind political freedom, without white rule."

Aunt Beatrice declared fervently, "They should exile all of them!" She pursed her lips. "Sukarno can't do much harm now. They'll never let him go this time."

"Will they keep him locked up for the rest of his life?" Mama asked.

"If nothing out of the ordinary happens, I suppose so." Aunt Beatrice wiped her mouth with her serviette. "And I hope nothing out of the ordinary will ever happen here."

Papa stared sadly at his empty dish. "*Ach ja*, I wonder if we'll ever have real peace and harmony in the Indies."

As if refusing to hear another word about the nationalists and their evil deeds, Aunt Beatrice announced with finality, "It's time for the *kumpulan*."

Mama did not go to the church service. In spite of the fact that she liked traveling, she was tired. Or perhaps it was the tension that existed between Aunt Beatrice and her. Jasmine and Danny stayed with her, and all three of them went to bed early.

Dozing off Jasmine heard a *tong-tong* in the distance. Faint, hollow beats that bounded like rubber balls through the forests and over the *sawahs*. When the sounds stopped, she heard only the soothing hiss of the kerosene lamp on the veranda. It belonged in this bamboo world, together with the reassuring "*Tokeh*" call of the gecko lizard.

The next afternoon at teatime they all sat in a circle around the low table. For some hours clouds had grown together into a solid grey blanket.

"It sure looks black," Jasmine said.

Aunt Beatrice looked out of the window, then busily fussed over the tea tray.

Amin closed the last of the windows, which gave Jasmine a feeling of security. She liked rain, but when there was too much lightning and thunder, she was happy to be in the house. Now it looked like a storm was brewing.

Native men and women passed the house, the wind twisting their sarongs around their legs. The forest trembled, and the *alang-alang* grass bowed to the superior force. Lightening flashed like a spear. A bird moaned plaintively. A dog howled.

Lea came into the room with a stack of folded tea towels. She opened a drawer of the buffet and put in the towels. As she straightened out the things on top of the buffet, she smiled at Jasmine, and then looked up when there was another bright flash of lightening. She stayed beside the buffet when the rain broke loose in splashing streams, in the forest and on the roof. Waterfalls came down from the roof into the yard. The chickens had come up on the veranda.

And he brought in animals, two of each kind. Two by two they came as the Lord had told them. And God locked the ark, with all eight of them safely inside.

Jasmine felt safe.

"I hope there won't be *bandjirs*," Aunt Beatrice said at supper time.

"So do I," Mama said, and some of Jasmine's safe feelings left. *Bandjirs* often ruined *dessa*s, *sawah*s, roads and bridges, even sweeping people to their deaths.

It rained through most of the night, but in the morning the sun shone brightly, but the cheery morning was disturbed when Nusomo brought news that a small *bandjir* had destroyed the foot bridge over one of the brooks.

Chapter Twelve

Mountain Kingdom

December, 1941

Now that Aminoto had asked him to take over the working of his fields, Sukandar felt some release from futile *Merdeka* dreams. The work would keep him too busy to worry about meetings.

Aminoto, on the other hand, had decided to be more involved. His uncle studied the histories of other nations who had fought for independence. He wrote articles about it, and went to every meeting. He had saved enough money to be able to do that. Sukandar suspected that his uncle missed his wife who was still in the leprosarium, and that concentrating on other things helped him to forget his loneliness.

The sun had broken through the night mists. With the morning fresh around the house Sukandar felt a strong sense of purpose. Ripening rice fields glowed dull golden in the valley. Those belonged to others. Aminoto's property was neglected, and needed much work. While waiting for Aminoto to come and show him what he wanted done, Sukandar sat down on a flat stone, his fingers playing with the new bamboo flute he had cut. He had not played for a while, but now he felt the need for playing new songs. He had willed them to come, the songs, which he knew lived in him.

He moved the flute along his palm and thought of the dreams he used to have of some day becoming a leader. Of course he now realized that it had been his mother's dream more than his. Had that really been he, Sukandar, who had aspired to become a leader like *Bung* Karno, or like Mohammed Hatta? The latter had not been much talked about in meetings, because it was *Bung* Karno who carried the charisma of leadership. Mohammed Hatta belonged to the leaders who favored cooperation with the Dutch in order to gain independence peacefully. He was cautious and advocated a gradual process of education of the masses, so that they would be able to carry the responsibility of independence.

With *Bung* Karno, who advocated a drastic change, the time for caution seemed to have passed. The rebellious nature of the movement forced the Dutch to take their own drastic measures. Thousands were exiled to New Guinea, Sumatra and other places. Hundreds more were confined in detention centers. Yet, when mass arrests took place, not a single weapon had been found, no bombs, no dynamite, and no preparations for a military coup.

Of course these were not the weapons the Dutch feared. What they feared were speeches in gathering halls, and articles in magazines, much more powerful weapons, and the only means open to the people. Now even those were forbidden.

Sukandar had been so deep in thought about political matters that the song which had begun to be born had shriveled. But when he finally got up to walk to the small house, suddenly the song was there, and his fingers started to move over the holes in his flute. It was a slow, lilting melody, gaining in strength and intensity, until the final notes leaped joyously from beneath his fingers. It was a song of hope. He, Sukandar, king of this mountain kingdom, had created his own anthem.

The mountains drew a line against the horizon and the sun sprinkled the brook with thousands of sparks. He looked at the mountains, the place where he wanted to make a home. In Tenang he would not be his own master. Here he could proudly say, "Look what Sukandar has accomplished."

When Aminoto came toward noon, Sukandar told him, "It's a beautiful place. It will be good to live here but it looks so much like a wilderness."

Aminoto nodded. "I will help you clear the wild growth. You have the brook with plenty of water, so you will not have much trouble reworking the *sawahs*."

After the noon meal Sukandar stood with Aminoto overlooking the property. "We should start right away," Aminoto said.

With Aminoto's help Sukandar threw himself into the work enthusiastically and found enjoyment in it. Aminoto, on the other hand, seemed restless, and often talked about the plans of the nationalists.

He talked about Sutan and Alimin and this upset Sukandar because he had to admit that he missed the companionship of his friends, the sense of belonging to a group. He had to guard against sliding back into the *Merdeka* mentality. Even thinking of those meetings depressed him.

But after Aminoto had gone back to his house in Tenang, Sukandar began to feel lonely. The rains which filled the *sawahs* were a blessing, but when it rained so heavily, Sukandar had doubts about living in such an isolated place. They were after all in the middle of the wet monsoon with constant threat of *bandjirs*.

In the third week of December Sukandar went to the *passar* in Tenang. He had started out early, but the rains were coming earlier every day. He had thought of taking the bus which he had done with Aminoto, but he did not have the money for it. He had often caught a ride on a *grobak* or even a truck going to the *passar*, but none of those had passed him.

Halfway to Tenang, when the sun was near its highest point, he heard the rattling of an ancient engine struggling up and down slopes. With steaming radiator, an old Ford stopped beside him. The native chauffeur turned towards Sukandar. "Where are you going?"

"Tenang," Sukandar said, impatient to be on his way.

"Do you want to ride?" the man asked, waving a hand at the seat next to him.

Sukandar hesitated a moment, then got in beside him. At the rate he had been walking he might miss the *passar* entirely.

The Ford rattled into operation and the driver shouted, "What's your name? Where are you from?"

"I'm Sukandar. I live up in the mountains." He pointed behind him.

"I'm Sastro" the friendly driver said. "I am chauffeur for the *Tuan* Doctor. My *Tuan* is away and gave me a few free days."

"He allows you to drive his car?"

"He trusts me, since I've been working for him for many years. He assumes I'm going too visit my relatives."

"Aren't you?"

"No, although I do have relatives in Tenang which I visit on occasion."

Sukandar wondered why Sastro's *Tuan* Doctor did not have a better car, but he did not ask. Some Dutch doctors worked for a small salary so that they remained relatively poor.

Sastro drove his noisy vehicle into Tenang where Sukandar got out.

The *passar* was refreshingly noisy after the mountain silence. Sukandar felt himself immersed in pungent smells, and familiar noises with a sense of belonging. He walked through dim spaces, here and there broken by glaring patches of light.

Large rattling trucks arrived, bringing more vendors from the *dessa*s, men with shoulder poles, women with baskets on their heads, full of vegetables and fruits; young women graceful in their colorful clothes; older women with red *sirih* lips.

From a vendor he bought a portion of rice and shrimps in a banana leaf. He ate it with his hand. He had just spent another dime on a cup of weak coffee, when Alimin walked up to him. Sukandar greeted him, and after asking about his health he fell silent. He felt uneasy because he knew Alimin was still involved with meetings.

When Alimin invited him to come to his place and see his wife Talitha, Sukandar reluctantly agreed. They set a time, and Sukandar continued his walk through the *passar*. He was annoyed with himself, but he could hardly refuse. After all Talitha was his cousin.

When Sukandar entered Alimin's house that evening, there was a meeting in progress. He did not really want to stay, but out of consideration for Talitha he sat down on a chair.

Of course Aminoto was there, who had apparently been talking when Sukandar came in. Aminoto had just returned from Surabaya, the birthplace of the *Merdeka* movement. He greeted Sukandar.

Another meeting! Repetitive and futile words, which became disjointed fragments.

Aminoto: ". . .the Dutch . . . prohibited meetings . . . ."

Pak Suyono: ". . . in 1928 . . . a solemn promise . . .'One people, One flag, One language'. . . ."

Pak Kromo: ". . . People's Council . . . concern . . . radical nationalists . . . hostility . . .Dutch authority. . . ."

Aminoto: ". . . arrests . . . penalties . . . ."

Pak Suyono: ". . .maximum penalty . . .seven years . . . ."

Pak Kromo: ". . .inspired the people. . . ."

Words and phrases echoed in his mind as in a sinister cave. *Merdeka! . . . Revolution! . . . Insh Allah! . . . Allah Akbar!* . . .

Sukandar looked from one face to another, and wished fervently that he had not come. Having been away he no longer could stomach the idea of revolt against a Government which had done the best they could for the people. How could his people not feel grateful for that? He wanted to put his fingers in his ears, but that looked silly. To shut out the voices he concentrated his thoughts on his fields, which didn't help very much. He opened his mouth, starting to say something entirely different, but both Alimin and Sutan joined the chorus.

Sutan said, "Christians don't favor independence if it forces them to oppose the Government. They believe the people should respect their Government no matter what."

Alimin nodded and said, "The Dutch think Muslims are godless heathen who are difficult to convert, but they do have compassion for them." He looked at his wife Talitha who had been sitting on a cot against the wall.

Sutan's and Alimin's comments seemed irrelevant to Sukandar, for freedom and independence should have nothing to do with religion, but *Pak* Kromo apparently did not agree for he referred to Allah once more.

"Allah, the Infinite, Almighty, Omnipresent Being has been guiding us every step of the way and he will guide us to freedom."

Aminoto made an irritated gesture. Sukandar knew his uncle was impatient with *Pak* Kromo's constantly invoking Allah's involvement. Aminoto preferred action. "That should not be our only concern. We have to make some plans if we are to succeed."

Sukandar had always been close to his uncle, but now he looked at him as if he were a stranger.

Alimin solemnly stated, "*Insh* Allah! We will succeed!"

Sukandar suspected that Alimin had said that to annoy Aminoto.

No one had anything more to say, and the meeting broke up.

Sukandar appreciated Alimin's invitation to stay, but he refused and went with Aminoto who had more room in his Tenang house. He was sick of it all and felt as depressed as he had expected to be. He made up his mind never to attend another meeting, hoping no one would pressure him about it. He wanted to accomplish something different.

Not until he was back in his mountain kingdom did he feel the depression lift. It was such a happy release that he grabbed his flute and played his newly created anthem.

Chapter Thirteen

Bandjir!

December, 1941

Early one morning Jasmine and Yvonne sat on the top step of Aunt Beatrice's house. They had been at the Mission a few days and Jasmine wondered if Sari had come. When an ugly-looking *gladakker* ran up the path barking, Jasmine jumped up. Sari! She ran down the steps to Sari, who grinned at her.

Jasmine hugged her friend. "I'm so glad you came!"

"My mother wanted to talk to Lea," Sari said. "I hoped you'd still be here."

Sari's mother smiled. She was carrying Sari's brother in a *slendang*, a long baby-wrap, in front of her. "I will look for Lea. You talk to Jasmine, Sari." She walked towards the back of the house.

Fifteen minutes later Lea and Sari's mother came out of the back building. Lea said to the girls, "The *'nDoro* told me I could visit with you a while."

Jasmine and Sari sat beside Lea on one of the veranda steps. The rain had left a chill in the air, and Lea shrugged herself more closely in her shoulder cloth.

Sari's mother sat down on the steps too and loosened the *slendang* from her shoulders, laid it on the floor and put the baby on it.

Sari said to Lea, "Sukandar went to stay at your parents because we are at Uncle Aminoto's house which is very small.

Jasmine had found out that Sari's mother was Aminoto's sister. Sari had told her that her mother was annoyed with Aminoto for encouraging Sukandar in what she called unlawful rebellion against the Government. She asked Lea, "Are your parents still encouraging him to work for *Merdeka*?"

Lea shook her head sadly. "Yes, they do." She looked worried. "I hope he's not going to get into trouble."

"Are you going to see them?" Sari asked.

"Yes."

"Can we come?" Sari asked.

"If it's all right with your mother."

Sari's mother nodded her approval and Sari asked, "What about Jasmine and Yvonne?"

"Let's ask their parents." Lea went in, followed by the three girls.

They found Mama in the living room with Aunt Beatrice, who was knitting furiously. Mama looked sulky, and Jasmine wondered if those two had had a spat again. Mama and Aunt Beatrice did not get along, and Jasmine was sure it was because Aunt Beatrice blamed Mama for Papa leaving the Mission.

Lea turned to Aunt Beatrice. "I would like your permission to visit my parents and relatives."

"All right, Lea." Aunt Beatrice looked at Lea kindly, with a faint smile on her thin lips.

Papa came in. "Quite a gathering here. What's going on?"

Lea explained and Papa said, "I trust my girls to you."

Lea gave a light bow, and Sari and Jasmine grinned at each other.

Aunt Beatrice said, "You can certainly trust Lea."

Jasmine could kiss her, and then the thought of kissing Aunt Beatrice made her giggle. She told Sari, and Sari whispered, "I could kiss her too." Both girls burst into giggles as they left the room.

Sari's mother had put the baby in the *slendang* on her back again and said that she would start out to prepare Aminoto's meal.

They would stay overnight at Uncle Aminoto's house, and the next day to Lea's parents. Jasmine packed some things, but Yvonne didn't want to come after all. Jasmine suspected her sister did not feel like walking that much.

An hour later they were ready and walked down the path.

Jasmine was worried about staying at Aminoto's house. What if he did *Merdeka* things while they were there?

"Does your uncle live in his house now?" she asked. "I thought Sukandar was working his field."

"He does, but once in a while Aminoto likes to come back, at least when he is not traveling. He does that a lot lately."

Sari said, "He spends a lot of time studying too. He wants to know the history of this country and our people, so he can help the *Merdeka* cause."

Jasmine thought he was stupid to be involved in that, but she did not say so. In spite of her fear to go to the house of a *Merdeka* person, she felt happy to be included in Sari's family. She felt she was living like a native now by walking through the *dessas* and forests.

Uncle Aminoto's house was on a slope, not far from a river and with a brook running nearby. The path to the house was slippery in places. They stopped in front of the veranda, where Sari's uncle greeted them with a brief nod. Sari's mother came out with the baby, smiling widely. They sat down on the steps.

Jasmine felt a little more comfortable with Sari's mother than when she was in the *kampong*, and she openly admired the baby. He grabbed her finger when she held it in front of him. "What's his name?"

"Elijah," Sari said.

Sari's mother explained, "Our family always gives their children names from the Bible, and Elijah was a great prophet."

"Elijah!" Aminoto said. "Great prophets and leaders have always come and gone, and there is not much distinction between them. Take Sukarno. Some people on Bali believe that he is the incarnation of Vishnu, the Hindu god." He nodded gravely when they all looked at him. "Yes, whatever place he came where rain was needed, the rain came."

Sari's mother said, "We get plenty of rain here. We don't need to pray for more."

"*Bandjirs* can ruin the fields you and Sukandar have worked on so hard," Lea said. "Then you wouldn't want to stay here anymore," she added with a twinkle in her eyes. She turned to Jasmine. "I am always teasing my uncle, because he seems to try to be in Tenang, Surabaya and here at the same time."

Uncle Aminoto nodded. "You're right of course, but you know that I have to be in Tenang and Surabaya on business, but I do like to stay with Sukandar now and then." After a brief silence, he added softly, "And I miss Sugi . . . I feel closer to her here."

Sari's mother shook her head while pushing rice into the baby's mouth, as Jasmine had seen her do before. Jasmine was not sure why she looked troubled. Was it about Aminoto and *Merdeka* or about her sister-in-law being ill? The woman changed the subject. "You were fortunate you haven't had a *bandjir yet*."

Uncle Aminoto ignored that and disappeared to the back of the house.

Lea watched him go with a worried look, but Jasmine was glad he had gone. She felt almost as uncomfortable with him as with Sukandar.

They went into the house and Jasmine looked around curiously. There was a large poster on one of the bamboo walls. A man with a black *pitjih* on his head.

"Who's that?" Jasmine asked.

Sari looked up and said nonchalantly, "Sukarno. He was the leader of the *Merdeka* cause."

"Really?" Jasmine remembered Aunt Beatrice's nasty remarks about him.

"You won't tell anyone about the poster will you?" Sari sounded worried suddenly. "Uncle Aminoto could be in trouble if the Government people found out."

"Of course not!" Jasmine was irritated. Anyway she doubted the Government would care. Sari probably thought that Jasmine might say something to Mama or Papa.

Sari grinned, and Jasmine's irritation disappeared. "Let's go outside," Sari said, and they left the room, after promising not to go too far.

They went further than they intended, and it was dark when they came to a *dessa*. The houses had bird cages hanging from the edges of roofs. A few sheep and a goat lay side by side in a pen. In the center of the square was a *waringin*. On the threshold of one of the first houses sat a young woman. "*Malem baik*," she mumbled shyly.

"*Malem baik*," Jasmine and Sari returned the greeting as they passed. The girls walked away from the square, past other houses.

An owl hooted; a dog barked. The bamboo huts in the moonlight, the jungle, and the *tong-tong* beats, all seemed to be hiding a threat. Suddenly Jasmine was afraid. "Let's go back," she whispered.

"Not yet. I'll show you something." This sounded ominously familiar, and Jasmine felt a heightened tension. It was like that time in Sari's *kampong*. But she didn't want to be a coward.

The girls walked back to the square, and crouched beside a house. In front of the house was a fire shining on the faces of men. Another circle of faces! Mostly different ones from those in Tenang, but Sukandar was there and Uncle Aminoto. There were women too, some forming a straggly circle around the men. Others sat against the nearest houses or close to the *waringin*.

Yes, they were really there, talking about *Merdeka* of course. She wondered about Sari's fascination with the meetings, and why she was so eager to show her. She nudged Sari. "A *Merdeka* meeting?"

Sari whispered, "Yes, for the *dessa* people."

"Is that why Sukandar came?"

"Well, whenever he's staying at his parents, they expect him to go to any meeting wherever it is and since Aminoto is at his house, Sukandar goes."

Jasmine marveled at Sari's lighthearted comments. Sari knew that her relatives could be arrested and exiled.

Sari put her fingers to her lips. "Let's listen."

Aminoto, smoking a *strootje*, mumbled something.

"What's he saying?" Jasmine asked.

"The *blandas* have to go," Sari murmured.

Jasmine's irritation was now greater than her fear. "They're always saying the same thing. Can't they think of something different to say?"

Sari said, "I think they're just trying to encourage themselves since they can't really do much now." And, as if trying to make Jasmine feel better, Sari added, "One of the older men said that the Dutch have done some good things."

"How nice of him," Jasmine whispered sarcastically.

"Aminoto does not agree. He always says that the Dutch have offered us little these past three centuries."

Jasmine looked at Sari. She had said 'us' as if she agreed with the *Merdeka* ideas.

The men were silent for a while and Jasmine's irritation turned to anger. A wild longing to dash forward and shout took hold of her. This was monstrous! She was going to stop it! Then she realized the stupidity of that. She was distracted by a boy who shepherded three *karbauwen*, water buffaloes, into the *dessa*. A cloud passed in front of the moon. As she peered into the darkness she felt a hidden threat creeping up then slinking away. The fire crackled crisply, spreading an orange glow over the people and up to the nearest trees. But a chill had come down from the mountains, so that the old men snuggled closer into their shawls.

"Long live *Merdeka*!" One of the young men suddenly shouted. It startled Jasmine's attention back to the circle.

"*Insh Allah!*" As Allah wills, an older man said.

"*Allah Akbar!*" *Pak* Suyono's eyes rolled up so the whites showed.

Jasmine forgot Sari beside her. She had been watching Sukandar who got up, then slipped quietly away, leaving a gap in the circle. He disappeared into the darkness. Jasmine wondered why he had left. Was he not as interested in *Merdeka* things as he liked people to think?

The rest of the circle dispersed as well, leaving Jasmine cold and anxious. "We really should go," she urged.

Sari followed her, as she hurried back to Aminoto's house, her eyes filling with tears. The Dutch had to go, flag and all? Red and white was *Merdeka*. Blue belonged to the Dutch.

Jasmine could hear Mr. Breda's voice loud and clear. Where were the Dutch power, their might, and their former glory? Four ships had come to conquer the Indies. Now the Dutch did not have much more than a coconut shell navy. Not enough to defend them if the Japanese came. What you don't look after . . . .

Jasmine thought of Marto. She was beginning to fear her more than Sukandar. To relieve her uneasiness, she turned to Sari. "I'm glad Marto isn't here."

"Me too. Marto is becoming meaner all the time. I think her parents are encouraging her. They believe the *Merdeka* cause is a righteous one."

"What about Sukandar?"

Sari said, "I have the feeling Sukandar is beginning to have doubts about *Merdeka*."

"He's beginning to feel his cause is not as righteous as he thought?" Jasmine knew she sounded sarcastic, but she felt that Sari was right. She thought of Sukandar leaving early.

"I think so, and I wish Marto would give it up. She's getting more brazen all the time. Even my mother thinks so."

"Your parents know about Marto and *Merdeka*?"

"Yes, because they overheard Marto say she hoped the Japanese would come soon, and get rid of the Dutch. Marto thinks the Japanese will help the *Merdeka* people."

When they arrived at Aminoto's he was already home, arguing with Sari's mother and Lea. It sounded like a continuation of the meeting in the *dessa*. Jasmine wished she'd stayed at the Mission. She was happy Lea was here.

"The Dutch have done good things," Sari's mother said.

"Many good things," Lea agreed.

"But too little, too late." Aminoto said. "We need a revolution."

"A revolution will cost many lives, Uncle Aminoto," Lea said. "And you might all be exiled."

They were silent for a few moments then Sari's mother said, "I think you will have to count the cost before you start anything so foolish." Jasmine could hear the disapproval in her voice, and she loved Sari's mother.

"*Merdeka* will be worth the cost." Aminoto's face was grim. He pointed at the poster on the wall. "Sukarno was not afraid. He spoke his mind. "*Saudara, saudara*, brothers and sisters," he would say, "the time for polite petitions is past. We have become a soft nation, without a will of our own. Now is the time to demand our rights."

Sari's mother interrupted. "But what good is *Bung* Karno now, exiled for life? You ended up without a leader."

Jasmine was becoming frightened again, as Aminoto continued his impassioned speech. "I would rather die than not fight. I'm no longer young, but I will fight till my bones no longer support me."

Aminoto still looked grim when they settled down on their mats for the night.

Early the next morning as Lea, Jasmine and Sari were about to start out, Sari's mother decided to join them, to see her sister-in-law.

They arrived at Lea's parents two hours later. Their *dessa* looked like most *dessa*s. About twenty or thirty houses with tiny gardens, palms and bamboos. Bird cages hung from the edges of roofs, and chickens picked at worms.

Sukandar was sitting on a log in the front yard, playing a bamboo flute.

Looking at him, Jasmine examined her feelings. Sari had told her that he had dreamed of some day becoming a leader like Sukarno. Did he still believe that? He stopped playing and slid his flute along his palm.

Lea and Sari sat down on the top step with Jasmine in between them. Sari's mother had gone inside with the baby. Sukandar sat a step lower and started to talk to Lea. "How is your work at the Mission?"

"I enjoy it," she said.

"I can't understand how you manage to get on with the lady of the Mission. I don't like her, and I'm sure she doesn't like me."

"The *'nDoro* is a good woman." Lea insisted.

Bandjir!

He shrugged.

"Many think that the Dutch have everything they want and have no troubles in life, but that's not so." Lea spoke urgently as if she wanted to change Sukandar's mind. "I wish you could be at peace with the way life is. Remember Sukandar that love is the greatest, love towards everyone."

He nodded, but still did not seem convinced.

There was clattering of dishes inside the house, and children's voices. Sukandar's mother came out, and called them in for lunch.

After Lea's mother had served rice and *sayoer*, soupy vegetables, they talked some more, but Lea's father was silent and seemed overcome with some emotion. Jasmine wondered if he was happy about Sukandar working for *Merdeka*. Sari had said that it was mostly his mother who encouraged him.

When it was time to leave, lightning forked above the mountains, and thunder rumbled. A fright trembled through the forest. There was no breeze and the heat was stifling, although the sun had disappeared behind massive clouds. It's going to rain, Jasmine thought, and the thought of a possible *bandjir* disturbed her.

When they came to a *dessa*, partly hidden by clusters of bamboo, the thick clouds had piled up to form a dark blanket. Another flash and boom, then the rain broke lose, and pelted Jasmine's body like stones. The others were ahead of her, hurrying to the river and the bridge.

Half an hour later there was another sound above the deafening rain, a dull thunder which made the ground quake.

Bandjir! The river would not be able to hold the masses of water from higher up the mountain.

They labored on over the slippery mud, rain pelting their shoulders. Sari and her mother were beside Jasmine now and Lea a little ahead. When at last they reached the river, Jasmine stared in consternation. This could not be the river she had walked by this morning! The water was a strange yellow, dragging along green plants. Whole jungle trees, complete with branches and roots, raced past.

Sari's mother, holding the baby tightly, looked frightened. "The bridge is out."

Then Jasmine saw the lopsided pieces of the collapsed wooden bridge they had used earlier to cross what had been a placid stream.

"We'll have to use the next bridge." Sari's mother stopped and clutched the baby tightly.

Sari and Jasmine slithered further down the path. Suddenly the ground they stood on began to sag. Both girls pulled themselves up on exposed tree roots.

Then behind them Sari's mother screamed. They turned and Sari shouted, "Mother!"

The part where Sari's mother had stood had broken away more and sagged towards the wild river. With the baby in one arm, Sari's mother had grabbed the root of a tree, which hung dangerously over the river. She gave another scream.

For a frozen moment Jasmine thought, *the curse!* Sari had told her that many Muslims believed there was a curse on people who rejected the Muslim faith.

Then, NO! They were *not* going to die! She fell on her stomach halfway over the edge of the break. It crumbled. She reached down, could almost reach the baby's arm which was raised as if he wanted to reach her too. He was screaming.

Desperately Jasmine stretched her arm . . . a little farther. *If only I can reach his arm . . . .*

Then she felt it, as it swung up. She grabbed it and pulled with all her might. "Let him go!" she yelled, not even sure Sari's mother would understand. She must have for she loosened her grip on the child. Jasmine kept on pulling, pulling. She hoped not to pull his arm out of its socket.

Sari had gotten hold of her mother—pulling. Lea had rushed back to help her. A huge tree shot past and touched Sari's mother's foot. She screamed then started praying, "*Bapak kami yang ada di sorga!*"

As Jasmine crawled up the slippery bank with the screaming baby, she thought, I've got to pray too. "Our Father Who art in heaven. . .!"

Finally she stood on safer ground, out of breath, wet and shivering, with the screaming baby tightly in her arms. She glanced towards the river to see what the others were doing. A few minutes later Sari and Lea joined her with Sari's mother between them. The latter was totally exhausted.

Lea said, "Let's find shelter in the *dessa* we just passed."

It was a nightmare, walking through muddy puddles, clods of clay, uprooted plants and stones. Trees had been knocked down across the path, parts of which had been washed away.

When they reached the *dessa*, they found a *pendopo*, a half-walled shelter, where they joined some people standing around a fire, warming themselves.

Jasmine handed the baby to his mother, who hugged him fiercely, then she joined Sari and Lea near the fire in the center, their dresses steaming. Except for the crackling fire and the heavy droning of the rain, there was no other sound. Sari and Jasmine looked at each other. Jasmine blond hair and Sari's black hung dripping wet along their faces, Jasmine knew her hair looked darker when wet. She nudged Sari and said, "We look alike now."

Still subdued Sari smiled and nodded. "Good!" Then she hugged Jasmine. "You saved my brother!"

Jasmine, a little embarrassed, said, "It just happened, I wasn't thinking . . . ."

"You cared, and you prayed." Both Jasmine and Sari brushed tears from their eyes.

Beyond the poles of the *pendopo* the curtain of rain hid the forest and the houses. There seemed no end in sight, as if this violence had to continue into eternity, shaking the flimsy shelter, bombarding the roof. Jasmine felt defenseless in a land which seemed to reject her. She went to one of the half walls, but when the rain splashed in she pulled away. Puddles formed on the floor.

Sari's mother had slumped down in a corner, the baby on her lap. Her hair had come loose from its knot and was glued around her face. Jasmine went to tell her to sit by the fire, but she shook her head.

Bandjir!

Lightning flashed again and the *pendopo* lit up brightly. Thunder crashed. The baby whimpered, and Sari's mother called loudly, "Elijah!" She pressed the child against her breasts. *"Bapak kami yang ada di sorga!"* Then she slumped sideways. Jasmine, Sari and Lea rushed over to her. "What's the matter?"

Jasmine stared at the baby. His lips had slackened, his head rolled back and then she saw his strangely rolling eyes. She closed her own eyes. *"Bapak kami* . . . Our Father!"

When she opened her eyes, the baby's eyes were normal, as he looked at her, smiling.

"Mother!" Sari shouted. She knelt beside her mother, shaking her shoulder. Slowly the latter opened her eyes, and stared at them. Then she became violently alive. "Elijah! Is he dead?" She peered into the baby's face, then slumped down with relief and started to cry. Tears running down her cheeks, she said, "I thought he was going to die but I called on God, and my son lives."

"Yes," Jasmine said.

Lea folded her hands and closed her eyes. When she opened them again, the rain had turned to a drizzle, and she said, "We must leave."

As they walked away from the *pendopo*, the rushing sound of the rain was still in Jasmine's ears. Her dress clung limply to her skin.

She walked beside Sari who carried the baby. Her mother seemed totally worn out.

Again they waded through mud, and over uprooted plants and stones. The last clouds disappeared. When they finally reached the edge of Aminoto's field, they stood still. The pleasant brook had turned into a hostile river they stopped and stared at the ruined fields. Sari's mother put her hand to her mouth. "The rice! The gardens!"

The house still stood, but strangely wet and forlorn against the slope. They hurried on, and when they entered the house, they found everything intact. The girls helped Sari's mother undress and get settled with the baby.

Lea decided that they should stay at Aminoto's again, because she wanted to make sure everything was well with Sari's mother and the baby. Although the woman was cheerful, she had experienced a terrible fright. Also they were too tired to take to the road again.

The next day Aminoto contemplated the ruined fields and shook his head. He believed he could still salvage some of the things, but when Sukandar came he said, "I can't afford to start over. I'm going to Tenang and find work there.

It was late afternoon before Lea and Jasmine left to go back to the Mission. Darkness descended soon and Jasmine breathed in the evening air, reveling in the magic of the moon shimmering over the palms.

This was again the land she loved. Her senses were honed to forest sounds, toads croaking, insects buzzing, the squeaking of *grobak* wheels to chase away evil spirits.

Beside the road stood some dim shapes with glowing points of cigarettes. They could not see the faces, but heard a soft voice.

"*Pundi?* Where to?"

"We're going west," Lea said in *Javaans*. Jasmine had heard Papa say this a few times.

The soft voices filled Jasmine with a longing to always be here. In spite of the horrifying events, she felt included in the life of these people.

When they got home, Papa and Mama said they had been worried, and they shook their heads when Jasmine told them about the *bandjir* and Sari's brother.

Jasmine had trouble getting to sleep that night. When she finally did she dreamed about a violent *bandjir* and Elijah and his mother being dragged down the river. She woke before sunrise, disturbed by the dream which had seemed so real.

Yvonne was awake early too, and they decided to go outside. They walked toward the open field where the new day glimmered behind the mountains. In a spathodea tree a bird welcomed the first rays with a song.

Dawn drained color out of everything, and the landscape looked pale and dull. Grey sunflowers and roses waited for the sun to bring out their colors. A layer of mist rested on the land further away and minutes later the horizon was on fire, turning the bed of mist into pinkish fluff.

Jasmine stopped to enjoy the sight, but when she thought of Aminoto's *Merdeka* talk some of her delight faded.

"I hate to think they're going to chase us out."

"Who will chase us out?" Yvonne asked.

"Never mind." Jasmine didn't want to spoil the morning with *Merdeka* trouble, but the candescent brightness of the morning had faded, and the first shimmering of heat rose up from the fields.

The next morning Sukandar came to the Mission. He seemed as nervous as Jasmine while he stood talking to Lea. She told him, "the *'nDoro* wants to talk to you."

"You know why?"

"No, but she seemed annoyed about something."

Sukandar looked tense. "Probably because I quit my job as mail carrier."

"Why?" Lea asked.

"Because. . ."

"Because what?"

"Never mind, but I'm sure she's going to tell me I'm ungrateful. Just because she helped me get this job doesn't mean I'm bound to it."

After a moment Sukandar walked to the front of the house. Jasmine followed at a distance, while Lea went back into the kitchen.

Sukandar stood in front of Aunt Beatrice, and when he stayed silent, Aunt Beatrice said, "I am concerned about the rumors that you are involved in illegal activities."

Sukandar looked at her and it seemed as if he was on the point of saying something, then changed his mind. He shook his head as he said, "I have handed in my resignation, *'nDoro.*"

"I see," Aunt Beatrice said after a brief moment.

Sukandar kept silent.

"I believe you're only seventeen?"

"Almost, *'nDoro*."

She shook her head, and for a moment it seemed there was compassion in her eyes. "If you need money, I will lend you some. You could perhaps rent a piece of land, and begin your own *sawah*. You can return the money, when you have harvested. . ."

"That's not necessary, *'nDoro*," Sukandar said, as he looked her straight in the eyes. "I plan to find work in Tenang."

"Then I can write to the Red Cross people. They might have. . ." She shrugged. "All right then." And after a brief pause she said good-bye."

Sukandar turned abruptly and walked away, while Aunt Beatrice walked back to the house with stiff steps.

The next day the Carters left the Mission.

Chapter Fourteen

On A Volcano

December, 1941/January 1942

*B*ack in Tenang it was as if they'd come out of an enchanted land to a place she didn't recognize any more. Although there had been the fright of the *bandjir*, she now had to face all the anxieties about war. With so many things going on, it would be a strange Christmas this year. Mama thought so too, apparently, for she said she didn't want to get a Christmas tree.

Jasmine understood how Mama felt. With the war on their minds, how could they celebrate Peace?

"Why not get a tree?" Papa asked.

"It doesn't seem right, with the war going on."

"We should try to give the children a joyous Christmas. We don't know what'll happen."

Mama shrugged listlessly. "I suppose you're right."

Jasmine was relieved Mama had changed her mind, for not having a tree would be sad. She helped decorate the huge tree *Kebon* had brought in. There were more than fifty candles on its branches, and some gifts under it.

They went to church where a missionary from Magelang spoke about the importance of remembering what Christmas was all about.

"Congregation, with all the wars and rumors of wars, there is a need to reflect on the truth that Jesus came in this world to show God's love for mankind."

After church Mama and Papa shook hands with many people, but they all looked serious, and for some strange reason that made this Christmas special. Everyone experienced the same anxieties, which made them easier to take.

That evening, the candles on the tree, lighted by Djaidin, ignored the war and shone as usual. Jasmine felt peaceful as they sang *Silent Night*, and *Shepherds in the Night* as they always did.

While they were unwrapping gifts, Jasmine could not shake the feeling that they were in a play and the peacefulness of Christmas fake, in spite of the missionary's words and of trying to pretend everything was as usual.

They did not get big presents, because there wasn't enough money. Papa's income had been severely reduced, because the Boys Home operated on charitable donations, and people had barely enough money to survive. But Jasmine was happy with the diary she got. It was light blue. Ellen and Yvonne had gotten one too, Ellen a green one, while Yvonne's was pink.

Jasmine knew Mama kept a diary. She had seen it on Mama's nightstand, and sometimes had been tempted to read it, to try and understand her mother. Jasmine had noticed her writing in it more lately. Mama did not seem quite as secretive about it and even wrote quite openly on the dining room table or at Papa's desk.

Yvonne wrinkled her nose. She whispered to Jasmine, "I think keeping a diary is stupid."

Jasmine looked at Mama to see if she had heard, but Mama had her handkerchief in one hand and sprinkled some drops of the Boldoot Cologne Papa had given her.

Papa spread the tie Mama had given him over his knees, and Danny seemed to be happy with his book of war stories. It was one of those Papa had kept in his bookcase, but Danny didn't seem to mind, or perhaps he didn't know that.

When Christmas was over, the year floated towards its end with increasing rain. Sometimes it seemed the great Flood was upon them. On the other hand, Jasmine began to think they were living on a volcano which was about to erupt.

On New Year's Eve they did not have *oliebollen*, sweet dumpling, topped with icing sugar, nor chocolate milk. They could not afford luxuries.

Like many people, Jasmine was still optimistic that the Japs would be beaten before they reached Java. But just as many people accepted that war coming to Java was inevitable.

Some people referred to the legend of Djoyoboyo, a native prince, ruler of the Daha Empire who had lived in the twelfth century. This Empire was the forerunner of the great Modjopahit Empire in East Java. Djoyoboyo had visions of white people coming to rule for a long time. Then from the North the *Orang Tjebol*, the little people, would come and conquer the Empire of the whites. The occupation of the *Orang Tjebol* would last a *djagung* period, after which they would disappear, and the great native Empire would come into its own again.

Djagung was corn and a *djagung* period meant the time it took for corn to ripen, about three months. But some said that the word *djagung* was not very clear, and that it might have been *djago*, rooster, and roosters matured in three years. Jasmine hoped it was corn and not rooster!

Even with danger looming closer from the north, hope and optimism seemed to grow. That was strange because propaganda films shown in dilapidated native *pendopos* brought news about attacks and lost battles in many areas.

One day at dinner Papa and Mama talked about the *Merdeka* movement and about Sukarno. Mama hated all this, but that day she seemed more interested than usual, as if she wanted to learn what had caused all the upset.

Ellen said, "We talked in school about the way the Dutch Government has kept the nationalists in line. They have treated them like children. They'll never get to govern themselves. No wonder they started to rebel. "

Papa nodded thoughtfully. "Actually, it's amazing that the Government allowed organizations like the *Budi Utomo*."

"What's that?" Ellen asked.

"*Budi Utomo* means Sublime Endeavor. Its purpose was for educational and social improvement. The Dutch Government instituted the Ethical Policy, which aimed at the same thing. So I suppose that's why the people were allowed this leeway."

"It was all for *Merdeka*, I'm sure," Jasmine said.

"Probably," Papa said.

"If the Japanese really come, do they expect the *Merdeka* people to work with them?"

"I think they would hope for that, and that's why they'll probably free Sukarno."

"That would irk Aunt Beatrice," Jasmine said winking at Yvonne.

Papa said, "Tokyo radio has been playing the *Indonesia Raya* anthem, so . . . ."

Mama laughed in a humorless way.

Jasmine asked, "Do you think the Allies will come before the Japanese attack us, if they do?"

Papa looked doubtful. "They're too busy in Europe and the Pacific is taking second place right now."

"If the Japanese did come, it would be for only three months," Ellen said. "Remember Djoyoboyo?"

"Three months? Three years more likely!" Mama prophesied darkly.

The following week, when the rain came down, forming puddles on the road, Jasmine remembered how she loved to squeeze mud between her toes.

Earlier she had stared for a long time at the orange glow in the darkening sky. It was a scary kind of orange, not like a sunrise after a rainy night. Their own people were burning the oil fields so the Japanese could not get at them.

With all the anxiety about war she felt like pretending to be a little kid again.

Yvonne walked in.

"You want to go outside?" Jasmine asked.

"It's raining,"

"We'll only go for a while, like we used to."

They put on their capes in the hall and took off their shoes.

As they stood in the streams of water, Jasmine lifted her face to the raindrops. She looked down and squeezed mud between her toes. She opened up her cape, but when her dress was soaked through to her skin, she thought of what Mama would say.

Yvonne seemed to have the same idea. "Let's go in."

In the hall they took their capes off. Their hair hung in strings beside their faces, and Jasmine's dress was glued to her body. She took it off in the bathroom.

Mama came in. "Do you want to catch pneumonia?" She looked more concerned than angry. She rubbed Vicks Vapo Rub on them with a liberal hand, until Jasmine's skin tingled. Now she was only too happy to stay inside and watch the rain through the window.

The next day Jasmine felt shivery, and Mama tucked her into bed, where Jasmine shivered even under three blankets.

When her temperature rose Papa said, "I'll send for Doctor Suhardi."

The doctor said it was pneumonia, and he gave her an injection.

Jasmine was sick for a week and when she was finally allowed to sit up in bed, Yvonne came to see her. "I saw Sari and she wanted to know what happened to you."

"Did you tell her I almost died?"

Yvonne grinned. "No, I told her you went into hiding."

"What else did she say?"

"She wanted to know if you're still getting lessons, like poor me."

"Yuck! Did the Japanese come yet?"

"I'm sure you would have noticed," Yvonne said. "But the news is not good."

"What happened?"

"The Japanese attacked Sibolga and Medan on Sumatra." Sumatra was one of the larger islands in the Indies.

Jasmine's eyes widened. "They're coming this way!"

Yvonne nodded gloomily.

After Yvonne left Jasmine felt no better than the news, and was glad Doctor Suhardi came in with Mama.

"How is the patient today?"

"Fine," Jasmine said. "Can I get up?"

"I'll have a look at you, then I can tell," he said, and smiled.

After he examined her, he said she could get up the next day. He took his bag, and left.

Dreary rains took over most of the afternoon, making the yard float in a dripping gloom, enough to make even Jasmine depressed. But when she walked into the hall the next day, Mama looked happy with a letter in her hand. From Aunt Hanna.

Mama wrote a lot of letters to Aunt Hanna, especially since she could not send any to Holland. Mama liked writing. Perhaps that was why she had given her girls a diary for Christmas.

One afternoon Jasmine saw Mama's diary on the buffet. She was alone in the house. Papa was in the workhouse. Ellen and Yvonne had gone with Mama to Grocer Wong's *toko*, and Danny was with Carl Smid, his friend.

Jasmine picked up the diary and plopped on a chair, feeling guilty as she glanced at the pages. She started reading at an earlier entry.

May 13, 1940
Dear Diary,

Rotterdam! Those bomb attacks reverberate in my mind like thunder and lightning. I told Paul, "It will be weeks before we know if they're still alive." He agreed, but I have the feeling that all these things don't seem to affect Paul, but as for me. . . . Overnight little pricks of fear have become stabs of worry, all because the Lion of Holland has proven to be flimsy cardboard. Holland has been crushed under the harsh truth of German airplanes, tanks and armies. What good has mobilization done? Did Jacob perish in the army?

Jasmine fingered the hard cover. She remembered Mama's worry about Uncle Jacob who had been mobilized. They had heard later that he was alive, and a POW. She did not want to read any more. She closed the book and stared out the window, where the rain governed. She thought about what she had just read about the Germans attacking Rotterdam. Was it true that Holland had been flimsy cardboard? *What you don't look after you will lose.*

When the Red Cross letters from Holland had arrived months after the Rotterdam attack, Mama had shouted at the top of her voice, "All alive!" Then she had burst into tears.

Since Pearl Harbor, Mama had sat beside the radio again, hurrying through the housework between newscasts, biting out crisp orders to the servants. Jasmine knew Papa was worried too, although he did not show it.

When Jasmine heard footsteps in the hall, she hastily put the diary back.

Mama came in and turned on the radio. It was hard to ignore the disembodied voice pouring war news into their dining room. War seemed such an impossible thing. In school you learned about wars in the past, but they had happened to other people, and were nothing to worry about.

Jasmine got up and went to look for Mopsy. It had stopped raining. Mopsy followed her to the gravel road, from where she could see the *sawahs* and the mountains. Sometimes in the morning the mist hid the mountains. Today they were all visible, and there was smoke above the Merapi. Life these days was like living on a volcano, which could erupt any time. Still, the mountains made Jasmine feel better. She envied Sari who would always live here.

She walked away from the gravel road towards the *sawah*, then stepped onto the slithery mud dikes, water close to their feet. The rice plants were getting so tall, that you could hardly see the water. A few steps behind her Mopsy flitted back and forth, delighted with the muddy water. He was no longer white but there was too much on her mind for her to care.

She realized that a lot of her doubt had started after Mrs. Van Waal's words about the defense of Java that time at the *passar*. You had to take care of what belonged to you. Ever since that morning, and the quarrel at home about Mopsy, she worried about everything she always considered her own.

Mrs. Van Waal's words had shaped a disturbing image, about losing a war and having the land taken away. Was it true that they did not belong here, had only pretended the land was theirs? But how could that be? She was born here too, so she was also a native. Could some day everything be taken from them? It was unthinkable, but perhaps not impossible. Many things happened, things you thought could never happen, like a war. Why not? God could unleash wars if he wanted to. And Mama believed it too.

Jasmine began paying more attention to Mopsy. The dog had adjusted well to the Big House, after a period of yelping piteously when left alone. On Sundays, when they went to church, they had to lock him in one of the bedrooms with the shutters closed, but one Sunday he escaped and followed them to church. Mama and Jasmine had to bring him back and missed the service.

Mopsy was smart.

The children always fed him pieces of meat or chicken at mealtimes.

Mama said, "I'm sure he won't eat bread."

"He will," Jasmine said, and took a slice of bread from the basket, ripped off the crust and reached down to Mopsy. He took it gently between his teeth, and Jasmine pointed triumphantly, "See! He's eating it!" As she looked at Mama, Mopsy moved forward and sat on the crust he had dropped just as gently as he had taken it between his teeth.

Mama glanced down at the dog. "He's not as spoiled as I thought." She reached for the liverwurst and gave him a piece. Mopsy wagged his hairy tail, sweeping the crust back and forth. Mama burst out laughing. "Hiding the crust, you little fraud!"

Although Jasmine laughed too, she hated being outsmarted by her own dog. She picked up the crust, and felt like jamming it down his throat. She threw it in the wastebasket instead.

Mama shook her head and looked at Mopsy. "How can you look so innocent after such dishonest behavior!" Mopsy wagged his tail.

A moment later Mama's face grew serious when Bandung Radio announced something about the war. The NIROM and Bandung radios kept broadcasting all kinds of news every day, none of it good. Germans were still wreaking havoc in Europe. Japan was moving south into Manila, Tarakan, Balikpapan, and East Borneo's oil fields. The radio told them nothing about the Allies coming, or about *Oma* Van Noren and the others in Holland.

In spite of the war, grownups went on visits as before. Each family invited others to come for tea, but now that most men were away, there were mostly women. One afternoon many of Tenang's women visited Aunt Greta Smid whose husband was a teacher. He did not have to go into the army because he had trouble with his stomach. Usually Jasmine stayed home, but when Mama said Sari could come, she decided to go. Yvonne and Ellen came too.

As the girls walked to the Smid back yard with their cups of tea and cookies, Sari said, "Your mother looks worried."

"Yes, she's worried about the family in Holland and about the Japanese coming."

Sari said, "I'm sure your mother's family is all right."

Jasmine curved both hands around her teacup. A fly sat on the edge, then started walking slowly around it. When it came halfway she pushed it off and put the cup on a concrete ledge.

Yvonne said, "It'll be years before we hear from anyone in Holland again."

"Yvonne!" Sari said. "Don't be so pessimistic!" She grinned, and Jasmine knew Sari did not really understand what it was like to have relatives so far away and in danger.

Yvonne said, "Germans wouldn't have gone through all this trouble to get Holland, then retreat. Besides, the Allies can't rebuild a decent army in a few weeks."

Jasmine was happy when Mama called them to leave. On the way she told the girls to go to Grocer Wong's store to get some flour. When they got there he did not look too happy. "War bad," he said. "*Japanee* come here—*Chinee* bad off."

On the way back home the girls decided to take another way home. This took them past the Van Doorn house and the swimming pool. They had to cross a *sawah*. One after another they balanced over the slippery dikes. The sun shone brightly on the plants, and a frog dived into the water. Here in the *sawah* Jasmine could forget about war and her constant worry about losing Mopsy and having to leave Java. She began to feel the old sense of belonging, and was more optimistic about the future, until she slipped and one foot went down into the water. There was a sharp pain and she yelped.

Yvonne helped her out and gasped when she saw the bloody gash in Jasmine's foot. With Jasmine limping between her sisters, the girls finally arrived home.

Although Mama looked worried, she still delivered the expected little speech. "Why do you always have to go into those dirty *sawahs*?" But her concern softened the sting. She made Jasmine sit on a lounging chair.

Still on the chair the next day, Jasmine was listening to Ellen's record *'Oh, Mammy Nye'*, blaring in the hall, when

Sari showed up. Sari smiled as she listened for a moment, but then threw a glance at the house. She looked anxious.

"What's the matter?" Jasmine asked.

After another quick glance at the house, Sari said, "There was another meeting last night and Marto was there. Afterwards she came to my house, and called me a traitor."

"Why would she come to your house? Were your parents there?"

"No, if they had been, Marto wouldn't have dared."

"What did you do?"

"I told her to go home, and then she told me to get rid of my *blanda* friend!"

"Perhaps she's mean to us because we're Christians."

Sari did not respond and there was a helpless look on her face.

Jasmine was surprised that Sari came to tell her this. Sari always seemed so sure of herself. For the first time Jasmine felt sorry for her friend, but didn't know what she could do to help. It was not easy to be a Christian here, especially for natives.

When Sari went home Jasmine was left with a sense of doom. It was fortunate that Mama's mood had improved, because of another letter from Aunt Hanna, inviting them to visit. Jasmine hoped they would go to the plantation soon. It seemed like a safe haven.

Chapter Fifteen

In the Gunung

January, 1942

*I*n the second week of January Mama finally decided it was time to visit *Gunung Didjalan*, Uncle Philip's and Aunt Hanna's plantation. Ellen and Yvonne complained loudly because Papa said they couldn't afford to miss any more lessons. They were to stay at the Van Doorn's. Now that the school was closed Mrs. Van Doorn was always home, and she had agreed to give Ellen and Yvonne lessons, since Papa was too busy. Part of his job was picking up some of the boys who had gone home for Christmas and New Year.

Jasmine and Danny had to come on the trip, because there was no one to look after them. Besides Mama didn't think a week without lessons was going to harm them. She told them what to pack, and soon they were on the long train ride. The plantation was near Bandung in West Java. There weren't many Dutch people on the train, mostly native Gov-

In The Gunung

ernment people, Chinese business men and some native women.

After the train they rode an ancient taxi which rattled over ruts and puddles past plantations and forests. On one side of the road rubber trees stood neatly lined up, like soldiers standing at attention. On the other side were deep ravines with waterfalls. The driver drove so close to the edge that Jasmine alternated between staring in terrified fascination and squeezing her eyes shut, but they made it through without incident.

Half an hour later the taxi sped towards a house, then skidded to a stop, spraying pebbles. Aunt Hanna ran out of the house and hugged Mama. They kissed and cried as if they had not seen each other for years. Then Aunt Hanna hugged Jasmine and Danny. Her grey eyes were kind. She looked a little like Mama, with that knot of hair at the nape of her neck.

After she led them inside, Uncle Philip entered through another door. He greeted them warmly as he sat down on one of the armchairs. He wore short khaki pants and a shirt with the top button undone. He stretched his long legs under the table, smiling at Jasmine. She grinned. She liked Uncle Philip.

Aunt Hanna poured tea, and they sipped it as they talked.

While *Djongos* Kassim, was clearing the tea things, they moved to the veranda and gazed out at the sky which had become a pearly sea with bulky clouds. The mountains, grey-blue silhouettes, seemed very close.

At bedtime Aunt Hanna took Jasmine to a bedroom which looked out over a river, and Jasmine could see the mountains in the moonlight. She lay in the narrow bed, snugly wrapped in her blanket, staring at the wall. There hung a painting, and she looked at it intently in the dim light. She had seen it before. Not this painting, but a picture like it. Then she remembered. It was in a book in Papa's bookcase. *Pilgrim's Progress*, that was it.

She had read the book and remembered the gloomy pictures of a man with a big sack on his bent back. Later he threw the sack some place, and there were crosses, and the devil and men with swords, fighting. She looked again at the painting with its dark hills, valleys and a lonely man. The crosses were in one corner, and bright light shone through an opening in the sky. But it looked like the man had a long way to go.

Jasmine closed her eyes, shutting out the depressing painting. Yet it was still in her mind, as she fell asleep. She dreamed about the darkness swirling around the man with the sack. Then the music came, soft, then louder, people singing, *Jerusalem. Hosanna in the highest!* Suddenly Jasmine was in front of golden doors, from which light streamed. The man behind her still struggled, but in front of her was heaven. Was she dead? Angel voices swirled in the music. *Hosanna in the highest...* but then they were gone, and the *bandjir* came. Cold, dark water. She plunged down into it. A hand managed to save her. A voice. "Jasmine, wake up!"

"So much water."

"You had a bad dream." Mama's soothing strokes on her hair calmed her.

Early the next morning Jasmine forgot the dream as she stood on the circular terrace in front of the house, with a thick hedge of jasmine shrubs. The sky was spotty with clouds, and the sun washed the slopes in a cheerful yellow. She sighed with happiness and drew a long sniff of fresh air.

That afternoon they had tea on the lawn. Uncle Philip, his long legs under the low table, tried to convince Mama that there was no place like Java.

Although Jasmine agreed with him, she wished he would keep quiet, because this kind of talk always bothered Mama. Mama pursed her lips, then sighed. "I don't know if we'll ever get to Holland again. . . ."

Jasmine asked Uncle Philip, "What about the nationalists who want *Merdeka*? Would you really like staying on Java if the *Merdeka* people took over?"

Uncle Philip shrugged, but Aunt Hanna, who had been sipping tea, said, "I really don't know much about *Merdeka*, but I don't see how these people could take over."

No one said much after that, and they sat till twilight, when the sky turned purple. In the *kampong* the guards began to light their night fires. Uncle Philip had explained that on most plantations there were guards to prevent theft of the rubber tins that caught the liquid from the trunks of the rubber trees.

When swarms of insects began to descend on them, Uncle Philip stood up. "Let's go in. Tomorrow I'll show you the plantation, and after that we're going to practice shooting."

Jasmine knew many people had guns, but she shuddered at the thought of holding one, let alone shooting it.

Mama said, "Don't include me in your plans."

Aunt Hanna said, "You never know when it will come in handy, especially since we're so isolated here. Why don't you try it, Beth? It isn't dangerous."

"Uh-uh!" Mama said. "I won't let anyone put a gun in my hands."

Aunt Hanna laughed.

The next day Uncle Philip showed them the plantation, and after teatime, Uncle Philip led them behind the house near the forest. He and Aunt Hanna carried guns. Mama and Jasmine followed warily, and Danny whined about not being allowed to shoot.

At first Mama had not wanted to come, but Jasmine had joined Aunt Hanna in trying to convince her to at least watch her performance, which was not the best.

"Way off center," Uncle Philip said.

Aunt Hanna laughed and turned to Mama. "Want to change your mind Beth?" And when Mama shook her head, "Consider it a game. We're not killing anyone."

A game. Jasmine shuddered. Guns were about war, evil.

She was glad when they got home, just in time for supper.

In The Gunung

That evening Jasmine sat on the veranda with Mama, reading a book under the hissing kerosene lamp. Danny had gone to bed. Uncle and Aunt were in the living room.

Jasmine felt a vague unrest. She kept looking up from the book. She tried to penetrate the wall of night outside the circle of light and felt a hidden threat approaching and retreating. She stretched herself in an effort to push away the uneasiness, and tried once more to concentrate on her book.

A few minutes later Mama got up, and walked down the steps to the lawn. Then she walked to the road, and Jasmine followed. The moon stood high above the mountains. It was eerily silent, which was strange, for there were always sounds in the forest. Jasmine walked beside Mama on wet leaves at the side of the road. She was surprised that Mama dared walk away from the house at this time of night. As they walked, Jasmine's unrest changed to fear, and she wanted to go back to the house.

A slope to the left of the road was covered with tea shrubs, which had been warm and familiar in the day, and were now pale as death. Under a coldly gleaming moon, banana leaves waved gently in the breeze. The whole landscape seemed to belong to another planet. And Jasmine felt alone in its endless secret.

Chapter Sixteen

The Cursed Ones

January, 1942

Sukandar walked along the gravel road without his usual jaunty step. He did not like going to the leprosarium, but his Aunt Sugi was there and it was his duty as her nephew to visit her from time to time. Sukandar felt pity for his aunt. She had lost her nose and her face was awful to look at with that hole. She should have come to the leprosarium much sooner.

The leprosarium was about five kilometers west of the Mission, and he knew the doctor who was one of the few white people he respected. If he were honest and less cautious he would almost admit to feeling some affection for that doctor, for he seemed to belong more to Sukandar's people than to the whites. He made no distinction between brown and white lepers. Of course there were very few of the latter, and a doctor was sworn to treat all human beings alike. Yet this doctor treated Sukandar with kindness and respect due an equal.

Some *tanis* passed him, waddling along comfortably on bare, splayed feet. Women back from the *sawahs* carried bundles of harvested rice. Others were carrying things on their heads from the *passar*. A small herd of *karbauwen* trudged lazily, neck bells clanging. One of the animals pulled a loaded *grobak*.

Soon Sukandar reached a *dessa*, where the *passar* was still in full swing. Women stood chattering cheerfully on the road. The young ones lively in their *kabayas* made of silk, with long sleeves and brilliant colors. Their shiny black hair was twisted into a knot at the back, held by curved combs. Older women wore more subdued colors. They talked with shrill voices while sweeping the smooth clay in front of their huts. Most of them had lips red from *sirih* quids.

His mind returned to *Merdeka*. It occurred to him that not all of his people would want the Dutch to leave, and did not concern themselves with *Merdeka*. The people were not unhappy, he could see that. Most of them seemed satisfied with the situation, and thought only of their daily concerns: enough to eat, a place to sleep, friends to talk to. Life went on smoothly, it seemed, and above the violent undercurrents the people enjoyed the blessings of Allah.

The people enjoyed as much as possible the things of the western world. But was the modern western culture better or worse than the old? The Dutch had their society halls, the planters as well as the city people, swilling beer, liquor, shouting coarse jokes. Then there were the theaters where they laughed and winked, kissed and hugged on the screens. When he had first seen such a film he had been disturbed by so much frankness. He had been ashamed, then learned to chuckle like his friends.

Yes, life seemed to flow smoothly. But sooner or later the undercurrents of unrest, fired up by dedicated nationalists, would surf up into a violent wave. It would be just like the volcanic outburst of the Krakatau in 1883, west of Java. The shock of that explosion was felt around the world.

As he left the *dessa* and soon approached the leprosarium, and he thought of Aunt Sugi again. The medication and treatment with the radiation lamp had done wonders. Even though she had lost her nose she would be able to go home soon the doctor had said. He believed lepers were shunned mostly because they looked awful, not because the disease was terribly infectious. The doctor had explained it to him one day, when he had visited his aunt. Still Sukandar had not totally lost his fear of the frightful disease that had changed his aunt's life so drastically, and he approached the dreaded wards cautiously.

The hospital looked somber. Native nurses in white shuffled noiselessly through the dim halls. There was a smell of disinfectant. A young doctor, with a stethoscope around his neck, walked hastily down the hall and disappeared into a room. A few wraith-like figures wandered by. A few more followed, a parade of phantoms, grey faces, feet, legs, some heads bandaged.

He came to a ward with two rows of beds. He glanced quickly at the screen to his right. He knew that on the bed behind it was the body of what once was a human form, now a mass of leprous sores. This man had been here for some years, his flesh slowly disappearing. According to the doctor it was too late to do much for him, but Aunt Sugi said that his soul was alive with the love of God. How that was possible, Sukandar did not know. It seemed more logical for God to reject such a person. Strange things happened all the time. That was supposed to be the miracle of faith.

In another bed lay a man without lips, and his teeth protruded like a skeleton's. Many lepers could no longer smile, because their skin had become too tight. Others could not see because the eyes were affected. But there was hope. The new radiation lamp. His aunt had benefited, for she was healed.

Sukandar walked to his aunt's ward. She was sitting on a chair beside her bed at the far side of the ward, reading her Bible. As he greeted her, he could not help staring at the gaping hole where her nose was supposed to be.

"It is good of you to come, Sukandar," she said, and pointed to a chair. He thanked her, and sat down. He rubbed his hands and did not know what else to say.

"How is your family?" she asked.

"They're well. Father and Mother send you their greetings. Mother said they will come as soon as they can get away."

She nodded. "My sister has a busy life. She's been blessed with a wonderful family."

"Yes," Sukandar said. It was as if he felt his aunt's pain of losing her sons so early. Her two sons had died of malaria before they could walk, and Aminoto and Aunt Sugi were still grieving over that. It was a delicate subject. He knew many people believed there was a curse on hers and Aminoto's life. Aminoto claimed that he did not believe in supernatural curses. Perhaps this was because fighting for freedom like the modern nations he admired had made Aminoto accept much of the western way of thinking, so that he more readily believed that diseases had physical causes. Many young people became that way. The old ways were not all good, they said, and they were optimistic enough to believe that Allah looked upon them with favor. This thought made Sukandar smile. When he looked up, his aunt was looking at him, smiling too, while her hands lightly stroked the Bible.

They talked a little more about Sukandar's family then Aunt Sugi said, "In two or three weeks I can go home. God is good."

"Yes," Sukandar said. "Uncle will be happy."

"Yes, Aminoto is a good man. Only. . . ."

Sukandar knew what she wanted to say. He knew she did not approve of Aminoto's nationalistic sentiments. The powers that are set over you, she believed, were instituted by the Almighty One. A fight to overthrow them would not remain unpunished, was her solemn conviction.

Sukandar asked, "Are you going back to your house in the mountain or the one Aminoto rented in Tenang?"

"Who told you about the house in Tenang?"

"Alimin."

Aunt Sugi said, "Alimin was here a few weeks ago." She paused. "He has changed."

"Changed?"

"Yes. I remember him as a sensitive and meek boy, like you." There was a long pause again, then his aunt went on. "Actually, both you and Alimin have changed, and I'm not sure I like it."

"Have I changed? In what way?" He was genuinely surprised.

"Both of you have allowed an element of rebellion to enter you. Sometimes I blame Aminoto, but I know it is my sister and her husband who are most to blame."

Sukandar shifted uneasily on his chair.

"Don't get me wrong. I love your parents, but they have instilled a spirit of rebellion in you." She smiled ruefully. "*Sudah*, I was the same way when I was your age. That is perhaps why all these sad things have happened to me. I was too proud and stubborn." She smiled.

"But Aminoto says. . ."

"Yes, I know what he says. But let us not talk about this any more. You must do what your conscience tells you."

Sukandar suddenly felt the need to talk to Aunt Sugi about his doubts and uncertainties. He took a deep breath then blurted out, "I no longer believe *Merdeka* is a good thing, at least not the way they talk about it at the meetings."

Aunt Sugi sat forward in her chair and he could see relief in her eyes. She said, "I'm so happy about that, but what made you change your mind?"

Sukandar tried to arrange his confused thoughts about this into some order which was difficult. "I'm not sure. It was a feeling I've had for some months that the idea of starting a revolution is wrong. Also, I've come to believe that the Dutch have done many good things and that most people here live a happy life."

Aunt Sugi nodded. "Yes, indeed." Then she added solemnly, "The most blessed thing the Dutch have done is to bring the Gospel to this country."

Sukandar nodded, too choked to speak.

Aunt Sugi said, "I thank God that your sister has become a Christian." There were tears in her eyes. "And Sari's family too," she added.

Sukandar nodded again. "Yes, I didn't realize it but I think Lea has influenced my thinking."

They were silent for a few moments then Sugi asked, "What does Aminoto say about this?"

"I haven't told anyone, not even my parents. I'm not sure what their reaction would be, but I know they'll be disappointed in me. As for Aminoto, I think he suspects how I feel."

Sugi laid her hand on his bowed head. "God bless you, my child."

He looked up and smiled at her. "Thank you."

They changed the subject, and Sukandar left soon after. Aunt Sugi's words had given him much to think about and her blessing had greatly cheered him. Yet her cheerfulness in the face of her deformity astounded him. Could the filthy disease attack the body, yet leave the soul intact? What was the source of her spiritual strength? She was not the only one like that here. In spite of pain and ostracism, many could still sing. The lepers had a choir. Hymns and distorted leprous faces did not go together. Suddenly Sukandar felt ashamed of his selfishness, his complaints and his failure to count his blessings. From now on he would try to accept whatever came his way, and try to see the good side of everything.

He was glad he had confided in his aunt. He was certain now that his aunt's beliefs were the origin of her serenity, and he was glad she could get out of the hospital and be home again so he could visit her more freely. Talking to Aunt Sugi had strengthened his belief that there were other things in life to strive for than political freedom. It was not in his nature to rebel, and he had only been doing what his parents wished.

Sukandar thought about what the elders expected of him—to spy on the lady of the Mission, and he was ashamed that he had ever considered doing such a thing. How it would have offended Lea – such a despicable thing to do, to read someone else's mail! But the most important thing was that he knew that fighting for a cause which would involve bloodshed was wrong. It would be much better to wait for the Dutch to grant them independence.

Chapter Seventeen

Merdeka!

January, 1942

*M*ama and Jasmine walked to the circular terrace in front of Aunt Hanna's house, and paused. Jasmine sensed acutely that something bad was about to happen when suddenly the formless threat took on concrete shape. A piercing scream was followed by the nearby sound of a *tong-tong*. Jasmine froze, then ran to the safety of the house, Mama right behind her.

Aunt Hanna sat in her chair, her face pale, and Uncle Philip walked to one of the windows.

"What was that?" Aunt Hanna looked at Uncle Philip.

"I don't know. I'll check."

"Please don't!" Aunt Hanna said, looking even paler in the kerosene light.

Merdeka!

There was shouting on the road, and another loud scream. It sounded as if it came from the yard. Jasmine, Mama and Aunt Hanna joined Uncle Philip at the window.

There was a gang of men with sticks, scythes and torches. The man who seemed the leader was the only one with a gun. They approached the house, yelling threats.

When Uncle Philip went out on the veranda, Aunt Hanna moved to join him, but Mama grabbed her sister's arm.

"I have to go to him. What if they hurt him!" Aunt pulled free, and Mama and Jasmine went with her to the veranda, behind Uncle Philip.

The shouting died down, and there was a tense silence until the leader spoke.

Jasmine didn't understand everything, but what she caught made her turn cold.

The leader, waving his gun said loudly, "Europeans are no longer welcome here. Asia is now for the Asians. All *blandas* have to leave as soon as possible. *Merdeka!*"

Uncle Philip took a step forward, and began to speak slowly and clearly.

"I understand your wish to fight for your *Merdeka*, but I came here to work for your people, to help build up the country, and it will not take long for *Merdeka* to come, in a peaceful way." He paused then continued loudly, "I am sure that you do not really want to harm anyone, for this is surely not Allah's will, who has blessed our country so richly, and who would punish anyone who breaks his laws."

A threatening grumble, raised sticks and *klewangs*, short swords.

Jasmine's breath stuck in her throat, fear like gall in her mouth. Aunt Hanna took a few steps forward and stood beside Philip, so open and unprotected that Jasmine wanted to pull her back. Mama seemed petrified.

Aunt Hanna began to speak haltingly, yet Jasmine was surprised how much of the language her aunt had already learned.

"I am a *blanda*, but I have come to love this country and its people, and soon the *blandas* will give *Merdeka* to the people, and . . ."

A chorus of mumbling disbelief rose from the ragged band, but they seemed hesitant to take action. Their eyes turned to the leader, who had lifted his gun. Jasmine stifled a scream, and then listened as in a trance to his words, slow and deliberate.

"The *Tuan*, as well as every other *Tuan*, has spoken the same words for years. Now the time has come to take our own *Merdeka*, because three hundred years of *blanda* rule is enough." He repeated this twice.

Uncle Philip resumed his pleading, and although Jasmine still admired his courage, she recognized the folly of it. He must know that sometimes people, no matter how calm they seemed, could break out into fits of violence.

But Uncle Philip seemed unruffled. "Is this your struggle for *Merdeka*, to harm your fellow creatures, the *blandas*, who have done so much for your country? You should all go back to you *dessas*, and work the *sawahs*, so that rice will grow abundantly, the tea and rubber, which brings wealth to our country. Think of your children. Do you want them to suffer want?"

The leader, his gun still pointing forward, said, "It is time that the *blandas* do the hard work, and the Indonesians tell them what to do. Allah, who is just, will avenge us."

Uncle Philip seemed to lose patience, and he said in a harsher voice, "I will report you to the *pelisie*, if you do not leave this yard right away."

They had listened silently but at his last words, a surly mumbling broke out. Many of those men seemed like boys trying to act in a difficult play. A few in the back seemed to have lost their appetite for violence, but the leader screeched, "We want *Merdeka* now! The *blandas* have to go!"

Uncle Philip said curtly, "The *Kompenie*, our Government, still rules here, and has the power to arrest those who do not obey its laws, and if you do not leave immediately I will telephone the *pelisi* and they will arrest you all."

The man completely ignored Philip's last words, and screamed again, "The *blandas* have to leave. Only then will prosperity come for our people. We can rule ourselves. You are no longer needed."

Jasmine was beginning to doubt the sanity of the man, when a great roaring broke out. She understood enough about the passionate feeling of these people to realize that once they broke loose, violence would wash over them like a *bandjir*. They could be killed right on this veranda. She hoped that Uncle Philip had enough authority to keep them in check, but she feared it was too late.

Suddenly the leader leaped towards him, firing his gun, but the bullet went up into the darkness over the trees. Before he could aim again, Uncle Philip had punched his fist in the man's stomach, so that the latter fell backwards on the grass.

Now it was Aunt Hanna who screamed, but Jasmine was unable to utter a sound.

A muffled groan came from the prostrate native, who tried to get up. Like a wild animal Uncle Philip threw himself on the man, who kicked and hit him, but Uncle Philip seemed the stronger. The gun lay a few paces away and the man tried to get it. The group stood in a trance.

Aunt Hanna screamed again.

Mama finally moved, and took a few steps closer to Hanna, who stood with her hand over her mouth, her eyes wide.

Jasmine looked away from Aunt Hanna to the eyes of the man beneath Uncle Philip. In the light of the torches those eyes were black with hatred. The man gave out a choked sound, but Uncle Philip's fingers seemed to be fused to the brown throat. The man's mouth opened, gasping for air.

"Philip, don't kill him!" It was Aunt Hanna. The man had closed his eyes, and all of a sudden Uncle Philip leaped away from him, staring at the petrified crowd.

Beside him the man on the ground croaked a few words, and then. . . .

Merdeka!

What happened next went so fast, Jasmine barely remembered every detail later.

One of the men in the group, who had a *klewang*, sprang towards Uncle Philip, and at the same time Aunt Hanna ran to her husband, her arms wide. She flung herself in front of Uncle Philip just when the man raised his weapon. It missed Uncle Philip, and the next thing Jasmine saw was Aunt Hanna sagging to the ground, and Uncle Philip bending over her.

Eyes wide with shock, Jasmine stood stock-still. Then she took a shaking step, saw the big gash in Aunt Hanna's neck, blood streaming. . . .

After a few seconds of stunned stillness, Uncle Philip, with an inhuman growl, picked up the gun and fired but the horde had already disappeared into the forest. Even the man on the ground, who had seemed near death a few moments before, was nowhere to be seen. Uncle Philip's shots disappeared into a dark void.

Mama was on her knees, beside Aunt Hanna, cradling her head and shoulders. Mama looked up and Jasmine saw grief burning in her eyes. Jasmine tried to swallow the lump in her throat, but it was too large.

". . . Don't. . . kill. . . them. . . ." Aunt Hanna's head sagged sideways, as Mama still cradled her and rocked her gently.

Mama whispered, "She's gone. . . .Philip. . .my sister. . . ."

Aunt Hanna had been the link between Mama and Holland, and now all she could do was clutch at the limp form. The sky was still full of stars and the kerosene lamp on the veranda streamed light across the yard, but the night seemed blacker than any Jasmine had ever seen.

The next thing Jasmine would always remember was Uncle Philip's look of desperation, while he carried his wife inside and laid her on the bed. He sat on the edge of the bed, and fumbled with a gauze bandage, trying to cover the gash.

Cold fear penetrated the room. A dim light came from a small oil lamp, which stood in the corner. Outside branches rustled in the wind. The clock ticked clearly and precisely against the silence in the house.

Uncle Philip stared almost pleadingly at the white face and the blood stained bandage, the bloodless lips, and the closed eyes.

Jasmine could do nothing except look. She tried to pray, but there was only a vast vacuum.

Mama sat on a chair by the bed, holding her handkerchief to her mouth. She didn't know that it was soaked in her sister's blood, which she was smearing over her tear-streaked face.

Uncle Philip bent more closely over the bed, as if willing life back into the limp body. He balled his fists, then grabbed the edge of the bed. He moaned.

There was a fine smile on Aunt Hanna's lips, and she seemed at peace.

Time faltered, as if the clock had skipped one tick, then Jasmine realized suddenly that this was a final farewell. Her hand curled in a tight ball.

Merdeka!

It rained on the day of Aunt Hanna's funeral. Ellen and Yvonne had come with Papa the day before. After the service in a small church, they went to the cemetery. Aunt Hanna's body rode in the car ahead. Behind them a long row of cars followed under the palms along the avenue. When they arrived, everyone formed a silent circle around the gaping grave. Jasmine stood between Papa and Mama with Uncle Philip on Mama's other side. Yvonne and Ellen stood beside each other, crying. Danny looked stunned. Mama cried, and Uncle Philip stood stiffly silent, head bent.

Six men carried the coffin, and the silence became oppressive, as the pastor stepped forward. He had white hair like Pastor De Waard. He coughed a few times, then began to speak with an old tired voice. Jasmine tried to listen, but his sentences came in pieces, as if he had trouble stringing them together.

"Like the grass, that is today. . . ." Some of his words seemed to disappear into the grave. . . . "This life, which God has taken to. . . ."

Jasmine listened but the words meant nothing. She hoped they would comfort Uncle Philip. She looked at Mama's tight face and swollen eyes, and wondered if Mama heard anything at all. Yvonne was rubbing her eyes, sucking in her bottom lip, but Ellen looked angry now.

Uncle Philip stepped forward when the pastor had finished, and thanked the people for coming. It had stopped raining and Jasmine tried to discover figures in the clouds. There was a lion, and Jasmine was just trying to imagine a sheep, when the pastor announced their final song. "Far above the stars. . . ." It was a poor, thin sound compared to Aunt Hanna's joyous laughter.

A few days after they got home Jasmine found Mama's diary open on the buffet. She wondered if Mama had written about Aunt Hanna. That thought resurrected all the horrors. It was as if there was a dead body in the house. She struggled against the pointlessness of it all.

"She's home in heaven," the pastor had said, but Uncle Philip had balled his fist, and Jasmine had done the same. She widened her eyes again in anguish at the memory.

Aunt Hanna had loved Java, saying repeatedly that she wanted to stay here the rest of her life.

And she had.

Chapter Eighteen

The Kampong

January, 1942

One afternoon shortly after they came back from *Gunung Didjalan*, Jasmine sat on her hassock by the living room window. The others were still napping, and she was happy to be alone. From outside came the doleful moaning of the wind, the soft rustling of the rain against the window.

The deep sense of grief and loss about Aunt Hanna's death grew. And anger against the people who had killed her aunt, like Sukandar and the *Merdeka* people. She had thoughts of taking revenge, which was silly for she knew Sukandar could not have been with the group on the plantation. Still, the resentment towards all natives would not leave her.

Although life seemed to go on much the same as before, there had been a break and she had to figure out in what ways this made things different for her. There still was no regular school. All there was to do was some boring things like knitting, doing school assignments Mama or Papa made them do, and of course playing with Mopsy.

As for Sari, after the events at the *Gunung*, Jasmine was confused as to her feelings about her friend, who was after all a native and whose cousin and uncle were involved in *Merdeka*. But avoiding Sari didn't really make much sense, since it was Marto who sympathized with the *Merdeka* cause. Jasmine wanted to ask Sari when and how Marto had become so hostile to whites, and why she even went to a Christian school. Jasmine also wondered if Marto was still bothering Sari. As for taking revenge on the natives, she knew she could not do it. It was not Sari's fault that some fanatics had killed Aunt Hanna.

As it turned out, she did see Sari but not the way she had planned. One afternoon a few days later, Jasmine and Yvonne were cleaning their bedroom. Miss Steen was coming to visit and Mama had told them to make sure their room looked neat. She had also sent Ellen to *Toko* Wong for some biscuits to go with the tea.

Jasmine was annoyed. "As if she's going to check our room!" Miss Steen had always been a nuisance. Mama did not like her either, for they lived in Miss Steen's house and the lady was very critical. Still, Mama had told the girls to come and greet her.

When they heard Miss Steen's voice in the hall, Yvonne and Jasmine heaved a huge sigh, made a face, and walked slowly to the living room. "Might as well get it over with," Yvonne said.

The Kampong

Ellen was already seated on the sofa. She probably liked Miss Steen least of all, for the lady had slapped her once when Ellen was in grade six. Danny sat by the window, on his best behavior. After all Miss Steen had been his teacher too. While they were drinking tea Jasmine asked, "Why don't you live in this house yourself, Miss Steen?"

Miss Steen who still lived with a friend, said, "It's too dangerous to live alone. Nowadays you never know what the natives might do." She blinked her eyes rapidly, and for a moment Jasmine thought she was going to cry.

"Most natives are good," Jasmine said.

Miss Steen looked at her disdainfully then started talking to Mama. She did not stay long, nor did she say anything about the house. After one cup of tea she left, not even waiting for Papa. Mama heaved a sigh of relief, and so did Jasmine. She and Yvonne went into the front yard and stood near the bougainvillea.

Talking about the natives had reminded Jasmine of Sari. When Yvonne said she'd thought up some practical jokes to play on the natives, Jasmine was not enthusiastic.

"What's up with you?" Yvonne asked.

Jasmine shrugged. "I don't feel good about it. Sari's father is *Kepala Kampong*, and Sari might feel embarrassed."

"We won't do it to her," Yvonne said, looking at the *kampong*.

Danny liked playing pranks while Ellen scoffed at such childish behavior, and told them they would get into trouble.

Yvonne, who had never been much into this kind of mischief, now seemed eager to do something.

Jasmine looked at her sister. "You have something in mind?"

Yvonne grinned and pointed at the *kampong*. "It would be fun to find out who else lives there."

Ellen came up to them. "You know you're not allowed in the *kampong*. The natives might not be trusted, now that Holland was beaten by the Germans, and the Americans were attacked by the Japanese. You never know what they might do."

Yvonne wrinkled her nose. "You sound like Miss Steen."

In spite of Jasmine's reluctance, she was irritated with Ellen. "*Ach*, you and your big ideas!"

Yvonne asked, "Can't trust the natives?" Then her face fell. "I guess there were some bad ones at *Gunung Didjalan*."

Jasmine said to Ellen, "You know you can trust Sari, and what about Lea?"

Ellen shrugged.

"The natives around here have never done us any harm," Yvonne said, looking cheerful again. "As far as I'm concerned, Miss Steen is much more dangerous." She grinned.

Jasmine thought of Marto, but didn't say anything. Ellen shrugged again, and went back into the house.

Finally Jasmine let Yvonne talk her into doing something, because Yvonne confessed that she hated one of the native girls in her class.

"Does she live in this *kampong*? Jasmine asked.

The Kampong

"No, but who cares." Yvonne could get up to real mischief sometimes. Or perhaps she was still angry about Aunt Hanna.

They found some horse droppings and wrapped them in a banana leaf, tying it with a piece of string. They entered the *kampong*, gave the package to a couple of boys, and ran back to the road.

Jasmine felt terrible. She hoped those boys would just throw it away.

Yvonne giggled. Of course Yvonne didn't have a friend living in that *kampong*, but the native children were sure to retaliate.

In the meantime Danny had found his own amusements. They saw him at the side of the road, his arms loaded with vegetables and fruit. At that moment Mama came out onto the road. Jasmine wondered if Ellen had warned her. To distract Mama they pointed at Danny. "He took things out of the road basket offerings." Natives offered things to their ancestors to appease them.

"Danny!" Mama said and looked around, as if spirits of native ancestors were there to punish them. She seemed unsure what to do at first, and then decided not to be too severe. Perhaps she felt that in this crisis concerning holy matters it behooved her to control herself. She took Danny's arm and said sternly, "Go and take all that back, understood?"

Danny understood. With a scowl at his sisters, he gathered up his loot and started for the crossroads. Mama and the girls followed. Angrily Danny arranged the items in the basket, and then pointed at the girls. "They put horse droppings in a banana leaf and gave it to some boys in the *kampong*."

"Girls! Is this true?"

They nodded in unison, and again Mama seemed to have difficulty controlling herself. "Don't you know that the natives are our neighbors, and are worthy of our respect?"

They nodded again, while Danny went back home.

"I want you to come with me and apologize to them."

They dared not object, and the three of them walked to the *kampong*. It was a significant moment, for Mama had never entered any native districts, even though this one was almost on their doorstep. But she seemed unsure what to do.

Jasmine was sorry about what she had done, and hoped she would not see Sari. But Sari's father was the *Kepala Kampong*, and he would be the most likely person Mama wanted to speak to. Jasmine's heart beat faster.

The place seemed deserted except for two boys and a woman, who chased after some geese, yelling, and swinging a stick until the fugitive fowl were safely in their cage.

The dirt road was red with *sirih* spittle. Yvonne and Jasmine, who were the only children with shoes on, carefully avoided the wine-colored phlegm, while the native children ran over it with bare feet.

Jasmine led the way to Sari's house, still feeling terrible. When they looked through the front door, they saw Sari's grandfather on a *baleh-baleh*, his skeletal bare knees against his chin.

"*Tabeh, Pak,*" Mama said. "We would like to speak to the *Kepala Kampong.*"

The old man looked at them, but did not answer.

After a few moments Mama said "He doesn't seem to hear us. We might as well go home." But just then a native boy walked into the yard, a basket with fruit on his head. He had a friendly face, and his large brown eyes looked straight at them. It was Sari's oldest brother, who had not gone to any Colonial school.

Mama said, "I think you should apologize to this boy. He can pass the message."

Mama explained, and Jasmine and Yvonne asked *ampun,* forgiveness. Jasmine felt foolish, but to her relief the boy grinned widely, and said, "*Tida apa, Nonya, nonnies.*" It doesn't matter."

"*Trima kassi.*" Thank you.

"*Baik! Slamat djalan.*" Fine! Goodbye.

Relieved that the ordeal was over Jasmine looked at Yvonne who giggled behind her hand. Jasmine soon did the same, for after all it had been fun to fool those boys with the banana leaf package.

Just as they were walking away from the house, Sari came from the back with a basket of clothes. Jasmine stopped giggling as Sari looked at her with a question in her eyes. Mama explained why they were there and Jasmine wanted to sink into the ground.

Sari said nothing. Jasmine hoped Sari was not angry, and wished she'd not been so stupid. After a few moments Sari nodded a greeting then went into her house.

As they walked home, the sun was setting in a bed of velvet colors. The warmth of the evening wrapped itself around Jasmine, and she began to feel better.

After the meal Mama called the children in the living room, where Papa sat behind his desk, looking serious. The three of them stood in front of the desk, with Mama behind them, as if she was afraid that they would run away.

"Mama told me what happened this afternoon." Papa paused, as if he wanted to give them time to reflect. "You know that what you did was wrong, and I can't understand what made you do it. The natives in that *kampong* have not done us any harm, and they deserve our respect."

Yvonne nodded solemnly. Jasmine thought of Marto, but kept silent.

"People have different ways and religions," Papa explained, then turned to Danny. "Do you realize that they put those baskets on the crossroads as presents to the spirits of their ancestors? Even though we don't believe the way they do, we must not offend them."

Danny nodded, subdued, but Jasmine asked what she had wanted to ask a few times before, "Aren't you angry about them killing Aunt Hanna?"

Jasmine saw pain in her father's eyes, but he simply said, "Those were a small group of bad people, and you can't blame others for what happened at *Gunung Didjalan*."

"Did they punish the people who did this?" Jasmine had been thinking a lot about how that incident had been possible. Of course a lot of men were in the army, and many things were kind of mixed up. But there must have been something they could do. She was not sure if Uncle Philip even knew any of the *Merdeka* men who came to the plantation. Had it been in the newspapers, or did anyone ever find out about it?

Papa said, "I know that they started investigations right away. The authorities are still searching for the killers, but according to Uncle Philip, without success."

"Maybe they're protected by the natives," Danny said.

"Perhaps," Papa said, then he added, "But what concerns us now is *your* behavior, and I hope I can trust you not to do anything again like what you did this afternoon."

Mama left the room, now that the speech was over. Papa looked at them across the desk, and to Jasmine's amazement he winked at them, and whispered, "It was a bad thing to do, but . . . I did something like it when I was a child."

In spite of Papa's words, Jasmine left the room in a subdued frame of mind, regretting most that she may have hurt Sari's feelings.

Late one afternoon, a few days later, they returned from a visit to the Van Doorn's place. Even in the *dokar* Jasmine could not forget the tense atmosphere during their visit, and life felt like precariously balancing on a tightrope. They could expect the Japanese to land on Java any time Mrs. Van Doorn had said and Jasmine imagined hearing the boom of cannon and massive explosions where oil wells and reserves were being destroyed. The first time they had heard these explosions, Papa had been writing at his desk.

"How can you just sit there," Mama had said. "Don't you hear the bombing?"

"Not bombing. They're destroying our oil wells and other supplies so the Japanese can't get them."

"Are they planning to surrender?"

"Of course not. It's just a precaution."

But now in the *dokar*, under the lurid glare in the sky, Jasmine was sure that hell had come to them. She shuddered, and looked out through the back opening into the falling night, in which the glowing disk of the sun slid behind the earth.

Jasmine sat straight on the bench. Her brains refused to function properly. She could almost hear the countless hordes of soldiers in a tramping march, with bayonets aimed at her. Eyes wide, hands clasped tightly, she looked at the faintly glowing horizon, where her hope was sinking.

She looked at Papa, who had crossed his legs. She wished he would say something, but they rode on in silence. They entered the leafy tunnel of the Cattle Lane, the gravel road that ran alongside the vanilla orchard. The overarching branches hid the sky from view, and the tension eased until they reached the end of the Lane.

There Jasmine saw something so strange, that for a moment she forgot her fear. At the roadside stood the Chinese from all the *tokos*, some of the richest in town, doling

The Kampong

out rice and clothes to *kampong* people. Grocer Wong was there. Jasmine was aware that he had been afraid, for he knew what might happen to the Chinese if the Japanese came. But giving things to the natives might be because they were afraid the Japs would confiscate their stocks.

Jasmine leaned over to have a better look. In the light of the glaring torches Grocer Wong's small eyes looked sad, matching the droop of his mouth. He scooped rice from a sack into waiting bowls, held up by the natives, who walked away happily.

The *dokar* had stopped. Jasmine saw Sari and her mother and brother. Sari was holding a bowl and Grocer Wong put rice into it. Then Jasmine noticed Marto who came forward, holding a bowl in front of Grocer Wong. As soon as he had filled it, Marto threw down the bowl, spilling all of the rice. Then she looked straight at Jasmine. She put her thumbs against her ears and wiggled her fingers mockingly. When she marched off she jostled Sari. Sari almost fell over, and the rice spilled out of her bowl.

Jasmine felt like jumping out of the *dokar*, running to Marto and punching her nose.

Sari bent over, trying to rescue some of her rice. Grocer Wong waved her over and when she was close to him he put more rice in her bowl, smiling at her. Sari managed a sad smile.

As the *dokar* moved on, Jasmine's scattered fears crystallized. Marto insulting Grocer Wong showed that perhaps the *Merdeka* people hated the Chinese just as much as the

Japanese did. She had heard about cruelties done to the Chinese. A nameless sensation swelled in her chest and as she remembered the ever cheerful and kind Grocer Wong, she knew the end was near.

The next day she went to Sari. She wanted to apologize for the trick and for having had bad feelings about her. Standing in front of her friend who stood on the porch, Jasmine blurted out, "Sorry I haven't visited you and also sorry about the poop in the banana leaf."

Sari grinned. "Oh no, it was hilarious! I just didn't want to laugh with your mother there. Of course the boys you gave it to were angry." She giggled. "You should have seen their faces!"

Jasmine heaved a sigh of relief then said, "I wonder what Marto would have said."

As the girls started walking toward the gravel road, Jasmine told her she had seen what happened at the side of the road. "I saw you and also what Marto did."

Sari nodded. "Marto hates Chinese and Christians. She's a real *Merdeka* fanatic."

"But why did the Chinese give away rice? I couldn't figure it out."

Sari thought for a moment then said, "I think they're trying to get the natives on their side, hoping they will help them when the Japs come."

Jasmine nodded. "That makes sense, but come to think of it, they also might want to give all their stock so that the Japanese can't get their hands on it."

The Kampong

The girls walked on in silence, and when they came to the Big House Sari said, "I hope you'll come again soon. I'm getting bored with doing laundry and washing dishes."

Jasmine grinned. "I should come and help you, but my parents know about meetings and all that, and they're not sure what is going on."

"Why don't you just say that you want to help me do dishes and laundry. They might feel sorry for me," Sari teased.

"You're right, they might! I'll see you soon." With that Jasmine went into the house feeling greatly cheered.

Chapter Nineteen

The Wayang Kulit

January, 1942

The third week of January Papa provided a distraction. He had mentioned wanting to see a *Wayang Kulit* show, and finally decided to do it. He would ask Mr. Boon to come, because he knew a lot about the *Wayang*.

Jasmine made a face, but realized that she could not do much about Papa's decision. Once, when she had said something about Mr. Boon, Papa had become angry. All people are worthy of our love and respect, he had said.

Jasmine used to be friends with Ruth Boon, but not since she'd become friends with Sari. It was not that she hated Ruth, but it was her resentment against Ruth's father, since he was always making fun of her curly blond hair, when she wanted it to be straight and black like Sari's.

Because she felt uneasy about Mr. Boon being there, she asked Papa if Sari could come along if she wanted. Sari knew

The Wayang Kulit

a lot about the *Wayang* too, at least more than Jasmine did. Papa agreed, but Jasmine had not had a chance to ask Sari. She did not see Sari much now that there was no school, and Papa was strict about going into *kampongs*.

The *Wayang* shadow plays were popular, Sari had said. While telling the story, a man called the *dalang*, moved the puppets in between a lamp and a screen so that their shadows fell on it. From where they usually sat the audience could only see the shadows, and not the colorful puppets. This did not sound too exciting. But Sari had also said that *Wayang* shows were sacred and depicted war between good and evil people. *Merdeka* people liked *Wayang* legends, because it was about fighting enemies.

Jasmine tried to remember where she had heard about the *Wayang* stories. It had been Mr. Breda, when he was teaching about Dutch Colonial history. The Hindus had come to Java in the second century, before the Buddhists and Muslims and long before the Dutch. There were two Hindu epic poems, the *Ramayana* and the *Mahabharata*. There were also Hindu temples on Java, like the Prambanan where the *Ramayana* characters were carved in stone. These were older than the Borobudur with Buddha's life etched in stone.

When they arrived, Jasmine was surprised that something sacred would take place in an old shed. Kerosene lamps lit the space and the dirt floor. Mr. Boon was there already, but Jasmine was surprised Ruth and Louisa had not come.

Jasmine tried to drop Mr. Boon from her thoughts. She could do nothing about his being there, but she planned to avoid him. He was going to spoil everything, she was sure of it. She even preferred Sukandar although he was a *Merdeka* person who wanted to chase the Dutch out. She shook off the irritating thoughts, and listened to the sounds of the night which lulled her into feeling that this evening was going to be significant.

Natives sat on the dirt floor or on wooden crates. Ellen, Yvonne and Jasmine found some unoccupied crates to sit on, away from most of the audience, while Danny, Papa and Mr. Boon stood beside them. Jasmine looked around her curiously. In front of a large white sheet was the *gamelan*. That was an orchestra made up of large bells in different sizes, some xylophones and cymbals. The sounds that came from these instruments were kind of monotonous and sometimes strident.

Between the *gamelan* and the sheet sat an old man. Beside him were a chest and a banana trunk, which lay flat on the dirt floor. Jasmine whispered to Yvonne, "Who's that?"

"I think that's the *dalang,* who's going to tell the story," Yvonne whispered.

The *dalang* mumbled something, opened the chest and took out the *Wayang* puppets. These were intricately carved out of stiff, flat buffalo hide and brightly painted, each representing different characters from the legend. The old man's skinny, wrinkled hands held them reverently, dusted them carefully, and stuck them in the soft trunk of the banana

The Wayang Kulit

tree. The puppets looked strange, standing in a row, mockingly protruding their noses. From where the girls sat they could see the actual puppets as well as their shadows which fell on the sheet.

Mr. Boon explained, "The story he's going to tell is from the *Ramayana*."

His words opened up a whole strange world of heroes and demons. There was a fight with wild movements of shadows, increased droning of the *gamelan*, and clattering weapons. An ugly puppet with a cruel grin ran off the screen. Two others followed.

Jasmine recalled more of what Mr. Breda had said. The mythology of the Hindu epics had become part of the thought life of the natives of Java. That didn't have anything to do with religion, but had become an art form like the *Wayang* puppet plays. The plays were so popular because every native on Java saw himself in a particular character in the *Wayang*. The secret of inspired nationalist speakers like Sukarno was that they touched the hearts of the people by comparing the plight of the nationalists to the struggles of the *Wayang* characters. The *Ramayana* stories involved fights against an enemy, in the case of the nationalists, the Colonial Dutch. Mr. Breda believed that characters such as Gatutkatja which Mr. Boon had mentioned, was Sukarno's hero, because Gatutkatja always rose up to fight again after defeat.

Mr. Boon's voice intruded into Jasmine's reverie, as he translated. "Gatutkatja is standing in front of the Evil One. He's getting the worst of it, he is beaten. But that won't last long. He will rise up again. He will be victorious. One cannot restrain a hero forever. Gatutkatja has risen up again. Gatutkatja is standing once more. He has killed the Evil One."

The *dalang* droned on while his hands handled the puppets with skill and precision, making their arms and legs move stiffly at their knobby joints. The monotonous Javanese chant was mingled with the sound of the *gamelan* instruments.

Jasmine, elbows on her knees, watched the shadows move erratically, and felt the deep mystery of this hour. She translated these strange, glottal sounds by way of the shifting shadows on the brightly lit screen, past the odd movements of the stiff puppets, into a language all her own. She was in an enchanted land. Kerosene lamps threw eerie blotches of flickering light through the shed, where grotesque shadows chased each other along the walls and ceiling with jerky movements. The mystery found its reflection in the circle of dark faces all around her.

Her feelings, not consciously shaped into thoughts, sensed a kinship with these ghostly beings. Through the light and shadows, the soft, sometimes strident sounds, she felt a bond with the people sitting here. She was part of it all in a way she had always wanted, but did not understand.

During the intermission, Papa bought the children satay at a *warong*. While Jasmine was chewing her satay, she suddenly saw Sari, on the other side of the shed. Beside her stood Sukandar, looking solemn yet intense. Maybe he was

The Wayang Kulit

thinking about how close he was to winning the *Merdeka* war.

Jasmine was just going to walk in Sari's direction, when Mr. Boon put his hand on her shoulder. It was distasteful, but it was best to suffer it, with Papa so close. Maybe Mr. Boon would buy them something too. He had done that a few times before because he did not know all the bad names she had called him.

But it was odd, she wasn't hungry anymore, and the satay tasted like kapok. She turned her back to him. He had done it, spoiled the whole evening. *Always be polite to everyone, Jasmine. All people are entitled to respect.* The last time Papa had said something like that he had smiled at her, but she could tell he really meant it.

After a few long minutes of conversation between Papa and Mr. Boon, the play resumed, and thankfully Jasmine could retreat to her spot next to Yvonne.

Papa seemed rather distant towards her on the way home, and the next afternoon he sat behind his desk while Jasmine stood beside him.

Papa said, "You seem to dislike Mr. Boon Jasmine. Is it because he's an Indo?"

She gritted her teeth. "I don't dislike him because he's an Indo."

"Then why?"

"He always calls me curly girl."

Papa smiled. "Is that all?"

"Isn't that enough? You know I hate these curls!" She grabbed a handful of hair.

"I'm sure he doesn't mean to be hateful. In any case, no matter what people do or say, you must still respect them. You're not a little girl anymore, Jasmine, and I expect more mature behavior from you"

Jasmine nodded. "I'll try to be nice to him," she promised.

"Good. It's not always easy to think of others instead of ourselves."

She just had to forget about Mr. Boon! Enough awful things happened in the world, although it still irked her that Papa had taken Mr. Boon's side. Yet she had to bow to Papa's wishes in order to keep his affection. What could she expect in this hostile world if she were not sure of that? Of course there was always the love of God. The world could sink, but God was holding everything and everyone in his hands. But you still often felt defenseless, a piece of fear at the edge of God's wide fields. Life was not as simple as you sometimes thought. It seemed as if you could travel to the future without obstacles, but that was not so. One thing was sure, it would be much easier without people like Mr. Boon.

Chapter Twenty

Confrontation

February, 1942

During the early part of February Sukandar lived in a state of total confusion. Whenever he looked at the devastation caused by the *bandjir* which had left Aminoto's fields in ruins, he had tried to piece together what had happened.

He remembered leaving Tenang the day after the meeting at Alimin's. Lightning had forked above the mountains, and the thunder was deafening. Thick clouds had piled up and he recalled vividly his anxiety, an unusual thing for him who was so used to the elements. He had stopped in a nearby *dessa,* where he joined other people in a *pendopo.* Continuing his journey had been difficult. He remembered being shocked to see the large sections of the paths which had been washed away, trees knocked down across others. Then the most frightening memory, the dull thunder of an oncoming flood. A *bandjir*!

For the first time in his life Sukandar had felt defenseless in a land which he deeply loved, but which had seemed to reject him. The rain which had filled his *sawahs* was now his enemy. When at last he had come to the river he had stared in consternation at it and at the swollen brook which had turned into a river. His rice fields! His gardens! Destruction of all his work!! He had sighed with relief when he saw the house still standing. He had found Sari's mother and brother, Sari's Dutch friend as well as Aminoto there. They had told him about their fright at the river, but he had been so upset that he had barely listened.

He had tried to repair the damage, but his heart had not been in it. He no longer felt king in his own kingdom. Aminoto had helped as much as he could, but his heart had not been in it either. "I'm going to find work in Tenang," Sukandar had told his uncle, but he had not succeeded yet. Aminoto had invited him to stay at his place in Tenang, but Sukandar felt he could not impose on Aunt Sugi, who had just come out of the hospital, even though she had said that she felt better if she had him there since Aminoto was away so much.

He was on his way to try finding work once more. He had come to enjoy the long walks, although he began to feel like a homeless wanderer, a pilgrim. He had caught a ride on a *grobak* and even a truck going to the *passar*. So he had made good progress.

He thought of the news about the war Aminoto had reported. The first Japanese air attacks on Java had happened in Surabya, and Magelang, and they had increased as the days went by. Most of these attacks were aimed at Java's harbors and airfields. A strike force had been put together from Dutch, American, British and Australian cruisers and torpedo boats. This squadron came under the command of the Dutch rear-admiral Karel Doorman. The Japanese had attacked this fleet, heavily damaging the United States cruisers *Houston* and *Marblehead,* and to a lesser extend the Dutch flag-ship *De Ruyter.*

Sukandar shook his head about the way people behaved. He hoped to avoid a lot of what the war brought here on Java. Yet everything around him was so peaceful. The little white church, pinned against the mountain among the green, pointed its tower up to the sky, as if showing where help and hope could be found.

He had walked for two hours under the burning sun, and was getting tired when not far from Tenang he heard a familiar wheezing and rattling. Before he turned to look he knew who it was. Sastro with his *Tuan's* Ford. Sastro stopped and grinned.

"Hello, friend, do you want to ride again?"

"It's remarkable how you always know where to be at the right time," Sukandar said, as he got in beside Sastro.

"How have you been?" Sastro asked, "Are the corn, the rice and bananas growing?"

Sukandar shook his head. "No, a *bandjir* destroyed the fields."

"That's bad luck. It will take a while to grow your crops again" Then Sastro asked, "What will you do in Tenang?"

"Go to the *passar*, and also try to find work."

Sastro nodded then shifted gear, going up a steep slope. Soon they entered Tenang, where Sastro stopped the car. He rolled a *strootje*, lighted it and produced puffs of smoke.

"Are you going to the *passar* too?" Sukandar asked.

Sastro shook his head. He sat up straighter, yawned and stretched. "I have to be at a meeting tonight, and I still have some errands to run."

"What meeting?" Sukandar asked cautiously.

"A *Merdeka* group. Have you never been to meetings, where the Faithful gather to talk and make plans for *Merdeka*?"

"Not any more," Sukandar said, then asked, "Which *kampong* do you have your meeting?"

The chauffeur mentioned it.

"A friend of mine lives there," Sukandar said. "He works for the cause!"

"What's his name?"

"Alimin."

Sastro grinned. "That's where we're having the meeting." Sukandar said. "His wife is my cousin."

"Why don't you come with me?"

"No, not tonight. Besides, I also want to see Aminoto's wife. He's my uncle, and very much involved in *Merdeka*, but he probably won't be at your meeting tonight. He's in Surabaya, and my aunt is alone."

"All right. I'll see you some other time then."

Sukandar got out, said good-bye and turned the corner to go to the *passar*. He entered it with the familiar sense of coming home. A new family had grown around him. There was not just the buying and selling, but the feeling of togetherness, the mystery in soft voices, smells and noises. There was darkness and dirt too, and an amount of suspicion of cheating, but it was all carried up by a sense of family. He bought some juice from a vendor, drank it greedily, then bought the most needed items. His thoughts were with Alimin, Aminoto, his parents, and also Sastro, all still so full of certainty that their cause was sacred, the total conviction that they would be victorious in the end.

He passed one of the *passar* sheds then wandered down *Passar* Street with warehouses and a number of stores. Most were Chinese grocery stores, *tokos*. The Chinese were business people who owned stores and imported most of their wares. Natives mostly sold their produce at *passars*. Toko Wong, the largest store in town, was on Main Street and as Sukandar passed it he could see wares exposed on shelves along the walls. They were stacked on the floor too. Bags of flour and rice, sugar, spices, and household items.

As he wandered through Tenang he stopped at a *warong* and bought some satay to pass the time. He did not want to go to Aunt Sugi too early. When evening came and the sinking sun spread its colors over the sky, he walked to Aminoto's *kampong*, and soon reached his house. One of the lamps on the veranda wavered weakly with a crooked flame. He knocked on the door, and Aunt Sugi opened it, smiling at him as he entered. They sat down on wooden chairs around a round table, an open Bible lay on it, and above it hung a naked light bulb.

"Is Aminoto still in Surabaya?" Sukandar asked.

"He went there, but he said he'd be home today. He's late, and I'm glad you came. He's been to Surabaya several times to talk to some of the leaders, or get more books for his articles. I'm not sure." She shook her head and Sukandar could tell she still felt distressed about her husband's activities.

"I got a ride with a young man who said there was going to be a meeting at Alimin's house. Will Aminoto go there if he comes home tonight?"

"No, I don't think so." She paused then continued with a slight smile, "Alimin said that Aminoto is their inspiration."

Sukandar nodded. "I do believe that's true. Aminoto has so much knowledge."

They talked a little more about Aminoto then the conversation swerved to battles being fought. They tried to encourage each other not to lose hope that everything would come out all right. Aunt Sugi reached for her Bible and said, "I pray constantly about all this, but especially that Aminoto may see the light."

Sukandar did not know what to say, and when Aunt Sugi asked, "And what about you? Do you have a Bible?"

"No, but I've been thinking a lot lately about the Bible stories I learned in school. Especially the Christmas story."

Aunt Sugi nodded. "Yes, it's amazing that the Son of God came to earth." She leafed through the Bible then said, "Here it says, *'Jesus said, I am the Way, the Truth and the Life, and no one can come to the Father except through me'.*"

Sukandar said, "I suppose Aminoto doesn't like you to read the Bible."

Aunt Sugi said thoughtfully, "I don't think he's such a devout Muslim as he appears to be. For him the movement is more a political matter. And it's probably the same with Alimin."

They were silent a few moments when there was a noise outside, and Aminoto walked in. He smiled at Aunt Sugi as she served coffee. It was obvious he was happy to have her home from the hospital.

After some general comments about his trip he turned to Sukandar. Looking sternly at his nephew, he said, "Why are you not at Alimin's? You must know there's a meeting there."

"I'm sure you know already how I feel about that, Uncle. What else is there to say?"

"Yes, but I still don't understand. Haven't you forgotten what the Dutch have done to us? We've become a weak and defenseless people."

Sukandar faced his uncle with determination. "The Dutch may have done things wrong, but they've changed since the Ethical Policy in the beginning of this century. Also, they've brought the Good News in this country, a message of love."

Aminoto said sharply, "I believe you've been influenced by your sister. Are you thinking of becoming a Christian too? You, become an Infidel?"

Sukandar answered defiantly, "And what if I do? My sister is the most loving person I know, understanding and forgiving. Why should I not want to become like her? Jesus told his disciples to love your enemies. Does the Koran teach that?"

Aminoto did not answer that question, but shook his head sadly. "I am disappointed in you for leaving the sacred task you have been destined for. I can't understand the reasons behind this decision. But I still respect you because I know it was not cowardice that moved you. And, besides, you are still my nephew, and family is important."

Aunt Sugi looked relieved, and smiled at her husband. It was clear that she was happy Sukandar was no longer in the movement.

The rest of the evening passed in a friendly atmosphere, although it was inevitable that the war would be one of the main topics of conversation. Aminoto always had an unlimited store of memories and could tell interesting stories about the past, but tonight his mind was on the present and the immediate future, including the *Merdeka* cause.

"We'll get into a lot more trouble before we're free. Europe is embroiled in a flaming struggle for survival, but there's not only Hitler and Mussolini. What will concern us more is that Japan has joined them in the Pacific, and they are now after our resources. The Dutch are too weak too resist them.

We'll all suffer on account of the Japanese, but after they're beaten, we'll be free."

Sukandar asked, "What makes you think that if the Japanese evict the Dutch, that they will just leave and turn the whole country over to us?

Aminoto answered, "No, we don't think that will happen, for the Japanese would stay here as long as they are able to hold on. But after they have been defeated by the Allies, which seems a very likely possibility, seeing that the United States has great military power, then we will firmly declare ourselves independent."

It sounded like a prophecy. Sukandar grimaced. "I hope we don't have to suffer too long."

Aminoto looked at him. "Not too long. According to Djoyoboyo there will be an end to the reign of the *Orang Tjebol*, the little people from the North, in other words the Japanese, and then the Empire will once more belong to our own people." He shrugged and looked sad. "If only *Bung* Karno were free to inspire the masses. The spirit has gone out of many people since he was exiled."

They were silent while Aunt Sugi served more coffee and *kwe kwe*. Sukandar refused the latter, for he hated this soybean cake.

Aminoto went on, "*Bung* Karno inspired confidence. It was not practicality the people needed most. It was hope, and *Bung* Karno gave us hope. When *Bung* Karno was studying in Bandung he began to give public speeches. He said that the Indies should have a national identity, and be called

Indonesia, and the people Indonesians. This was not allowed because the Colonial Government was worried nationalism was going to get out of control. Now they have successfully paralyzed the movement by exiling our leaders."

Sukandar thought of the *Merdeka* efforts. Some months earlier he would have been involved, which seemed so long ago. The *Merdeka* people and the Colonial Government were at war with each other, but the opposing parties were horribly unmatched, like Goliath with a giant spear over against a puny David without even his slingshot and pebbles. God had seemed to be on the side of Goliath. Would he finally side with David?

Aminoto was more optimistic. "Our movement is like a volcano. If the crater is plugged too long, a violent explosion cannot be avoided. One of the few times the outside world heard about us was when the volcano Krakatau burst in 1883. That outburst will be nothing compared to the groundshaking *our* movement will bring about. Then The Hague, the center of Colonial power, will truly quake with fear."

It was getting late, and when Aunt Sugi said she would like to retire, Sukandar spoke, "I wanted too ask if I could sleep here. I had not planned too stay this late and. . . ." He was reluctant to explain that he did not like to stay at Alimin's.

"Of course," Aminoto laid an arm over his shoulders. "I'm sure you'll find work here. It's good to see you more regularly, and Talitha would like that. After all she's your cousin.

"But what kind of work is there? All I have done is field work, and carried mail. I do not have special skills."

"There are so many Europeans who need servants. They change servants all the time. Also, you can always try the Public Works. Roads, power lines always need repair and they need many laborers. Most of the Dutch men have been mobilized."

Sukandar smiled. "I'm sure you're right, and I'll look into that tomorrow."

Lying on his sleeping mat Sukandar thought about finding work in Tenang. It was true that he had enjoyed his independence in the mountains. At the same time, he liked the bustle of Tenang, and had missed people around him. Part of him had liked to belong to the group, because all his friends were involved in it, but so much of their leisure time was spent thinking and talking about *Merdeka*.

He sighed, and realized he had to confront the truth, make firm decisions about what he wanted out of life. Even his parents still did not know that he no longer wanted to become a leader of anything, let alone lead a group into a revolution. Yet, in spite of his misgivings and Aminoto's disapproval, he knew he had made the right decision. Something else would soon fill his life, he was sure.

Chapter Twenty-one

The Accident

February, 1942

Jasmine stood by the hedge, squeezing the handlebars of her bicycle. Mama didn't like her riding her bike to church, but Jasmine hoped to see Sari later, and didn't want them to know about it.

The others were already in the *dokar*. "Jasmine!" Mama made an irritated gesture, but Papa laughed. "She can follow us."

Jasmine got on her bike and rode beside the *dokar*.

At the church people were walking in through the wide-open doors. Jasmine put her bicycle in the stand and joined them.

The church was small and there were chairs instead of pews. The nicest things in the church were the windows with colored glass, red, white, blue, green and orange. Orange

The Accident

was her favorite color, like *afrikaantjes* or a Dutch banner at royal celebrations.

She sat down beside Yvonne, and turning a bit she saw Sari with her parents and brothers. Pastor De Waard went to the pulpit. After having his congregation sing two hymns he started his sermon.

"The love of God, Congregation, brings blessing. Man cannot live when there's no love."

Jasmine squirmed. These words touched a raw nerve, for hate and anger still boiled whenever she thought of Aunt Hanna.

". . .If we love God and our neighbor, he will bless us. Who is our neighbor? Everyone we come in contact with, every race, color and creed. . . Where there is no love, people perish. . ."

Perish? Many people had perished in Noah's Flood. Would there be another Flood?

". . .Yes, the love of God encompasses all. . ."

How could she love people like Marto and Dorothea? And Sukandar? Or Mr. Boon?

". . .Amen!" The pastor's hands came down after the blessing and they filed out, leaving behind the dying organ tones.

Jasmine blinked a few times in the bright sunlight reflected on the concrete square. She went straight to her bicycle. She did not want to wait for the others. She knew Papa and Mama would not want her to go to Sari as she planned. That's why she did not walk up to Sari who was with a group of people in front of the church.

Jasmine got on the bike and rode away from the church. She turned right at Station Street. A few other bicycles swerved skillfully along the path beside the road, tinkling warnings with their bells. She did the same.

She rode on, deep in thought, watching the front tire. How it happened she could never remember exactly. Suddenly there was a native man walking towards her. Sukandar!

He kept walking, head bent. She didn't slow down, but slanted off from the asphalt to the side of the road. She tried to avoid crashing into him, but she couldn't control her bicycle. It jumped over rocks and ruts, dipped into holes and slipped on gravel. She panicked as she came close to him. When he looked up in surprise, it was too late for him to jump aside. The next moment the bicycle rammed against his legs.

There was a flash of white clothes, brown arms and legs, a face, dark brown eyes. Jasmine slid onto the gravel alongside the street, and the bicycle rolled a few crooked feet further, after the steering bar punched her stomach like a steel fist. Her knee was bleeding, her stomach hurt.

Sukandar made a move to help. She looked up into dark eyes, and could see that he was upset. She ignored his move to help, and felt her eyes filling with tears. Through her tears everything was under water, and as she started walking without her bike, she sensed that he was watching her.

The Accident

She felt dizzy, and her knee hurt. The poplars along the road seemed to sway back and forth, but as she kept walking the trees stopped wobbling. Her legs knew where to go. Back to the church.

Although she couldn't think properly yet, she knew something had changed. She had thought she hated Sukandar, but knew it wasn't true. The memory nagged: dark eyes staring at her in astonishment, and yes, concern too. She couldn't escape them. It seemed as if she had looked into his soul, discovered all his deepest feelings. She began to tremble all over. Through her confusion the dark brown eyes followed her, and behind them stood a relentless power. *Merdeka!*

The minutes went by slowly as she kept walking.

Congregation, love is all. . . Where there is no love people perish. . . perish . . . perish. . . .

Oh God, help me.

She was not far from the church when she saw Sari, without her parents and brothers. Jasmine was so happy to see her that she forgot about ever having had bad feelings at all.

Sari saw her and walked over. "What happened?"

"I fell off my bike." She couldn't possibly talk about Sukandar now. She walked with Sari, away from the church. The *dokar* was not there, probably taking the family home.

"Where's your bike?"

Jasmine pointed vaguely.

"You'd better get it before someone steals it."

"It's wrecked."

"I'll help you get it home."

They were both silent as Sari helped her walk the bike to the house, then said good-bye.

In the meantime, Sukandar was walking towards Alimin's *kampong*. He had planned to go to the Town Hall to ask about work, but realized it would not be open on Sunday. He could not stop thinking about the girl with the bicycle. Sari told him her name was Jasmine. He saw again those blue eyes filling with tears. It seemed to him they had looked into his soul, discovered all his deepest essence, his will to do good, to strive for peace and freedom.

When he thought of the blond girl, he hoped the Dutch would not be beaten. He had come to realize how much the Dutch had done for his country. The missionaries, the doctors and all those who worked for the welfare of his people were all persons who cared about what happened here. He did not think the Japanese would be kind to the Dutch nor to the natives. All they wanted was to expand and get hold of vital resources. He began to walk faster, and not until he arrived at Alimin's did the uneasy feelings release him.

In spite of his conflicting emotions, Sukandar was glad to be back in Tenang. What he liked less was that he could not avoid seeing the men who were still faithful to the cause. Even when there was no official meeting, every visit with his friends or relatives these days turned into a heated discussion about the war and about how the Japanese could help them get free from the Dutch.

The Accident

With the Japanese attacking Java and other islands, it looked like the war which Djoyoboyo had predicted had come. The little people from the North were on the warpath, although most of the fighting took place in big cities and on the Java Sea. The Red Cross had organized Civil Defense activities and drills, and there was much to do.

Sukandar had succeeded in finding work with the Red Cross. He liked this work, such as making stretchers from bamboos even though it would only be temporary. Sooner or later the Japanese would leave, or the Dutch would surrender. And what would happen afterwards?

He did his work conscientiously. The headquarters of the Red Cross was in the house across the road from Sari's *kampong*. The family of the white girl lived there. He saw her more often now without Sari. Perhaps the time would come when he could talk to her without feeling nervous. He wanted to get to know her, a member of the people he so long had despised. All he had to do was wait patiently for an opportunity.

Chapter Twenty-two

Sonny

February, 1942

$\mathcal{P}$apa and Mama had not said much when she showed up with a bleeding knee and the handlebars twisted. Papa asked what happened and Mama had an "I told you so" look on her face. Jasmine had just shrugged and gone to the bathroom. Anyway, Papa and Mama had other things on their minds. They were going to take in refugees. In the middle of December Japanese planes had bombed Pontianak on Borneo, and many people had evacuated to Java. Most families in Tenang had taken in refugees.

But that was the least of Jasmine's worries. She had heard from Sari that Sukandar now worked for the Red Cross in Tenang. She remembered Sukandar's talk with Aunt Beatrice and that he might be working in Tenang, now that he was no longer a mail carrier. Jasmine was nervous about seeing him again.

Sonny

After the attack on Pearl Harbor the authorities had been looking for an appropriate place for head quarters for the Red Cross. The Big House had been chosen as it was one of the larger houses in town, and they had asked if the Carters were willing to have this set up. Since most of the responsibility would fall on Mama, the family had been surprised that Mama had agreed. She seemed full of newly discovered energy. She had reluctantly admitted that the reason she had not been able to handle the Boys Home was her fear that one of the boys might harm her children. She had not wanted to admit this, so she had said it was the work. Jasmine suspected that Mama had felt useless, and now wanted to be involved in the war effort. Her mother seemed to have accepted the inevitability of war, and she was the kind of person who normally liked to volunteer, especially in an emergency.

The Red Cross work involved civil defense measures. They had built two bomb shelters, a trench covered with tin sheeting *Kebon* had dug out in the yard, and one in a bedroom that was more like a comfortable little den. It was built of several double beds on their ends and extra mattresses. Papa thought this shelter was kind of flimsy, but they had been told to make it this way. Of course the walls of the house were constructed of cement and stone. When the civil defense drills alarm bleated over Tenang, they were supposed to drop whatever they were doing and go to the nearest one, usually the one inside.

A Garland of Emeralds

They were getting pretty good at getting to the shelter fast. These shelters and drills took on graver reality when they knew that they would shelter a family who had been chased from Borneo, where the Japanese were attacking, and many people had to flee for their lives.

The Hansen's arrived a few days after the accident, a mother and twelve-year-old boy called "Sonny". His real name was Johan Maxwell. With a name like that it was no wonder he proved to be a horrible pain in the neck. He had a pale face, brown hair and eyes, and fat lips.

After the first polite nothings, they had tried to engage him in real conversation, but Sonny only wrinkled his nose and sniffed. They kept trying to be nice to him, as Papa had told them, but that became more difficult every day.

"Sonny's a spoiled brat," Ellen said. Yvonne and Jasmine teased him whenever they could, but when Papa heard about it he was angry. How would they feel if they had lost a father in the army, and a sister, and had to leave home to go far away?

Some things about the war were fun, like the outside bomb shelter, which was an ideal place to play. But now the Hansen's were here with Sonny always pestering them the fun went out of it. The quarrels with him increased, and Jasmine felt the tension between Mama and Mrs. Hansen grow as well. Papa kept the peace as best he could, but he was not always home. Jasmine knew Papa thought Sonny was spoiled, but he would not say so.

Sonny

Sonny stuck to them like a parasite, and he had the sneakiest ways of starting quarrels. He thought he knew everything about the war and the Japanese. He bragged about what he would do to them if they came to Tenang. "The Japanese have no business here," he said. "When they come here I'll butcher them!"

"Ugh," Yvonne said. "You couldn't even butcher a bird."

"Oh no? You wait and see."

"You're going to be the one to be butchered," Ellen said.

Yvonne said, "They'd get their soldiers, cannon and guns and start shooting. Bang! Boom! Then they would drop a bomb and finish you off!"

They had been standing near the back buildings, and had not noticed that clouds had gathered. Thunder crackled threateningly behind Tenang, and it rolled out, growling along the mountains to the ocean. Cannon? The sun came through the clouds, making the windows glow, as if behind them the rooms were on fire.

In the meantime Sonny kept airing his arrogant opinions. Yvonne was testing Ellen on her history lesson, a homework assignment for Mrs. Van Doorn, who still gave Ellen and Yvonne lessons for a few hours a day. Sonny commented on Yvonne's questions and Ellen's answers. "All that nonsense about Holland's heroes! They're nothing but paper dolls."

Jasmine thought back to Mr. Breda's history lessons, and regretted not having appreciated them more. Ellen looked annoyed. "William of Orange was a mighty man."

"He was not," Sonny said.

"You know nothing, Sonny," Yvonne said. "William of Orange fought for Holland's freedom."

"Does that make him mighty?"

"Sure," Ellen said, "leaders of countries who make them free are always mighty."

"It's all lies teachers tell us."

"It's in a book, stupid," Ellen said. "About the King of Spain who conquered Holland."

"So, let him have it," Sonny said indifferently. Ellen was really angry now. "Holland had a right to be free! What business did the King of Spain have in Holland? None whatsoever!"

Sonny mimicked with a high twangy voice, "William of Orange was a mighty man, leader of his people. He made Holland free. Long live Holland. Long live the Prince of Orange."

"The Prince of Orange is dead, you stupid!"

"Good!"

"You're impossible, Sonny," Yvonne said. "Your Ma has spoiled you rotten."

"Oh, shut up." Sonny snorted and walked away.

"Okay, tattle to your Ma."

"I will."

"I hope a bomb falls on you."

"Hee hee." Sonny grinned.

It was best to pretend Sonny wasn't there, and this was not too difficult, if you were clever about it. Although this strategy worked well most of the time, it was at mealtime that he could not be avoided. Sonny was a fussy eater and his Ma never failed to announce what a tender stomach he had. She often said he did not have to eat porridge, and when she did Jasmine noticed Mama's chin jut out, and her lip curl in the familiar way. Mama was angry, but would not come out with it.

Jasmine knew every expression on her mother's face. A strained face with quivering rounded chin and wet eyes meant Mama was about to cry. A blazing face with rounded eyes and compressed lips meant that she was annoyed with one of the servants. A jutting chin and curling lips meant that she was about to speak her anger. It was this face she showed frequently when Sonny was around. Jasmine hoped Mama would give Sonny a spanking some day, perhaps when his mother was not around.

In spite of what Papa said, Jasmine felt that he was often impatient with Sonny too, but in the name of peace and quiet did not want to say anything to him or Mrs. Hansen. Besides, he kept saying that the Hansens had suffered enough.

It was the incident with Sukandar that changed Papa's mind about Sonny.

The Breda's had come to visit, including Dorothea. She and Sonny were obnoxious individually, but together, they were a horror! Sonny was bragging again about beating all the Japs single-handed.

Dorothea said, "The Japanese are an extremely aggressive race. They should be eliminated."

"Dorothea knows some fancy words!" Jasmine grinned at Yvonne.

They were on the patio at the back of the house, when a Javanese man walked towards the back buildings, and started to work on the stretchers for the Red Cross. With a shock Jasmine recognized Sukandar. It still bothered her that she had crashed into him that Sunday, even though it was because she had lost control. She knew she had been wrong in even thinking that he had anything to do with killing Aunt Hanna. Sari had told her that sometimes certain natives just went *mata glap*, berserk. Jasmine knew this was rare, because most natives she knew were kind.

For a few moments she stood open mouthed, expecting him to glare at her angrily, but he started working without looking at the children, plugging the ends of the bamboo stretchers with pieces of wood.

"I wonder why he's doing that," Danny said.

"To keep out rain water." Sonny curled his fat lips.

"You think you know everything," Ellen sneered.

"More than you, anyway." Sonny said, his hands in his pockets.

"Ha, listen to Ma's boy," Yvonne said, and mimicked in a high voice, "Oh Sonny, my little darling, don't go out in the rain, you'll catch a cold."

Sonny pushed out his jaw. "Watch it, I'll tell my mother."

Jasmine taunted, "Ma! The big bullies are teasing again! Yeah, right! We're not afraid of your Ma."

Dorothea wrinkled her nose. "You're all quarreling about nothing, and you don't even know yet what that man is plugging the bamboos for. Why don't you ask him? He's glared at us a couple of times." Dorothea took a few steps towards Sukandar, and said, "Hey! Stupid *Inlander*!"

Jasmine held her breath, but Sukandar pretended he had not heard anything.

"Shut up, Dorothea! Leave him alone. Can't you see he doesn't want to talk to you!" Ellen was angry, Jasmine could tell.

When Sukandar looked at Sonny, the latter glowered back. "Look at yourself, dirty *Inlander*!"

Sukandar returned to his job, but Jasmine felt fear coil inside her. She was glad when Mama came out with bananas. She gave one to each of them then went back in.

Sonny threw his peel in Sukandar's direction, who ignored it.

As the children walked back to the passageway, Jasmine looked at Sukandar, who got up out of his squatting position and started to walk to the kitchen which was in the back building. He had only taken a few steps when he slipped on Sonny's peel.

Sonny giggled. "Hee, hee, he slipped." For a few tense moments Jasmine watched Sukandar's face, pulled in a venomous grimace. Then he disappeared into the kitchen.

"Why did you have to laugh at him?" Jasmine really hated Sonny now.

"That was awful, Sonny." Yvonne glared at him.

Sonny giggled again. "He looked so funny."

Danny threw an angry look at him. "Who do you think you are! He's worth ten of you!" Then he walked off.

Jasmine stared after Danny, and felt respect for her brother for the first time. She had always been convinced that he was only concerned about himself.

When Sonny and Dorothea walked to the front yard, Jasmine turned to her sisters. "Let's go to Sukandar and apologize. I don't want him to think we're as detestable as Dorothea and Sonny. He's Sari's cousin, you know."

Ellen and Yvonne agreed and together they walked to the kitchen, where they found Sukandar standing by one of the windows. When they came closer, he turned around and faced them.

Jasmine stepped a little closer, facing him squarely, while gathering courage. "We want to apologize for the behavior of our guests."

Sukandar didn't say anything, just looked, as if he was trying to decide if she meant what she said. Then he nodded.

Encouraged by his mild attitude, Jasmine said, "I also want to apologize about crashing into you that Sunday." She looked at his face, still anxious, but he smiled slightly and said, "It was not your fault. I was daydreaming."

His reaction gave Jasmine courage to ask him what she really wanted to know.

"I know you were involved with the *Merdeka* movement, people who want to get rid of the Dutch. Why do they want *Merdeka* so much? Don't they have a good life?"

He looked at her as if deciding how much to reveal. Finally he said, slowly, "They want freedom for themselves, their own Government. They believe that this country should be ruled by the natives and not by white Colonials." He paused a moment then added, "I do believe the natives should run the government, but I decided to leave the movement, because it's turning to violence, and I don't believe in that."

Jasmine couldn't help feeling surprised, and she said, "I'm glad to hear you say that, for I was born here and I've always thought of this as my country." She looked at his face, which seemed to soften.

After a few moments he started talking again. "I was in the kitchen when you had that argument about the king of Spain. That convinced me that the Dutch are not being honest. They wanted to be free, didn't they?" He added, "Don't get me wrong. I don't hate the Dutch. They've done many good things which have benefited this country. But isn't it natural for a people to want to be independent?"

Ellen nodded. "You're right, of course, but the Dutch have been here so long that it's hard for them to change their idea that they belong here."

Jasmine found it more difficult to agree, because she was born here and always thought of this country as her own. She simply could not think of Holland as her country. Yet, she could understand the feelings of *Merdeka* people now. She was about to say that to Sukandar when there was Dorothea's mocking voice behind them. "Your own Government? You'd make a mess of things! You can't do it!"

Jasmine turned around to face Dorothea, and threw an angry glance at the obnoxious girl. It was people like Dorothea and Sonny who gave the Dutch a bad name.

Sonny joined them too, snickering.

Jasmine looked with dislike at Sonny and Dorothea, and wished Dorothea had stayed home and Sonny in Borneo.

They said good-bye to Sukandar, and entered the house strangely silent.

Later in the evening when she asked Papa about the bamboo plugging, she told him about Sukandar and Sonny and Dorothea making fun of him. She said they had apologized to Sukandar and Papa nodded his approval.

Papa explained, "The wood plugs are against rats," then added. "I'll talk to Sonny tomorrow."

At breakfast the next morning they all sat around a pan of steaming oatmeal standing in the middle of the table.

Sonny whined, "Do I have to eat porridge, Ma?"

Papa answered instead of Mrs. Hansen. Jasmine could tell he was angry. "We all eat what is served."

Mrs. Hansen pursed her lips, and Mama disappeared behind a cloud of steam after she lifted the lid. The big ladle scooped the bowls full of porridge.

Mrs. Hansen said, "I don't see why Sonny should eat this if he doesn't want it."

Mama looked determined, as she scooped on. Silence, except for the ticking of the clock on the buffet. Tick, tick, tick. Tension stretched. Jasmine could hear the leak in the attic drip, which drew her attention to the rain outside. Tick, tick, tick. All heads were bent over the bowls.

Sonny

Mama had reached Sonny's bowl, but he picked it up. "Not me!" He looked at Papa. "You're not my father, and I don't have to do what you say."

Papa's jaws tightened, but he did not say anything. Jasmine hoped that Sonny would not say any more either. Mrs. Hansen still sat with pursed lips.

Finally Papa said, slowly, "While you live in this house, you'll live by its rules, and I expect you to show respect for any person who lives or comes to work here."

"For that dirty *Inlander* too?"

Then everything went fast. Papa's chair flew back against the wall. He jumped up like an enraged lion, walked around to Sonny, boxed his ears twice then punched him on the shoulders. Sonny bawled. Mrs. Hansen got up to protect him.

Papa lifted his hand as if to slap her in the face, and Mama cried out, "Paul! Don't!"

It turned into a big fight. The table wobbled when Jasmine and Yvonne got up at the same time. Danny crawled under the table. Jasmine went up to Sonny and hit him on the head with her spoon. It sure felt good. It was as if she was taking revenge for Sukandar.

What frightened her was that Papa seemed to have lost control of himself. She had never known him except as patient and kind.

Sonny was running around the table, Yvonne after him. Ellen sat on her chair as if paralyzed, and Danny's head protruded from under the table now and then. Mama stood against the wall, her hand against her mouth. It was like a bad dream.

Then Mrs. Hansen and Sonny fled from the room as if the Japs were after them. Their bedroom door slammed. Mama wailed, "Oh Paul! What now?"

Papa was breathing hard and said in a voice Jasmine had never heard from her father, "It was time someone disciplined that boy." He sat down. "Let's eat," then forgot to say grace, and no one reminded him.

They ate in silence, but Jasmine found it hard to swallow the thick porridge.

Mrs. Hansen and Sonny stayed in their room all day, and Mama worried about them not eating.

Jasmine began to realize that Papa was angry with Sonny mostly because he had been nasty to Sukandar, and the porridge had only been an excuse. She loved Papa more than ever, and was glad she had found an explanation for his strange behavior.

She did not see the Hansens until the next day, but she knew Mama and Papa had gone to them and made peace. Jasmine was already in bed when Mama had come to kneel beside it. It was so strange to see Mama in that position that Jasmine felt uneasy. Not only that, but she could tell that Mama had been crying. Neither of them said anything for a while, then Mama got up and sat on the edge of the bed.

"What's the matter, Mama?"

"Nothing. It's all right."

"Are you sad about the Hansens?"

"Yes, but not in the way you probably think."

"Can't they live somewhere else?"

"Perhaps they will, but I want to talk about what happened. Papa and I always taught you that we should live peaceably with everyone, and we've not been good examples with Sonny and his mother."

"You couldn't help it. They're horrid."

"Jasmine!"

"Well...."

"I know how you feel, and that's why I want to ask you to be especially patient. We might have war right on Java, and that could mean dreadful times. We must do our best to love each other."

Mama got up and kissed her goodnight.

Jasmine could not sleep for a long time after that. The worry about war was like a disease that spread to all people. She would try harder to be kind to Sonny and his mother. This thought did not bring relief, only a strange sense of sadness.

Chapter Twenty-three

The Shelter

February, 1942

It was hard to stick to her resolution to be kind to Sonny. He was as pesky as ever and Jasmine was angry that Papa had asked him to join the choir he had started. Jasmine loved the choir practices in the dining room around the organ.

But it was not Sonny who caused problems, but Ruth and Louisa Boon. One afternoon, when they practiced harmonizing, the children were more restless than usual, and Papa more irritated. He sat on his stool, giving directions, when Ruth and Louisa Boon pushed each other, then began an argument. Jasmine did not know what it was about, and the girls ignored Papa's warning.

"It's not!"

"It's so!"

"It's not!"

The Shelter

"It's so, you stupid, shut up!"

This was too much for Papa. He slammed the organ shut, got up and said, with his last bit of polite dignity, "This is enough. We won't sing this afternoon, and you can go home." He walked away from the organ and out of the room with quick, short steps.

The children stood very quiet, impressed by the unexpected outburst, until Jasmine whispered to Louisa, "It's all your fault!"

Jeannie Werda added, "If my mother hears about this, she won't let me come anymore. You're ornery."

The Boon girls shrugged and followed Papa through the door, sisterly side by side.

After Papa had canceled the choir Jasmine went to see Sari. She was fed up with her Dutch friends, and wished Sari could be in the choir. It still bothered her that she had crashed into Sukandar. After all, he was her cousin, and Sari was special.

Sari seemed nervous.

"What's the matter?" Jasmine asked.

Sari pulled her towards the hedge around the house. "There's going to be another meeting at Alimin's."

Jasmine felt a cold tingle along her spine. Sukandar! And Marto? They might be there! Even though Sukandar had said he was not with *Merdeka* any more, the *Merdeka* people could be planning all kinds of things! "I'd better go home."

"No, stay!" Sari urged. "I want you to see Talitha."

"Your other cousin?"

Sari ignored Jasmine's ironic tone. "Yes, and Alimin's wife. She's expecting a baby. She became a Christian, we think because she and Lea are such good friends."

"I can't stay long. My parents don't know where I am."

When the meeting started, Jasmine and Sari sat on a tree stump hidden behind a rain barrel. They could see and hear the men in the circle around the fire in front of one of the houses.

Aminoto smoked a *strootje*. Alimin sat beside him, in white slacks, but Sukandar was not there.

Jasmine whispered, "Is Sukandar not in *Merdeka* any more?"

"No he isn't," Sari whispered. "But Uncle Aminoto is trying to get him to change his mind. Sukandar is afraid he or someone else will talk to his parents, before he does."

"Why would he be afraid to tell his parents?" Jasmine asked with a puzzled frown.

"If you knew his mother you would not ask that." Then she added, "I think Sukandar hopes to talk the people out of using violence and causing bloodshed."

The men were silent for a while, and Sari whispered names, including that of Sastro, Doctor Jansen's chauffeur. A woman came out of the house with refreshments.

"That's Talitha," Sari whispered. A few more young men came to fill the circle. Then Jasmine's eyes widened in shock. Their *kebon* was there! What was he doing here? She looked at Sari, but Sari did not seem surprised. Had she known? Jas-

The Shelter

mine remembered Sari's question about their servants. But *Kebon*? The one servant she liked best!

The old man, *Pak* Suyono arrived, and everyone listened respectfully to him. "Many things are happening. We need to organize and train ourselves in the better use of *klewangs* and *krisses*. There aren't enough guns."

Sari explained what he was talking about.

Jasmine's apprehension grew. "Who are they going to fight? The Dutch or Japanese?"

"Who knows!" Sari sounded worried. "You know about the trouble near the Mission?"

"Who told you?"

"Talitha. That's why she moved here. She's worried about Alimin, and doesn't like him to work for *Merdeka*. She's sad he's not a Christian."

They were silent as the men went on talking.

"The war could last many months," *Pak* Suyono said. "Our fate is in Allah's hands."

Aminoto said, "The Dutch made us a people of coolies, soft in spirit as kapok and weak of will as fried bananas."

"They're all imperialists." Sastro said. "They. . ."

All of a sudden the girls noticed Sukandar behind them. Sari asked, "When did you come?"

He did not answer, but stepped forward and approached the circle. He spoke in answer to Aminoto's remark. "What do you think we can expect from the Japanese? Japan began the war because they needed coal and oil, and whatever else. You're wrong to think they're coming to help you."

Aminoto made an agitated movement, waving his *strootje* as he turned on Sukandar and argued vehemently. "We may not be first on their list, but they will certainly beat the Dutch and then, when the Japanese have lost the war and leave, we will have our opportunity, because it would take the Dutch years to build up enough strength to stop us."

Everyone was silent, then Sukandar spoke again. "From what I've heard about the way the Japanese have treated, and are still treating the people in the territories they've conquered, they may be much worse than the Dutch."

Aminoto looked at him and made an irritated gesture. "I can see that you would rather have the Dutch stay here forever!"

"I believe it is possible to come to independence in a peaceful way." He started talking fast. "I'm totally against violence and lately the discussions have been more and more about revolution."

Pak Suyono said in a calm voice, "Why are we arguing about this. You know very well that every time in history a nation wanted independence, the only way that came about was through a revolution. The United States is a prime example."

Sukandar shrugged, pressing his lips together.

Jasmine remembered his words that time at the house. He must certainly mean what he said, if he went against the opinions of the older men. Young native people usually respected their elders. She felt more cheerful until Aminoto started talking again.

The Shelter

"They say the Japanese are about to land on Java. There's an Allied fleet on the Java Sea. There are reports of plunderings on the north coast, and some of the Faithful have stirred up the people to make trouble for the Dutch."

Was this for the cause of *Merdeka*, or was it to ease the way for the Japs, Jasmine wondered, and her fear returned. At first no one had taken the Japanese seriously. The papers were full of cartoons making fun of them. Of course *Merdeka* people hoped that the Japs would help their cause, for after all, the natives were Asians waiting to be freed by other Asians.

As the moon weaved its rays around the squatting figures, and the talk circled around the struggle for *Merdeka*, Jasmine was fiercely glad that Sukandar was no longer part of the group.

Pak Suyono threw a disapproving look at Sukandar then spat his chewed *sirih* quid into the center of the fire. He wiped the dripping blood-red saliva from his lips with the back of his hand, and moved his legs beneath him. He got up and the meeting ended.

Sukandar stayed in Tenang doing work for the Red Cross and came to the Big House often. Jasmine was nervous every time she saw him, especially when Sonny was around. Thank goodness Dorothea and her family had moved to Magelang. Jasmine hoped never to see her again. Too bad Sonny was still around!

One afternoon Jasmine saw Sukandar look at him, then spit on the ground. Jasmine hoped Sonny saw that, although she doubted that he would care. As for herself she felt that their apology had helped make Sukandar change his mind about *blandas*. She didn't think he hated Christians, because Lea was one. Sari had said that Sukandar knew many Christians were sincere like Lea. Suddenly Jasmine longed to see Lea's kind face, and hoped they could visit the Mission again soon. That thought perked her up a little, but she was still depressed the rest of that afternoon.

The only good things about the war were still the shelters. There were curtains against the "walls" made of stand-on-end beds. An old organ they had brought down from the attic stood in one corner with a stool for Papa to sit on. Jasmine almost longed for the alarm to sound, so that Papa could play while they were waiting for the "All Clear" signal. Yet when one rainy afternoon she heard the mournful air raid sirens her first reaction was fear.

When she entered the shelter Sonny was already there, sitting astride the organ stool. He leaned one cheek in his hand, his mouth hanging open stupidly.

"Can I sit there, Sonny?" Papa asked.

Sonny stared at him, got off the stool, and plopped down beside his mother.

They all sat in a half circle around the organ, while Papa was playing a tune. Mama's rattan chair stood next to Mrs. Hansen's and the children sat on the rug; Yvonne with a piece of embroidery, struggling with needle and thread; Ellen with her nose in a book, her right hand on *Mata Hidju*. Danny was trying to fix an old radio. Sonny held his sulky face in his hand, elbows on his knees. Jasmine was just thinking she should

The Shelter

have brought Mopsy in too, when she heard him whine, and she pulled him in.

The wind howled against the roof, rattling the windows like machine guns. They could see glimmers of lightning flash through the room. One loud crack of thunder drew Sonny out of his sullen mood. "That's a good one." An even louder clap made Jasmine think the house would come down.

Papa stopped playing when a deluge of rain battered the roof. God had judged the world in Noah's time, when the water destroyed everything. Noah had been in the Ark with his family, safe on the wild waves, with all eight people inside plus the animals.

Now the sea stood hollow and high all around them. It was a blessed adventure, for they had the Father's Son on board. A song began to sing in Jasmine's head, as she looked out over the violent sea and the scum-crested waves with courage.

She smiled as she listened to the thunder rolling. *Peace, be still, and the storm passed*; all eight of them were safe in the shelter. Suddenly Jasmine thought about Lea and the storm that afternoon on the Mission. There had also been eight of them. The noise outside lessened. Jasmine pressed her eyelids tightly closed, and imagined Noah's rainbow.

"Play something Paul," Mama said.

Papa began to play one of Jasmine's favorite songs. The tune made shivers run along her spine.

Leave your future to a loving Father.
Trust him ever, he will guide your ways.

Restless heart, oh see his light come nearer,
Night shall end and bright shall be your days.

Jasmine swallowed away a lump as she looked at Mama, whose lips trembled. Nasty thoughts disappeared. A warm feeling filled her, even for Sonny and his mother. After all, they'd been chased from Borneo by the Japs. She felt like protecting them.

She was so lost in reverie that she barely noticed the singing was over. She got up with everyone, when the All-Safe siren sounded, and started to walk out. She was rudely awakened by Sonny's strident voice, "Hey, you're stepping on my toes, stupid!"

Quickly she moved aside and stared at him blankly a few seconds. Then all old resentments surged back. That ape! That. . .! And she had wanted to protect him! Then she saw Mama press her handkerchief against her trembling lips, her eyes full of tears. A searing pity for Mama blotted out thoughts of Sonny. As she made up her mind to help Mama all she could, she was sadly aware that the fragile, tender mood of the past moments had cracked.

Towards the end of February a letter arrived from Aunt Beatrice. Papa frowned when he read it.

"What is it?" Mama asked.

"She says there's trouble in the area, and she wonders if we would consider coming to see her."

"What kind of trouble?"

"She didn't say, but apparently some of the residents are acting out of character."

"You want to go?" Mama looked resigned.

"Yes, I think we should."

Chapter Twenty-four

Lea

March, 1942

It was not until the beginning of March that Papa could get away. Ellen and Yvonne protested when he said they would stay with the Van Doorns again and continue their lessons. Mama packed Jasmine's and Danny's school books, but Jasmine hoped she would forget about them at the Mission.

It took some days for Papa to make arrangements to find a replacement at the Boys Home. His usual person was ill. Papa was worried about Aunt Beatrice, and as soon as he had found someone they boarded the train.

When they arrived at the Mission, Nusomo, the *guru*, came out of the school with Sukandar. What was Sukandar doing here? He seemed to be traveling back and forth a lot. Then Jasmine remembered that Sari had said he came to the Mission area as often as he could to see his parents and Lea.

Nusomo greeted the family and Sukandar bowed his head lightly. When Papa, Mama and Danny started walking towards Aunt Beatrice's house Nusomo asked Sukandar how he was, and why he had come.

"I heard there was trouble in the neighborhood and my parents may need me. Also, they want to know if Lea's all right. They know there may be danger for Christians."

Nusomo looked worried. "It's too dangerous to go to the *dessa* now, because of the *rampokkers* in the area. Lea suggested your parents come to the Mission until the trouble is past, but they refused. As for you, what can you do to help your parents?"

Sukandar shrugged. "Not much perhaps." After a few moments of silence he added, "I'll go and see Lea now."

Nusomo nodded, and Sukandar walked away. Nusomo started to walk towards Aunt Beatrice's house and Jasmine followed, thinking that Nusomo was right. What could Sukandar do? How could he protect anyone? Being a Muslim he might not be attacked himself, but if whoever wanted to harm Christians knew that he was trying to help his sister, he would be in trouble. Suddenly Jasmine began to worry about him.

They arrived at the house where Papa stood by the veranda steps. Still looking worried Nusomo said to Papa, "There are *rampokkers* close to the Mission."

Papa looked grim. "The *'nDoro* wrote about some trouble, but I wasn't sure what it meant."

"Because of the rumors that the Japanese are close to Java, some natives are trying to take advantage of the situation. Of course that has happened before, but now I'm sure fanatic Muslims are involved."

Papa shook his head and Jasmine's anxiety grew. Fanatics meant violence.

They joined Mama and Danny in Aunt Beatrice's office. The latter sat at her desk and asked, "What now, Nusomo?"

"Do you have a lot of money here?'

"Why do you ask?'

"You should not wait to get yourself and your possessions to safety."

"Why?"

"The Japanese are close to Java, and I believe some natives will start plundering stores and homes."

"Do you think they'll come here?" She seemed absent-minded, and Jasmine couldn't believe she was calmly arranging her papers when there was trouble brewing. Yet Aunt Beatrice had seemed worried when she had written to Papa. She must be pretending. Although Jasmine was irritated about Aunt Beatrice's calm, part of her admired her courage.

Nusomo seemed agitated. "Anything can happen."

"No one has ever done us harm. I don't see why I should suddenly. . . ."

Before she could finish there was a knock on the door.

"Come in," Aunt Beatrice said.

A man barged into the room, disheveled and wide-eyed. Without greeting, he blurted out that droves of natives were plundering the stores and the houses of the Chinese in a town east of the Mission.

There was a stunned silence. Aunt Beatrice sank back in her chair. Her shoulders sagged a moment, but she straightened them again. She looked at the man and said, "You must warn the police and the Assistant *Wedono*. They should be able to do something." *Wedonos* were native heads of districts who worked together with their Dutch counterparts.

"It has been done," the man said.

"Good."

Nusomo urged once more, "Will you let me take your things? Everything will be safer in my house." He hesitated then added, "And I wish you would come."

Aunt Beatrice shook her head. "I can't abandon the residents, and we have medical supplies here." She agreed to let Nusomo take some of her things, and the Mission money, then got up and stood behind her desk. She reached for her Bible, read a few passages and prayed.

Nusomo turned to Papa and Mama. "I think it would be better for you to come to my house. You and the children will be safer there."

Papa hesitated, but Mama said, "We will."

They went to their rooms to get their suitcases. When they came back they followed Nusomo, who was carrying Aunt Beatrice's money, some papers and most of her clothes.

Jasmine was really frightened now. They were the only Europeans here, for the doctors lived farther away. There was no telephone and no car.

Outside there were no other people to be seen. It seemed they had all left the Mission. It was inky black and it started to rain. Nusomo led them to his barn. "It's safer here than in my house."

They put their suitcases on a wooden platform, and sat down beside them. Nusomo left, but came back ten minutes later with some blankets and pillows. That night they slept on the hard boards, on a thin mat. This was the way most Javanese slept. Turning from one side to another, Jasmine wondered how they could stand it.

The next day was Saturday and Doctor Jansen came by. He had heard of the trouble and wanted to see what he could do to help. He told them Aunt Beatrice still refused to leave.

Jasmine peeked through the bamboo wall and could see the chauffeur Sastro behind the wheel of the Ford.

When Papa said he did not want to leave while Aunt Beatrice was still at the Mission, the doctor left. As the sound of the engine faded, Lea came in.

Jasmine was so glad to see her that she ran up and hugged her. Lea put her arms around her, smiling. As they were talking, Jasmine sensed Lea's anxiety. Lea said she was worried about Aunt Beatrice, but could not persuade her to leave either. Finally Lea said, "The *'nDoro* has no idea what is going on, but there's new danger.

Papa asked, "*Rampokkers?*"

"No, they are leaving the area, but I heard rumors that fanatic Muslims have declared *Jihad*, Holy War, and their priests are telling the Christians that whoever will not embrace Islam, will be killed and all Christian influence will be destroyed."

"Are they close to the Mission?" Mama had gotten her handkerchief out and pressed it against her nose.

"Not yet," was all Lea said but Jasmine could tell she was upset. Lea stayed for a while longer, then left, saying that she would come to see them later.

It was scary not knowing where the Japanese were. They hadn't gotten any newspapers, Aunt Beatrice's radio didn't work and no one else had one.

They were sitting in Nusomo's living room on Sunday morning, the eighth of March, when the mail carrier came in and said he wanted to go into town to see if he could get food, and perhaps a newspaper. An hour later he came back, excited. He had heard on the radio that the Dutch capitulated in Bandung, the army's headquarters.

They all stared at him in silent consternation. Mama had her hankie against her nose again, and Jasmine had an 'It can't be happening' feeling. The Japanese had won, and could be here any time.

Mama looked at Papa and said, "What about Ellen and Yvonne? We should have stayed home. We must go back."

Papa looked worried too, but he said, "They'll be all right. Nothing much is going to happen there for a while, now that the fighting has stopped. We'll go home as soon as we know Beatrice is safe."

It was hard to tell what Nusomo was thinking, but he invited them to dinner. His wife was helping their *kokkie* set the table and bring in the food. They ate in silence. The news about the army capitulating had seemed to depress them all. They stayed at the house and had tea later.

That evening, as they were getting ready to go back to the barn, they heard a loud banging. It sounded like it came from Aunt Beatrice's house. Nusomo went to the front and Papa followed him. Jasmine and Mama joined them. A group of men were forcing their way into Aunt Beatrice's house.

Aunt Beatrice, an oil lamp in her hand, and wearing a nightgown and slippers, spoke to them, her voice loud and clear. "Who are you? What do you want?"

The men did not answer, pushed her aside, and entered the house. Soon they came out, carrying things one by one into the yard. Everything, including furniture, was thrown onto a growing pile. It was not until the men began dragging out medical supplies, that Aunt Beatrice started walking toward them putting up her hand, trying to stop them. Most of them ignored her, but one came up to her. "Dress yourself like a native. Be one of us."

Jasmine thought that was a crazy thing to say. But Aunt Beatrice did not seem surprised at the man's statement, for she turned to face him. "Dear man, I have no such clothes." Apparently she understood their way of thinking, and even in her sodden nightclothes she looked dignified, not at all afraid for her personal safety. Or perhaps she was just not thinking straight!

"What's going on?" Papa asked.

"It's what I feared," Nusomo said, with a grim face.

"Feared?" Mama wiped her forehead.

"It is as Lea said. Some Muslim priests came to the Mission and threatened to kill the residents unless they recanted the Christian faith and became Muslims. They would also be killed if they helped the leader or invited any Christians into their homes. They're showing that property of Christians should be confiscated or destroyed."

"What about you? You'll be in danger!" Jasmine looked at *guru* Nusomo with new respect, because he knew and had still helped them.

He shrugged, and turned to look out again. "I'll be all right."

Aunt Beatrice had followed the men in. It was still drizzling, and the yard was muddy.

"We should do something to help her," Papa said, and started to go out.

He was just outside the door, when Aunt Beatrice came out of her house again, her slippers almost disappearing in the mud, and her nightgown clinging to her legs.

Nusomo seemed strangely reluctant to go out and help her. Although he had tried to get her to come to his house, it was clear that he intended to stay away from the Mission house now that those men were there.

Papa came back into the living room, a helpless but firm look on his face. He said to Mama, "You and the children go back to the barn."

"You're not going to the house are you? You'll get killed!" Mama said, fear in her voice.

As Papa ushered them into the barn he said, "I'm going to get Beatrice. I don't think Nusomo dares do it, and we don't want him to get into trouble." Then he walked in the direction of Aunt Beatrice's house.

After about fifteen minutes Papa returned to the barn, holding an oil lamp. "You'll be safer here," he said over his shoulder, and to Jasmine's relief a disheveled Aunt Beatrice followed him, almost falling over the threshold.

Mama put her arm around Aunt Beatrice's shoulders and led her to the platform. She gave the dazed woman a blanket and pillow, and after a few minutes they all settled down to sleep, as pigs squealed on the other side of the wall.

When they woke early the next morning, Aunt Beatrice had already left the barn. When they looked though the door opening, they saw her close to her house. She stood still, staring ahead.

Jasmine saw why, and gasped. "The house!"

Gaping holes where windows had been. The door ripped out. In front of the house all Aunt Beatrice's possessions had been thrown in violent disorder. Clothes and books, chairs and paintings, tables and china, all heaped on the muddy grass. Aunt Beatrice stepped over the shards of broken flowerpots while some of the residents were standing at a safe distance, watching silently.

Papa looked grim, and Mama's face was ghastly white. Jasmine grabbed Danny's hand. She could see Lea standing with the residents, who seemed as reluctant as Nusomo to help. They must be petrified. Jasmine wondered where Sukandar was. Had he gone to his parents already?

Papa called loudly, "Come back here, Beatrice before they hurt you."

Aunt Beatrice did not respond, and Jasmine noticed that the silent crowd across the road had grown. Suddenly there was another sound, a wailing. "*'nDoro, 'nDoro!*"

With a shock of recognition Jasmine saw Lea's frail figure come forward, throwing a sheet at her mistress. She walked back quickly when a man approached menacingly. Aunt Beatrice draped the sheet around her body, but when she walked to the house, Papa left the barn and started towards her.

Jasmine let go of Danny's hand, and followed him. When they approached the house, Aunt Beatrice seemed to come out of her daze and started shouting, "You evil men, how could you . . ."

Jasmine put her hand to her mouth. Someone jerked her shoulder. Danny. "Let's get out of here!" he hissed. "I don't know what's the matter with Aunt Beatrice! We'll all get killed."

A man with a *klewang* in both hands approached Aunt Beatrice.

"Come on!" Danny grabbed Jasmine's arm, but she squeaked, "We can't just leave her! And what about Lea, she's there too."

Suddenly there was a hoarse cry. Lea ran towards Aunt Beatrice again, shouting, "Run, *'nDoro*! He will kill you!" She screamed again.

Someone else shouted, and it took a few seconds for Jasmine to realize the words came out of her own mouth. "Aunt Beatrice! Run!"

To Jasmine's consternation, Lea confronted the looters. She shouted at them in *Javaans*, and seemed to be telling them what they were doing was wrong.

Two more men came up, threatening her. One spoke in Malay and Jasmine caught the meaning of what he said. It was something like, "Java is for the Muslims and all Christians will be killed. You became a Christian and if you continue in your heresy, you will also be killed."

Lea shouted, "No! I will not become a Muslim! Jesus Christ is the Son of the living God, and your Allah is a false god!"

The next few minutes would always remain a confusing memory for Jasmine, if she dared think of them at all. One of the men turned and grabbed Lea's arm while another turned on her with a *klewang*. Lea struggled to get free. He let go of her, while the man with the *klewang* turned to Aunt Beatrice. Lea shouted, "*'nDoro!*"

Just then Jasmine saw Sukandar walk up from the entrance gate. He stopped to stare at the scene, then ran to his sister. But Lea was close to Aunt Beatrice now, raising her arms in front of her mistress. Then the man turned to her, raised his *klewang*, and a second later it came down on Lea, drawing a bloody gash from her left shoulder to her breast, slicing her white *kabaya*. Lea slumped to the ground.

Aunt Beatrice gave a strangled cry, too stunned to move. Papa ran up, grabbed her arm, drew her away and walked in the direction of Nusomo's house.

Jasmine stared at Lea's body as the man with the *klewang* walked away. Sukandar made a move as if to follow him, but he turned towards Lea. A scarlet stain had spread over her *kabaya*. He bent over her, and touched her shoulder and hand. He shook his head as he rose and stood stock still for a few moments. He balled his fists. Jasmine sensed his consternation, grief and rage that one of his own people had killed his sister.

Jasmine was aware of a choking sensation as he looked up and faced her. For a few intense moments their eyes met. It was as if they finally understood each other. There was a flash of understanding, a brief connection. Suddenly she knew what he felt, how he felt. He knew that it was not right what these natives did to Christians, whether they were native or white.

Sukandar seemed to be making a crucial decision. When a man with a knife walked up to him, he ran towards Jasmine. As she turned to look for Danny, Sukandar grabbed her by the arm, pulling her into a run. Jasmine let herself be pulled. She had a last look at the heap of things in the yard, on top of which was Aunt Beatrice's Bible.

Papa and Mama stood with Danny and Aunt Beatrice at Nusomo's house. Nusomo gave them sheets, saying he would send for help. A young man stood with them. Alimin.

Jasmine was glad to see him, but wasn't sure why. She didn't really know him, only that he was Sukandar's friend, and had relatives in the neighborhood.

Sukandar pointed towards the trees. "We must run. Follow us."

Jasmine had never heard such authority in his voice. Even Aunt Beatrice didn't object.

As they ran Jasmine wrapped the sheet around her body, and the others did the same.

"Where are we going?" Papa asked.

"To the cemetery, *Tuan*. They will not follow us there."

"But Lea. . .," Jasmine said, looking behind her once again.

Sukandar pressed his lips tightly. Lea was dead! For the first time Jasmine felt real compassion for him, and forgot her own pain.

Sukandar and Alimin took them to the cemetery. For hours they huddled at the foot of a tree, one of the many weird looking ones there. No native would dare come here, especially after dark. Jasmine understood why Nusomo had given them sheets. It made them look ghost-like. Christians did not believe that the spirits of the dead would do them harm of course, but what about Sukandar?

Now that they were relatively safe, Jasmine thought back about the eerie scene at Aunt Beatrice's house. It was strange that they hadn't even seemed to notice the Carters. Perhaps that was why Nusomo didn't interfere, for that would have called attention to him and to his guests.

Aunt Hanna's death was eerily like the way Lea was killed. Jasmine pushed all memories of that from her mind, which was difficult right in the middle of a cemetery. Death was frightening, but here they were, moving about as ghostly yet living apparitions. The place of the dead had saved their lives.

Wrapped in the sheet Aunt Beatrice looked more pitiful than ever. Jasmine tried to undo all the unkind thoughts of many years. "Thank goodness you're still alive." She made it sound as sincere as she could.

Aunt Beatrice merely shook her head.

Yes, they were alive, but back there was Lea on the ground, dead. The ugly truth had begun to penetrate Jasmine's frozen brain. She heard Sukandar whisper, "Lea" a few times, and she never thought she'd be glad to have him there. Lea's brother, whom Aunt Beatrice had not trusted. They stood together, as if they'd always been friends.

Suddenly Jasmine wished Sari were here, but that was a selfish thought. Sari would be so shocked about Lea. Also, this was not the safest place to be even for Sari. Besides, Sari was afraid of cemeteries.

The next morning when the doctor's car came to take them to Tenang, Aunt Beatrice refused to come. She wanted to make sure Lea got a Christian funeral. She would stay with Nusomo.

Chapter Twenty-five

Moment of Truth

March, 1942

So the Japanese had landed on Java. The Allied Squadron under rear-admiral Karel Doorman had been defeated. Hospitals were filled to overflowing. Smells of Lysol, chloroform, groans, casts, Red Cross nurses, white and native, blood on limbs and heads. Wounded on stretchers from the *Prince of Wales* and the *Repulse*, from American ships, from invaded cities.

Pastors praying, priests offering last rites, the Lord's Prayer. . . . "Forgive us. . .for Thine is the Kingdom, and the Power, and the Glory for ever. Amen." All this went on while soldiers were creeping through *sawahs*, swamps, jungles, swimming in seas, marching through forests. Streams of refugees, mothers and children, through jungles, on ferries, bobbing between Borneo, Sumatra, and Java. Large empty houses. It was a sad panorama, Sukandar thought, but it was nothing compared to what he felt about his sister. A sorrow gnawed in his stomach at the sad waste of a beautiful life.

The most terrible moments of his life. The Mission. Lea losing her life to protect her 'nDoro. A man with a klewang. A hoarse cry. Lea running, shouting. "He will kill you!" The lady running, the man turning. The klewang slashing into Lea. White kabaya and scarlet blood.

He had stood rooted to the spot, in a nightmare. From Lea's huddled form he could not tell if she was dead. The man who had done this had walked away as if nothing had happened. Still stunned he had moved towards his sister, touched her shoulder, her *kabaya*. Another scream and he had run too, avoiding the scythe meant for him. He and Alimin had led the 'nDoro and the *Pandita's* family to the cemetery. Later he had brought Lea to his parents who had allowed a Christian burial after Nusomo spoke to them. Sukandar had stayed with his parents to comfort them on the loss of their daughter.

He shook off the agonizing memories with difficulty, and it was late in the afternoon when he started his journey back to Tenang. He did not feel safe, now that there were rumors about guerrilla bands, mostly made up of natives who had been in the Dutch army. It was believed they were led by AWOL Dutch officers. He would have to walk most of the night, longer perhaps, if he had to hide from guerrilla groups. The Japanese had thoroughly upset their lives even though they had not come here yet.

It was quiet. Only the wind played through the leaves. He was tired and for an hour he sat on the grassy hill, looking at the sky and the trees. Everything had been created by the Almighty, including the people who made war on each other. The Almighty God was not only a God to fulfill personal desires or even the wish of Muslims to be free. Men had united in prayer to God for rain, which was for all people, but men should pray for peace and freedom for all people, no matter what creed they professed.

He stared ahead into the darkness, and walked for another hour. It was past midnight when he reached Tenang. His aunt and uncle had told him that he was welcome to stay with them. It did not seem to bother his uncle that his property in the mountains would revert to wilderness once more.

One evening he and Aminoto visited Alimin and Talitha and their new baby boy. They were sitting on the front porch. Sukandar tried to fathom what his uncle was thinking, he who had experienced so much in life. It still seemed strange that his aunt was a Christian, while Aminoto remained a Muslim.

Sukandar knew Aminoto strongly believed that young people should respect their elders, like *Pak* Suyono. Both *Pak* Suyono and Aminoto worked for the cause with fervor, although they differed in the way they viewed the cause. *Pak* Suyono saw it as a means to gain spiritual supremacy, while Aminoto was interested in political action. Sastro and Alimin were both as young as he was, yet Alimin had always been a much more ardent nationalist. Alimin found the old men at the *dessa* meetings tiresome. All they did was talk endlessly about wearing or not wearing sarongs and *pitjihs*. Alimin said he preferred the Tenang group, where the meetings were much livelier, and the young people were allowed to speak their minds.

Sukandar had agreed partly, but he knew that the fervor of the old men such as *Pak* Suyono was real. He had sensed the throb of revolution in them. What more could they do but talk? It was not totally useless, for it kept interest, hope and courage alive.

Anyway, he was happy that he had succeeded in distancing himself from the group, where talk was about things which had been discussed countless times. It was amazing that even these repetitions had the power to draw people. Here in Tenang they were seriously starting to talk about weapons. Of course that was because of the war.

A kerosene lamp hanging on a beam in the porch hissed softly as they remained silent for a while. Talitha had gone into the house to tend to the baby.

It became clear what Aminoto was thinking when he started talking. "Many things have been happening since the Japanese landed. There are rumors that guerrilla groups are active, somewhere in the forests."

Sukandar said, "I know. When I came back from my parents I was afraid to meet them."

Aminoto ignored that and said. "That should not concern us. What we need is stronger organization and to train ourselves in the better use of *klewangs* and *krisses*."

Sukandar wondered cynically how they planned to do that with the Japanese breathing down their necks. Then felt ashamed for he knew that the men of Java were no cowards. Many had joined the Dutch army and fought under white officers. Some of the *Merdeka* people had done that because they wanted to learn the methods of war. They had trained for months on the *alun-alun* in front of the *tangsi* in Magelang. *Pak* Kromo's group had gotten hold of more *klewangs*, even one gun, but they could not do much with one gun and only a few bullets.

Aminoto's voice intruded on Sukandar's thoughts. "It's obvious that unarmed you cannot defend yourself against a great number of soldiers who have all kinds of weapons. Nevertheless, all the armies in the world will not succeed in enslaving those who want to be free. We have tried to follow a policy of cooperation, but it failed to produce results."

"But what can we expect from the Japanese?" Sukandar asked. "Japan wants power. They started the war because they need coal and oil and bring their own kind of imperialism. We're mistaken if we think only the whites are imperialistic."

Talitha came to bring some refreshments, and while they enjoyed those, Sukandar's thoughts went back to the defeat of the Dutch. The Japanese had convinced them all of the superiority of their military. At first no one had taken them seriously, and the papers had been full of mocking cartoons. Now they knew better, and fighters for freedom were generally convinced that the coming of the Japanese spelled hope for them. Weren't they Asians waiting for delivery by Asians? It had become clear that the Dutch were doomed after American and Australian airplanes had disappeared.

The Red Cross chapter in Tenang had closed. Even though the war was still going on in other parts of the Indies, on Java it was over, and Sukandar had not found another job. He told his uncle one evening, "I want to see my parents. I know they're still grieving for Lea, and also. . . ." He hesitated.

Aminoto looked at him. "And also, you didn't tell them yet that you've not been involved in the fight for independence."

Sukandar looked at his uncle, and nodded. "I feel bad about hurting their feelings, especially my mother. But I'm sure they suspect that I'm no longer involved." He smiled slightly. "Someone may have told them. News travels as fast as the wind. It's *kabar angin.*"

But there was more that bothered him. He had felt their pain at Lea's loss and wanted to assure them that he still greatly respected them even though he had disappointed them. They had always been astounded by Lea's devotion to the *'nDoro* more than to her becoming a Christian. His mother had once said that if the opportunity arose, Lea would give her life for this Dutch lady, and had failed to understand such fanaticism. Now this prediction had become reality and they were suffering.

It was not until the following day that he left Tenang, once again walking the road he had walked so often. Most of the time he did get rides, mostly from men with trucks, sometimes from a Dutch planter.

He remembered the visit to his parents at the last *Lebaran* when his life had gone at an even pace according to a plan. He had still been sure of himself then. Perhaps it was because during *Lebaran* all the *dessa* people went to pray on the mosque square, and he had always been part of it. Sukandar reflected guiltily that he had not prayed very much. The direction of his life was still too uncertain for him to think clearly.

He also remembered with nostalgia the celebrations they had at the last *Lebaran*. During the day everyone visited friends and relatives, and *selametans* were held. Everyone gave gifts; there was a spirit of goodwill, and the poorest got extra gifts of rice, money or clothes. Most important, *Lebaran* was the time to ask forgiveness of people you had wronged. He knew deep in his heart that he wanted to ask his parents for their forgiveness for disappointing them.

When he arrived at his parents' *dessa*, and reached their house, he could see they had been expecting him, although he had not sent any message. His mother held him fast after he had finally told them that he had not done what they had hoped for him. His father put his hand on his shoulder, and said, "My son, you have always been a good son, and all I have always wanted for you is to find your own destiny. I know that you will choose wisely."

Sukandar's eyes filled with tears. They shared a meal, as they shared their mourning for Lea, who had followed her own convictions. All was well, at least in their family. Whatever else may still happen, they would bear it as a family.

Chapter Twenty-six

The Japanese

March, 1942

A week after their return from the Mission, Jasmine went to the *kampong*, and found Sari sitting on the front steps of her house, crying. Jasmine put her arms around her friend's shoulders. They sat together silently for a few moments.

"She was such a lovely person," Sari said, and Jasmine knew she meant Lea.

"Yes," was all Jasmine could bring out. The choked feeling was back in her chest when she thought again about that ugly scene at the Mission. To break the uneasy silence she said, "They smashed the house and all the medical supplies! It was terrible! And they threw Aunt Beatrice's things in a heap on the lawn. It's a miracle we escaped."

When Sari did not say anything, Jasmine continued, "I never thought I'd see fanatic Muslims at work, wanting to kill

Christians." There were again the vivid images. Aunt Beatrice sopping wet. Natives with swords, dragging things out of the Mission house.

Still silent, Sari nodded, wiping her eyes with the back of her hand.

Jasmine said, "If it weren't for Sukandar, we might have been killed."

"Sukandar's back in town."

"Alimin too?"

"No, and Talitha's really worried." Sari looked at Jasmine. "Did you know they killed the doctors?"

Jasmine gaped at her. "How do you know?"

"Sukandar told us."

After a few minutes Sukandar came out of the house across the street. Talitha followed and Sari said, "Let's go talk to them."

Jasmine greeted Sukandar diffidently. He nodded and sat down on the top step, slowly, like an old man. She wanted to know about the doctors, but was afraid to ask. After a tense silence, Sukandar began to speak. He told them how the doctors had been stabbed and then buried while they were still alive.

"How do you know all that?" Sari asked.

"Nusomo came to see me, for he knew that I was with my parents. Doctor Jansen had come by the Mission to see the 'nDoro who was still very upset. He had advised her to leave as soon as possible. It just wasn't safe to be there alone as a white woman." Sukandar was silent, lost in thought. "The next day Sastro came, totally upset, and told him what had happened to Dr. De Lange and Dr. Jansen."

Jasmine listened, not really believing. The doctors, who had only wanted to do good things here on Java, thrown into pits. As Sukandar talked, images came. Doctor Jansen's groaning Ford jumping over ruts, diving into potholes. Doctor De Lange, a friendly face, cheerful voice. She would never see them again. The doctors' cruel death erased her last doubt about the Colonial Government having collapsed.

When Sukandar finished talking, Jasmine turned to him. "Thank you for what you did for us."

He looked at her and said, "I'm glad I was there to help. Those men would sooner or later have come after your family."

She said simply, "You saved our lives! But I thought those men acted very strangely. Why didn't they come for us right away?"

Sukandar said, "They may have been in an opium trance. Sadly there still are too many who indulge in this vice. If they were sober they would have come after Nusomo too, for he was the teacher at that Mission."

Jasmine thought of the opium kit in Tenang. She'd never quite understood what that was all about. She was still thinking about that as Sari walked her home. Jasmine promised she'd come again soon.

At home Jasmine wanted to blurt out the news about the doctors, but hesitated, because Papa and Mama would want to know how she knew. The newspapers had not reported the killing which had happened in an isolated place. Also, some of the Dutch newspapers and radio broadcasts had been banned. The Japanese had started to take control of the media. So, if Papa and Mama asked how she knew, she would have to say that she had been at Sari's.

The next day Jasmine walked into the back yard, just in time to see *Mata Hidju* with a squeaking bird between her teeth. She caught the cat and tried desperately to free the bird, but the cat swung out her claw, tightened her bite and ran off into the bushes. Jasmine slumped down on the grass, feeling guilty. She should have tried harder to save the bird, and now it was too late. Tears came whenever she thought of that 'too late', and began wishing the cat were dead.

When Ellen found *Mata Hidju* dead under the hedge a few days later, she was inconsolable, and Jasmine's guilt about wishing the cat dead almost overwhelmed her. Of course it happened often that natives put poisoned food in the bushes, or the cat just ate some spoiled food. Sitting on the top step of the veranda, she watched rain drip from the roofs and drawing dark streaks on tree trunks. She had always loved rain, but now she could understand Mama's gloomy moods when grey clouds hung low.

Thinking about the deaths of the bird and *Mata Hidju* brought to mind the doctors and Lea. She decided to tell her parents about the doctors. Still nothing about the killing had been reported in the newspapers or radio. So at dinnertime she suddenly blurted out, "They killed the doctors."

They all stared at her open-mouthed. "The doctors?" Mama asked.

"Yes, Dr. De Lange and Dr. Jansen."

"How do you know?" Yvonne asked.

"Sari's family."

Papa wanted to know how they knew, and when this happened.

"Sukandar went to his *dessa* and found out."

Ellen asked, "Why didn't you tell us before?"

Jasmine shrugged, too choked to speak.

They finished the meal in silence.

After their naps, Mama asked Jasmine again about the doctors. "What did Sari tell you?"

Jasmine didn't want to go into the gruesome details, but she knew Mama and Papa had a right to know. "Sukandar found out from *guru* Nusomo that they stabbed them first then buried them alive." She almost gagged on the last words.

Ellen and Yvonne gasped, Papa looked shaken and Mama's chin started to bulge up. The doctors had been the first Dutch friends they had when they came to the Indies. The silence stretched for some time until Jasmine could not stand it any more. She walked out onto the veranda.

The happenings at the Mission faded as constant news about the Japanese victory poured in. They had marched into Batavia, the capital, on the first of March, after the battle on the Java Sea, when the Japanese Navy pushed through Doorman's fleet. The 'Java will stand' motto of the weakening Dutch Navy had echoed like the wailing of sirens.

On the eighth of March the Japanese had arrived in Bandung where the Dutch army capitulated and the Colonial

Government surrendered. The defense of Java had been like people playing at war. They had sat for hours in the shelter, but not a shot was fired near Tenang. Not a single bomb fell. The Japs had an easy victory and came with their motto: 'Asia for the Asians', which, Jasmine was sure, really meant, 'The Indies for the Japanese'. The radio had broadcast the last sad speech of the Governor-General, which ended ". . .until better days. Farewell." They had been at the Mission when that happened, but the speech had been in all the papers, just before the Japanese started banning Dutch media.

Papa and Mama were glued to the radio once more, and this time the children listened too. Tanks thundered into the big cities, bringing horrible reality: They're here!

Within a week the Japs were all over Java, entering every town and city, streaming out like a *bandjir*. In a way the radio announcer recounting these awesome events made them sound like exciting stories. And that's all they were until the Japanese came to Tenang the third week of March.

Jasmine felt apprehensive when she heard the news, yet at the same time she was filled with an obsessive curiosity and a determination to face the danger squarely. She also sensed a fear in Mama, who seemed nevertheless driven by the same morbid desire to see the victors march into town. Mama suggested they walk to Main Street to see them.

So they watched the Japs peddle into their lives on bicycles, wearing white surgical masks. That looked so strange! Jasmine was not sure what exactly she had expected, but certainly not these little men wearing gauze masks as if they

The Japanese

feared a pestilence. It was as if some undigested thing that had lodged somewhere in her body, had suddenly dissolved. She felt like giggling and nudged Yvonne. Seeing these soldiers ride through Tenang on stolen bicycles, she felt a strange kind of pity for them, because they looked so insignificant. When one of them faced her she dared look straight into his black eyes. She had the sensation of having just awakened from a long nightmare in which she had run along endless roads, breathless and weak-kneed.

They were ordered to go to the *alun-alun* to listen to a speech from the Japanese official who was in charge of Tenang. They went, and when Jasmine listened to the speech, she had to think back to the time the native Regent had given a speech on the occasion of Princess Irene's birth. It was eerily the same, except that this time the talk was about cooperation from the Dutch with the decisions of the Japanese rulers. One of the rules was that they were to call Japan *Nippon*, and that they had to bow whenever they came close to a Japanese soldier or officer.

In spite of this show of power, when they got home everything was the same as it was before, except that the Hansens had moved out. Jasmine was happy about that. Mrs. Hansen said she was upset about the Japs following them to Java, and that they were going to find a safer place to live. Jasmine was sure they had moved because Mrs. Hansen hadn't liked Papa's and Mama's attitude toward Sonny.

But the Carters were to get another refugee. One afternoon Ellen and Yvonne returned from the Boys Home with Papa, after their lessons with Mrs. Van Doorn. They were talking excitedly to Mama, who sat behind her sewing machine.

"Aunt Beatrice is coming, Mama!"

"What?" Mama looked at Papa, perplexed. "Why did Beatrice change her mind?"

Papa sank down in his favorite rattan chair. "I really don't know, but one of the nurses has heard from the Mission."

"*Babu* Noenoeng cleaned the front room. Beatrice can have that." The front room was where the Red Cross had been.

Mama turned to Papa. "Beatrice must have been greatly upset about the doctors,"

Yvonne was just asking, "Why didn't she come sooner?" when Jasmine shouted, "There she is!"

A *dokar* drove up and Aunt Beatrice descended, slowly and regally. When she walked up to the veranda, Jasmine noticed that her face was pale and drawn.

Papa and Mama greeted her, then Mama led her to her room, asking if she wanted tea.

"Later Beth, if you don't mind. I would like to rest first."

After Aunt Beatrice had settled down for a nap, Mama went back to the dress for Yvonne, white with red polka dots, like tiny Jap flags. The needle stabbed relentlessly into the red polka dots. Papa sat sideways on the balustrade, beside Danny's dangling body. No one spoke.

The next afternoon Aunt Beatrice's iron resolve broke. They were sitting on the veranda again, and when Aunt Beatrice talked there was a noticeable quaver in her voice. But

The Japanese

she said nothing about Lea or the doctors, not even about the destruction of her possessions. She had both hands over her face, when she blurted out, "I treated him so badly, and he saved my life!"

"Who, Beatrice?" Papa asked gently.

"Sukandar." After a brief pause she added, "And I feel so bad about Lea getting killed trying to protect me."

Then Aunt Beatrice sobbed openly. They all stared at her. This behavior was so completely foreign to Aunt Beatrice, that it took some time to take it in.

Papa said, "We can thank God for people like Sukandar and Lea."

Beatrice nodded, and Papa went on, "You must not keep blaming yourself. That will not bring Lea back."

Aunt Beatrice was still wiping her eyes when Sukandar walked around the bougainvillea arbor. He paused a moment, then walked slowly up to the veranda steps.

"What is it, Sukandar?" Papa asked kindly.

"I wish to speak to the *'nDoro* of the Mission."

Aunt Beatrice looked at him, and for the first time Jasmine saw uncertainty on her face. "Yes, Sukandar, what do you wish to speak about?"

"I know you cared about my sister, and she loved you and the Mission. I want you to know I'm grateful."

Aunt Beatrice said with difficulty, "I loved Lea! I'm so sorry I couldn't save her! I also want to thank you for helping us. Forgive me for not always treating you kindly."

"I forgive you," Sukandar said solemnly. "But I have often thought badly of you, although I know you have done a lot of good for my people and for Lea. So I must ask your forgiveness."

Jasmine was astonished. How difficult it must have been for him to admit this.

Aunt Beatrice said, just as solemnly, "I forgive you."

Sukandar said, "Thank you," then he added, "I'm very sorry about the doctors. They were good men."

"Yes, a terrible tragedy," Aunt Beatrice agreed. They all sat in silence, while Sukandar still stood on the steps. It was a momentous moment. Then Sukandar just bowed briefly and walked out of the yard.

Later that evening Jasmine had trouble shaking off the images of killings. She had learned a lot in the last few weeks. She had been afraid of Sukandar, but he had shown he was a good person. She had always disliked Aunt Beatrice, but now she felt pity because Aunt Beatrice was a homeless wanderer, a pilgrim.

Crickets chirped and the moon pulled a sparkling path across the wet palm leaves, as Jasmine reflected on the astonishing surprises in life. Would there be more?

Chapter Twenty-seven

The Arrest

April, 1942

Thinking about war had made everyone irritable and on edge, yet now that the enemy was among them, Jasmine lost some of her fear. Actually, the Hansens had been more trouble, and she was glad they had moved. That left Aunt Beatrice, who basically had not changed, in spite of her experiences at the Mission. She looked the same as she always did, her mouth drooping in a downward curve, and her forehead puckering into many wrinkles. Her back never touched the back of any chair she sat on, and she usually embroidered or knitted, driving the needles as if they were swords in a duel. She knew a lot about the Bible and prayed constantly, so she must love God. Jasmine only wished she were nicer.

One Sunday something strange happened after church. The pastor had preached about love again. He had told them how important it was to love even their enemies. He pointed out that the Japanese soldiers were perhaps longing to be home with their families. Jasmine almost began to feel sorry for the poor soldiers so far from their home.

Walking home, the grownups were busily discussing the pastor's sermon, and the girls trailed behind, looking for flowers. Jasmine was thinking about what the pastor had said, that human beings were all the same, with the same need for love.

By the time they passed the cemetery, the adults with Danny were way ahead. Two Japanese soldiers stood just inside the cemetery entrance, laughing and chatting. One of them had a camera. They did not seem afraid to go into cemeteries. Of course no ancestors of theirs were buried here.

"It looks like they are taking pictures," Ellen whispered.

"Of the cemetery?"

One of the soldiers gestured for them to come closer. Ellen hissed, "Don't go!" but Jasmine and Yvonne went up to them. One soldier kept smiling and beckoned to Ellen. He showed them the camera and pointed to a flower bed.

Ellen came, still cautious, but Jasmine and Yvonne showed their widest smile, especially when the soldier made strange noises while he took pictures.

The soldier with the camera touched Jasmine's hair. "*Mas Bagoes.*" A few moments later they gestured that the girls could go home.

The Arrest

When they told Papa and Mama, Mama looked worried, although they had found out that most Japanese liked children. But you could never be sure, of course.

Mama asked, "Why would they want pictures of you?"

Yvonne said, "I think they liked our red polka dot dresses, tiny Japanese flags."

Aunt Beatrice said, "I'm sure it's a propaganda stunt. They'll send them to Japan so everyone can see how well Japanese soldiers and white children get along."

Jasmine thought that sounded stupid, but who knew these days?

After supper on Monday there was banging on the door. Mama turned pale, and Aunt Beatrice showed her tension with a nervous twitch of her lips. Papa was at a meeting in the Boys Home.

Mama told the children to go to their bedroom, which they did.

Jasmine was frightened and excited at the same time. She heard Mama go to the front door, and open it. There were voices, talking to Mama in broken Malay.

Japanese soldiers! Jasmine crept out of the bedroom and sneaked down the hall, ignoring Ellen's frightened whispers. She came close enough to hear what the soldiers were saying. She was not sure if they were the same ones from the cemetery, but she hoped so. At least they were nice.

The soldiers wanted to see the *nonnies*, who lived in this house.

A Garland of Emeralds

Jasmine sensed her mother's fright. She had heard rumors about Japanese wanting white girls for their soldiers, and knew there were some Dutch girls who had been ordered to report. Mama stammered in Malay that there were only two old ladies and a little baby boy, and *Tuan Nippon* must have the wrong house, perhaps the wrong town.

Jasmine suddenly felt great admiration for Mama's courage to tell Japanese soldiers a bald faced lie. She only hoped that Aunt Beatrice with her passion for truth would stay away. The two *Tuans Nippon* looked suspiciously past Mama into the hall, and Jasmine pressed against the wall.

At last they left, leaving Jasmine with trembling legs, as she watched Mama on the threshold, waiting till she was sure the soldiers had left the yard.

Jasmine went back to the bedroom to discover Aunt Beatrice huddled with the others on Ellen's bed, her hands folded and her lips moving.

"They're gone," Mama said, and fell down beside them. "I thought I'd die!"

When Papa came home and they told him what had happened, he threw a worried look at Ellen and Yvonne. Ellen was fifteen and Yvonne fourteen. Papa and Mama said nothing more, but Jasmine knew they were worried about what the Japanese might yet do.

One afternoon in the middle of April there was another visitor. Jasmine heard voices, which sounded like Mr. Boon and Mama, on the front veranda. She peeked around the door and saw him sitting on Papa's favorite rattan chair, his

The Arrest

legs stretched beside the low table. It made her furious, and she almost jumped forward to drag him off. She had never been able to figure out why he upset her so much. It seemed silly to be angry at someone making fun about your hair.

His news obviously upset Mama. "Are you sure? Someone came to tell Paul all men had to report at the Resident's office for an important meeting with the Japanese officials."

"He won't be coming back. They took all of them to a prison camp."

Jasmine lifted her hands to her mouth.

"I can't believe it," Mama said.

"I wouldn't tell you if it weren't true, Beth," Mr. Boon said in an oily voice.

Jasmine leaned against the doorjamb not quite believing what she had heard. Yet it had to be true, for Mama seemed to believe it, for she had not even served tea.

"How about you?" Mama asked. "Did you not get an invitation?"

"Yes indeed, and I obediently presented myself."

"They let you go?"

Mr. Boon explained with a mocking smile, "They discovered that I was a Eurasian, and let me go." He settled himself more securely in Papa's chair, and lit one of his smelly cigars. "I wouldn't worry, Beth. Paul might be allowed to return home, because of the kind of work he does."

"I hope so!" Jasmine heard Mama's uncertainty, and saw that her chin began to bulge up. She herself had not quite taken in what they had been saying. Papa gone? Where? If she could believe Mr. Boon, Papa might come home again, and she hoped he was right, for it would be too much to bear if he didn't.

Mama pulled herself together. "Where did they take them?"

"Semarang."

"Semarang!" Mama rose and paced restlessly behind her chair. Semarang was a large harbor city northeast of Tenang.

Jasmine's thoughts raced. She wanted to challenge Mr. Boon but managed to stand perfectly still.

Mama put her hand over her mouth. "Oh no! He doesn't have a change of clothes!"

"You'll probably get a chance to bring him some soon, if he hasn't come home by then."

When Mama finally offered tea, he said, "Don't bother, Beth. I've stayed too long already."

Now that was the truth, Jasmine thought, as Mr. Boon rose. He shook Mama's hand, walked down the stone steps, and disappeared behind the hedge.

When Mama sat down again, Jasmine could read the anxious thoughts on her mother's face, and she longed to comfort her.

Mama did not say anything about Mr. Boon's visit. Jasmine was dying to tell her sisters and Danny what she had heard, but talking about it made the awful truth more real. It was not until they went to bed that Mama told them that Papa had been taken prisoner. She sat on the edge of Ellen's bed, and her eyes began to fill with tears.

The Arrest

Yvonne asked, "Why didn't Mr. Boon go to the camp?"

"He's an Indo," Jasmine said, hearing the bitterness in her voice.

"So what!" To Yvonne the coming of Mr. Boon with such terrible news about Papa and not having to go to prison too, was totally unfair. She did not seem to like Mr. Boon now either.

Jasmine felt sorry for Mama who looked as if she was about to cry. Jasmine's irritation about Mr. Boon, and her sorrow about Papa was drowned in Mama's obvious distress.

Ellen asked with a strange squeak, "Will we ever see him again?"

"Of course," Mama said, a little too hastily.

Jasmine became aware for the first time of a real ache, as if she had not known the horrible truth since teatime.

During the following days this ache about her father's leaving so suddenly stayed with her constantly, and she felt the shock of his sudden disappearance out of her life like an emptiness that nothing could fill. Yet alongside the ache, hope persisted that he would come back, as Mr. Boon had said.

While they were waiting for news about Papa, the Japanese became more entrenched on the islands. It did not seem so bad at first. The military government of Lieutenant-General Hitoshi Imamura was mild, and they said he might lose his job because of it. Jasmine hoped that Japan had no mean generals.

They couldn't have books and magazines with anti-Japanese things in them, or any portraits of members of the Royal Family. Jasmine had to think of the large portrait of Queen Wilhelmina in the classroom. Mama had hidden all pictures of the Royal Family.

The Japanese Emperor, Hirohito, also called Tenno Heika, King of Heaven, was now the supreme ruler of Java, and they had to do what he told them. Not all of it was bad. Tenno Heika's birthday was April 29, and he showed royal benevolence that day, at least the *Tuans Nippon* made sure the Dutch knew what a great favor their Emperor was showing to his subjects. In honor of his Divine Majesty's birthday they could visit Papa!

When they were all on the veranda having tea, Mr. Boon came to tell them what they already knew.

Mama said, "We heard, but thank you anyway for coming."

With chagrin Jasmine noticed that he sat on Papa's chair again. She nudged Yvonne, and wrinkled her nose. Mama said, "I've already packed some clothes, hoping for just such an opportunity."

This time Mama had not forgotten to offer tea and biscuits. The time for good cookies was over. Ellen helped her, since they had to dismiss Djaidin, the last of the servants.

They drank their tea in silence, until Mama said, "What a situation! Paul must be reeking by now."

Mr. Boon got up. "Now you have a chance to bring him some clothes." He left.

The Arrest

To Jasmine it was as if the last remarks made everything acutely real. Papa had always loved his baths, and he said he felt like a beggar if he could not bathe and change. Perhaps he did get a chance to bathe, but he had no clean clothes.

Ellen asked, "Do we have to pack our clothes too?"

"Yes, get your suitcases ready. We may have to stay overnight in Semarang." Jasmine tried to fend off the growing fear that after this visit, she would never see her father again. And failed.

Chapter Twenty-eight

A Hill of Trouble

April, 1942

Early in the morning of the twenty-ninth of April they left by train for Semarang. There were many families crowded into the train, from Magelang and other places as well as Tenang. Jasmine was not interested in talking to anyone. She was thinking about the times she had been in Semarang.

She remembered going to that city when she was little. The green hills, the harbor, an endless sheet of water, the Java Sea, glimmering in the sun. Mama had pointed to the grey horizon, saying that Holland was on the other side of all that water.

Jasmine had tried to pierce the horizon barrier, to imagine what Holland looked like. Such a wonderful country according to Mama, who had looked over the water with misty eyes, saying, "Some day we'll go back there."

A Hill Of Trouble

Jasmine had been uneasy then, but now the war had thrown up its own suffocating barrier. The war and the Japanese had changed everything. That became clear when they arrived in Semarang, and were told to walk from the station to the men's camp. The last time they had been in this city, there had been someone with a car, or they had hailed a taxi or a *dokar*.

They were overwhelmed by the music coming over numerous loudspeakers all through Semarang. It was the *Kimigayo*, the Japanese national anthem.

Jasmine was taking steps but her body did not seem to move forward much. But that was all part of this strange day, which stretched out like a dream. A hill of trouble lay before them, and it seemed they would never reach the top. And Papa.

Mama was slightly ahead, with Danny beside her. Ellen and Yvonne were walking ahead of them as were Aunt Greta Smid who clutched her baby girl in her arms. Three-year-old Herbie with Jan and Carl walked beside her. Aunt Greta was the only other woman in Tenang whose husband was in this camp. All other husbands were in military prison camps, probably mostly in Bandung or Batavia, because the military had been concentrated there.

Jasmine drew a shaky breath. "Are we almost there?"

Mama took a few more steps before she answered. "At the top of this hill is Papa's camp."

Papa. Jasmine swallowed the painful emotion, which had clogged her throat all morning. On this high hill the thought that Papa was not with them was ten times more bitter than how she felt at home. How was she going to live without him? He had not even had a chance to say goodbye.

When walking became a tired shuffling of feet, Jasmine tried to remember how many streets they had passed. Left. Right. Left. Right. She noticed that the streets with the *tokos* were behind them. In front was the smooth asphalt road winding up. Such a hill should be a pleasure to climb, not hot and high with the sun burning above her throbbing head. She stumbled over a rock.

Mama looked back. "Jasmine, don't daydream. That Japanese soldier is going to pounce on us for dawdling."

Jasmine's heart beat with quick little throbs. It was not a dream. After today she would not see her father again for a long time, perhaps never. She tried to absorb the shock of this 'never'.

They finally reached the top, where the dark-grey stretch of asphalt road continued, shaded by trees and with a tall fence alongside. They came to a gate where Japanese soldiers ordered them to line up on a large concrete square. Hundreds of women and children arrived from every direction. Jasmine was surprised to see so many people. But of course many women had come from Magelang and other places too. They put their suitcases down.

Yvonne was rubbing her hands. "I'm sweating like a pig."

"Me too," Jasmine said, while she trembled at the thought of seeing Papa in this strange place.

Close to the fence stood a few *waringins*, silently observing them. Did they disapprove of this unholy situation? Jasmine tried to shake off this stupid feeling. She was getting too old to pretend trees had feelings like humans.

They were made to stand for about half an hour, while the heat shimmered and the stench of sweating bodies pierced the nostrils.

Another series of jerky orders made them move slowly forward through the gate where they bunched together in fearful silence. Jasmine pinched her suitcase handle between her thumb and forefinger, as if that could give her courage. She swallowed noisily.

Ellen complained of sore feet. Mama was silent, and Danny seemed to sleep while walking. Aunt Greta and her family had joined them.

Yvonne was still rubbing her hands as if she wanted to squash something. Jasmine stretched her neck, but there were too many tall women in front of her. The crowd spread out and thinned, so that the men became visible. In their white suits they stood like crosses on rows of graves. Jasmine scanned the rows, but could not see Papa.

Mama craned her neck, and sweat moved with the ripples of her skin as she turned her head this ways and that. "I see him!"

"Where?" Jasmine whispered, standing on her toes.

"To the left, second row." Mama pointed.

Jasmine stared at the figure that was her father, and was almost surprised to recognize him. She had expected to find him stranger than the strangest relative in Holland, but she realized it was impossible for someone to change much in such a short time. She kept staring at him. He stood stiff and silent, as if he had really turned into a cross. She tried to control her shaking legs. She hoped she would not faint. A sense of dread filled her at the sight of bayoneted guns.

A Japanese officer on a platform began to speak. An interpreter translated that showing emotion in any form, such as kissing, crying or embracing, was not to be indulged in. That was a vulgar Western habit. The officer's snarling words went on for a while. He finished by saying, "You may go see your men now. You have half an hour."

Aunt Greta hissed, "They're crazy! Two days' travel for only half an hour!"

"You'd better keep that to yourself, Greta, or we'll get nothing," Mama whispered.

Carefully searching for their men, trying to keep their children quiet, the women walked forward. Mama and Aunt Greta walked side by side. Jasmine practiced her broadest smile behind their backs. She wasn't going to risk their safety by crying.

She was wondering what to say to Papa, but before she could think of anything, they stood in front of him. All she could do was look at him, as he stood there, smiling. His clothes were dirty and he looked tired. There was sadness in his eyes.

Mama grabbed his hand, and whispered, "How are you?"

"Fine. And you?"

"Don't worry about us."

Then Papa turned to Jasmine and smiled. He took her hand, and the next moment she hugged him, ignoring the "no embracing" order. As she put her head against his chest he became real once more.

"How are you, Jasmine?"

Ordinary words. Words he had spoken so often in their earlier life. Yes, how was she? She did not really know anymore, and felt herself drawn dizzily in the whirlpool of change. Even though she felt more like crying than ever before, she had to pretend happiness, for this was a different life.

"I'm fine. You too?"

"Yes, of course."

They were in a play, with parts that demanded they had to be happy. It was not too difficult, because everyone else on the field was desperately happy. Papa played his part well and chatted with them as if he were just on a short trip and would soon be coming home.

The only one who seemed his old self was Danny, who grumbled that he was tired and hungry and wanted to go home.

They walked towards a wide, gloomy hangar-like building with hundreds of thin mattresses on the floor. They were only allowed to look inside. Papa placed the suitcase on one of the mattresses. He took out clothes, soap, toothpaste, towel, toothbrush and hairbrush. There was also a small Bible, which he shoved under the mattress.

Papa came out and started talking to Mama again. Jasmine stood near the door apart from the others, and could not hear what they were saying. All she noticed was how much Papa and Mama looked like all the other couples on the field. As she watched Papa smile and talk to Ellen, Yvonne and Danny, she felt a strange relief for it seemed so normal. She walked up to them.

"Don't worry," Papa said, "Everything will be fine." Mama did not respond and Jasmine was glad he could pretend so well. This too was a strange relief.

It was at this point in her thinking that she saw a man kiss a woman and she held her breath, hoping no Japanese had seen it.

When their half hour was almost over, a Japanese soldier came to bark some orders in Japanese. Perhaps he thought they should know enough Japanese by now to understand what he was saying.

"I think he's telling us to go," Mama said, and held Papa's hand more tightly. Anxiously Jasmine watched Mama's chin bulge up and her lips quiver. Careful, Mama. Pretend just a little longer. As if her mother had heard the silent message, she created a crooked smile.

Another barked order, and the handshaking began once more. Papa shook Mama's hand so long and firmly that Jasmine's head began to move up and down in rhythm with the motion. She was still in a play, and it was best to get used to it and shake hands with him, like everyone else.

A Hill Of Trouble

While they walked slowly to the gate, Papa, with the other men, were ordered to stand in the center of the field again. Women and children gathered near the gate.

Suddenly there was a long drawn-out wail. A woman ran from the group with arms stretched forward, "Oh Robert, Robert!"

A Japanese soldier came forward and pushed the woman's chest, shouting angrily. She would not go and for a few minutes the two struggled. Then the soldier gave her a firmer push so that she fell to the ground, still calling, "Robert!"

A man came running from the line-up of bodies, his face contorted. "You dirty dog! Get your hands off my wife!"

His fist came very close to the face of the soldier, who moved back a bit. Then the soldier raised his gun butt and beat the man on his head and shoulders. Jasmine could not move. A terrible fear petrified her. She stood on wooden legs, straight and stiff, feeling her face draining, while a paralyzing cold crept through her body.

She wanted to groan, but only a choppy kind of fast breathing came. Trees wobbled, and she felt herself grow small as a marble, then larger than a house. She pinched her thighs, and held herself stiff, so that she would not fall over. Through her consternation she clearly saw and heard everything. Little Herbie Smid crawled on the grass on hands and knees, between people's legs. Ellen and Yvonne had turned pale. Mama and Aunt Greta stood stock still, Mama's right hand raised, holding a handkerchief.

The soldier's voice thundered and the man fell on the grass, holding his arm over his head, as the soldier kicked him, as if he never planned to stop.

Jasmine swallowed, but her dry throat could only bring out a hoarse whisper. "Do you see Papa?" It was the only important thing, to know how far Papa was from the soldier. The latter was still beating, when another white figure emerged from the rows of men, going up to the soldier, who looked surprised.

"Paul!" Mama's scream.

Papa? Jasmine could not believe this. Her heart was still ice, and her legs still wooden, but her eyes functioned perfectly. Papa's hand went up, as he tried to stop the beating. He shook his head. The soldier turned on him, and swung the butt in his direction.

Where was her fear? Her legs became flesh again, and they moved, one, two, three steps, faster, to Papa. He was in front of her, his arms over his head, warding off the strokes.

Jasmine saw his face. Vaguely she heard Mama scream, but she was burning with an uncontrollable urge to fly at the Japanese, to scratch his eyes out, and to beat his ugly nose to pulp.

Papa said, "Jasmine, go back! I'm all right. I love you!" He had spoken hurriedly, and then the butt whacked his cheek and he sank to the grass.

"You swine! Miserable ugly swine!" Jasmine shrieked, and flew at the soldier who gaped at her with wide, black eyes. Her hands moved and she scratched at his face, pummeled his shoulder and chest. He was not much bigger than she was, but he had a gun and when he moved his arm, the butt hit the side of her head, so that she fell on her knees beside Papa.

The first thing she became aware of was a thick silence. Only one barked command, and the boots walked away. Papa was on the grass, white and still. Was he dead?

"Papa," she whispered. He did not move at first, and she put a hand on his. To her immense relief he opened his eyes, smiled faintly, and squeezed her hand. "Forgive them . . ." He closed his eyes again. Jasmine looked at the other man. Was he dead? He was bruised and his eyes were closed. His wife was nearby, her hands against her face, as if the sight was too horrible. Jasmine's head hurt. She felt a bump near her left temple.

After the soldier had gone, some men came to carry Papa and the man called Robert into the barracks. When she got up slowly, feeling dizzy, soft, kind hands on her arms pulled her in the direction of the others. Mama was lying on the grass very pale. Was she dead? She wanted to ask Aunt Greta, who had pulled her away and still held her, but she dared not.

"She fainted," Aunt Greta said softly.

"Oh." That was not so bad. It had happened before. Jasmine put her hands to her face, for she did not want to see anymore. She did want to cry, but they were told not to. Or was it allowed now? Perhaps it was, for Ellen and Yvonne were both crying. When she looked at them, their tears freely on their cheeks, she burst out in tears too and felt the relief. "Papa! Papa!"

"Shh," Aunt Greta soothed, and pulled Jasmine against her soft side, where Jasmine sobbed against her dress. Mama stirred and opened her eyes, which stared up to the sky. When she saw Jasmine, she got up and hugged her so tightly, that Jasmine almost choked. Mama had never held her so tightly, and Jasmine was sure now that everything had changed. Nothing would ever be the same again. She looked up and saw sweat streaming from everyone's face and she wondered why they did not wipe it off. Fat, slow flies seemed the same, still teasing, as always, and the sun had moved along its trail in the sky.

Back home the following day the world was still as it had always been. Only two things were different. First, Mama had not noticed the bump on the side of her head. Jasmine lifted her hand to the sore spot and decided not to draw Mama's attention to it. Mama had enough problems. The second thing was that Mama sobbed loudly, her face in her hands, elbows on the table. Her sobs, usually quiet and subdued, were so open and forlorn, that Jasmine was sure this was the end of everything.

During the following days it seemed as if they were all waiting for something, not knowing exactly what. In this tense waiting were hope and despair, excitement and boredom, terrors and fears, and gloomy news on the radio. Burma occupied, a fierce battle in the Coral Sea, someone proclaiming that the age of imperialism had ended, Australia attacked. When were the Allies finally going to free them?

Jasmine was deeply despondent, certain she would never see her father again, and sometimes hate and anger flared like a flame inside her. How was she going to live without a father? A life without him seemed an insurmountable hill.

To escape the confusion of feelings, she sometimes went into the *kampong*. It was important to see Sari and talk to her, even though playing in the *kampong* had lost much of the usual thrill. The girls did a lot of serious talking. The topic of war and the fate of the Dutch were the most important concerns, and one afternoon Jasmine said, "I suppose it has started, what the *Merdeka* people wanted."

"Yes." Sari looked troubled. "It will take a while, because the Japanese are here, and I don't think they are going to give leadership to the *Merdeka* people, no matter what they promised."

"So nothing will happen until the Japanese are beaten."

"I suppose so." Sari nodded.

"I hope that happens soon."

"Me too."

This conversation left Jasmine with a sense of satisfaction. She was sure the Japs were going to get their just dues sooner or later. Of course the Dutch would be next on the list, according to the *Merdeka* people.

The feeling of hope gained ground. On returning from Sari, Jasmine was greeted by Ellen's breathless outburst, "You know what? Papa might come back!"

Jasmine repeated stupidly, "Papa?"

"Yes, dummy, Papa! Don't you remember him?"

"How do you know?"

"Mr. Boon of course. He came again."

This astonishing news took a while to sink in, but every day after the news of Papa's return, Jasmine waited on the road. Sometimes Yvonne joined her, or Danny.

One day she said to Yvonne, "I'm sure Papa will come today."

"How do you know?"

Jasmine did not answer, but heaved a big stone closer to the side of the road and sat down on it.

"Call me when you see him," Yvonne said as she walked back to the house.

"All right."

For an hour Jasmine waited. Come, Papa, come home.

The sun was hot, and the stone was hard. A while later the sun was still hot, and the stone much harder. Soon now.

A *dokar* came, its horse trotting friskily towards her. The *dokar* rolled past, but there was no Papa.

They had supper. Mama prayed before they ate, and they were still eating when Mama began talking. She talked as if what she said did not concern her. "No one knows where the rumor came from, but Papa won't come back."

"He won't?" Yvonne's face fell.

Jasmine kept eating.

After supper she walked into the hall, and looked at the ceiling and the walls through a blur of tears. How she came to lie on the tiled floor she was not sure. All she knew was that she was alone with the blackness of betrayal that had darkened everything inside her. She wanted to scream, "Papa! I want Papa!" It came out as a groan. What if she never saw her father again? The Japanese began to loom larger with their boots and gun butts.

She lay still for a long time, eyes blurry, pondering the dark future.

When Mama came in, Jasmine turned away from her. She did not want any comfort, and when Mama touched her shoulder, she jerked it violently. She put her hands over her face when more tears came, which dripped onto the tiles.

After Mama left, Mopsy rolled in like a white, hairy ball, and she turned her body until her face was beside Mopsy's floppy ear. He licked her hands and face, and gave a little whine. Jasmine lifted her hands away from her face and tried to look into Mopsy's eyes, but his hair hung over them as usual.

Then she hugged him close. "At least I've got you," she whispered under his floppy ear, and he licked her face again, then huddled closer. "You must stay with me always."

He licked her nose, as if to say yes. And that was again as it should be.

Chapter Twenty-nine

Asia for the Asians

May to December 1942

It was odd. Jasmine had thought everything would have changed without Papa, but life seemed to go on just as before. Yet at night, with the windows blinded, it was as if someone had died, and you had to walk on your toes and talk in whispers.

Death. No one could escape death. She wondered if Papa would die. Her throat tightened, and when rain and wind lashed the roof and trees, she thought it was death calling her. She had more nightmares than ever, but never any clear images. Only their fearfulness stayed.

In the daytime she played and worked as usual. She helped Mama wash dishes, and air the bedding, since all the servants were gone. She went to Sari; she fooled around with Danny, Yvonne or Ellen; she went to the Smids with Mama.

Between such happy moments the sad truth would worm its way up inside her. Papa was gone, and that thought would send her to her hassock near the window to recapture all the good feelings she used to have sitting there. Without success.

The dry monsoon came and it did not rain much anymore. Mama made a habit of complaining regularly, "I'll never get used to this manless world! I don't feel safe without men."

"There are lots of men," Ellen observed.

"Japanese and natives," Mama said disdainfully, as if they did not count. "What good are they to protect us?"

The girls helped Mama willingly with the housework, and often Jasmine trotted between Ellen or Yvonne and Mama to get food from the central kitchen which was set up near Tenang's Town Hall. With Papa gone there was no income at all. They still had some rice and canned food, but their stores were dwindling. They cleaned the house together and made a game of it, pretending that mattresses heaved onto chairs out in the yard for airing were elephants, and rugs, rolled up to be taken outside for cleaning, tunnels for a train.

It was during this time that Mama's courage grew like a banana tree. One day, when they had just returned from the central kitchen with their rice and *sayoer*, Mama complained about the manless world for the last time.

"Those thieves," she exploded, "they make me so angry!" She had been angry earlier about thieves stealing clothes off the lines, and that morning she had discovered a large hole chiseled in the thick stone wall at the back of the house. The hole had not gone all the way through, but the intention was clear.

"Why don't they go through the window?" Ellen asked.

Mama looked grim. "They're superstitious about going through windows." She shrugged, and went on, "In any case, that does it for me! I'm not going to take anymore of this nonsense!"

A few nights later the children discovered Mama's plan, which was very simple. Jasmine woke up because of a strange sound. She was not sure what it could be, but heard Mama rise in the next room, muttering soft imprecations, and Jasmine understood that the thieves must be back. She itched with curiosity, but was afraid to go by herself to see, so she woke Ellen and Yvonne, who were as curious as she was. As they tiptoed out of the room, Jasmine became afraid again, this time for Mama. What if they did something to her?

They found Mama in the dark dining room, lifting the blinds.

Yvonne asked, "Do you see them?"

This startled Mama. She dropped the blind.

"What are you doing out of bed?"

"We just want to see if the thieves are back," Ellen whispered.

Mama whispered, "I saw something near the back buildings."

"Are you going out?"

"Definitely," Mama said, and although Jasmine was happy that her mother had been delivered from her fear, she did not like the thought of her going out after thieves, who could be armed.

"Can we come?" Jasmine whispered.

"Only as far as the door." Mama went to the closet, from which she took a broom. Holding it tightly in her right hand she walked out the back door. From the doorway the girls watched her go in the faint moonlight. They waited tensely for a few minutes, then saw some dim figures appear from behind the back buildings, like ghosts around the corner. Mama's figure, wrapped in a thin nightgown, stepped purposefully forward, not in the least ghostlike. She began waving her broom, and the dim, ghostlike figures stopped slinking, and started running. Mama ran too, waving the broom, and yelling, "Woe to your bones, if you ever come back here again!"

Whether the thieves understood her or not, did not matter, for they scampered off at great rate. Jasmine shivered with fear, but also with excitement. When Mama had almost reached the spot from where the figures had emerged, another figure suddenly appeared, a small one on four feet, barking shrilly, and running as fast as its short legs could go.

Mopsy.

He caught up with Mama, and the thieves doubled their speed. But Mopsy reached the last one and tried to put his teeth in the heels of the man, who gave a wild shriek. Mopsy barked and ran until the last of the figures had disappeared into the vanilla orchard.

Mama came back with a tail-wagging Mopsy, both out of breath, and Mopsy's tongue hanging out as if he were laughing. Mama put the broom back, then sat down patting Mopsy on the head. "That'll teach them not to snoop around here!" She took a few deep breaths, and wiped her forehead.

"Good for you," Ellen said, "You sure scared them."

Mama looked pleased.

"Aren't you afraid without men anymore?" Jasmine asked.

"I suppose not," Mama said, as if surprised.

They talked a little longer about the thieves, and that they all deserved to be bitten by Mopsy, and how brave he was too. Just when they decided to go back to bed, Aunt Beatrice came in, a wrap around her nightgown, sleepy and curious.

"What's going on?"

When they told her, she shook her head sadly. "You never know what to expect," and it was obvious she was not thinking about the thieves. "The residents at the Mission were all so loyal, and now. . . ." She shook her head again, and mumbled something about unconverted natives.

Back in bed, Jasmine was excited about Mama's daring attack on the thieves. Mama had changed. Mostly it seemed as if life went on as before, but people did change. She should have been used to these changes by now, because so many had happened during the past year. They had upset even Aunt Beatrice, and yet, when the natives went crazy at the Mission, Aunt Beatrice had not been too scared to talk to them and walk across the cemetery. Of course natives were more afraid of spirits than of the Japs. Spirits could be angry ancestors, who would punish them if they did not give offerings.

But the Japs had the power to send people to camp, and camp was like hell, Mrs. Van Doorn said. She could know, for her husband had smuggled a letter out of his POW camp in Batavia. Papa inhabited a strange world called a camp, and they didn't really know what it was like.

Before they came the Japs had only been shadowy figures in a vague distance, but now they intruded into their lives with new rules. They were strange people, and it made Jasmine almost forget her hatred of them. For one thing, Dutch flags were not allowed. Even the natives could not use their own *merah-putih* flag. Only the *Nippon* flag, a red ball on white, was allowed. They called it 'kokki'. Now that was strange, to have a *kokkie* for a flag.

Worse was that they could no longer listen to the radio, except when it was Japanese or Malay. They could not sing their own national anthem, only the Japanese one, which was sad and slow, even though it had a perverse fascination for the children. Some radio broadcasters of the NIROM had been killed because they had dared to broadcast the Dutch anthem.

Almost everyone tried to fool the Japs, and instead of the Dutch national anthem they sang as often as possible the Dutch folk song, "*The Sun Will Soon Depart from Us*," which was all about a night without worries, after the sun had set. It all fit perfectly, but the Japs discovered the meaning and that was the end of it.

Their travel was severely restricted. They could not go anywhere except to shop, or go to the doctor and things like that. Ladies were not supposed to wear slacks, because eastern women did not wear them. They were told that all people on Java must show respect for the *Nippon* military men by bowing to them whenever any came in sight.

Alarms still went off once in a while, but now, instead of scampering into the shelters, everyone went outside, beaming with hope that it might be an Allied airplane, which would free them from the Japs.

Mama seemed to have taken the situation in stride, and she began to have a purposeful look on her face. Jasmine had not seen Mama's diary lately. She might have hidden it. Jasmine looked at the diary she had gotten for Christmas. She wanted to start writing in it, but felt a little foolish about it. Yvonne would think she was crazy. Jasmine fingered the little book, then opened it on the first smooth page. It was actually a shame to spoil it. Paper was expensive, if it was available at all. So what! She'd do it in pencil, then she could always erase it. She started to write.

August 20, 1942

I should have started my diary sooner. So many things happened since Pearl Harbor, after which we expected an invasion too, while hoping it wouldn't come. In February, not long before the Japs reached Java, they had thrown down pamphlets from airplanes. One had a Bible verse, changed to suit their purposes, something from the Second Book of Corin-

thians, ". . .behold, now is the accepted time, the time of battle; behold, now is the day of salvation." The pamphlet ended with something from Ephesians: "The grace be with you all, who love the Lord Jesus Christ indestructibly," signed, "Commandant of the Japanese fleet."

Another pamphlet told us that the Indies Government was nothing but a puppet of England and the United States. It went on saying that Nippon wished for the native peoples of the Indies to set up a new government, who would cooperate with Tuan Nippon. It was all propaganda, but now that Nippon had conquered the Indies, they could do what they wanted.

A third pamphlet told us that the Japanese would not interfere with freedom of religion. It all sounded so good, but now I'm not sure any of these good promises are going to be put into practice.

August 23, 1942

All the changes in the past months are overwhelming. New regulations etc. In April we had to change to the Japanese calendar. We're now in the year 2602.

We don't get dependable news, because we had to hand in our radio, and the Dutch newspapers have been banned. But we hear plenty of rumors. This means that there are people who have kept their radios, which is risky business, for the Japs have executed people who had radios. I'm sure many of these rumors come from the Boon's who still have their radio. Ruth told me. Strangely enough she clings to me and I'm not sure why. Sari and I often get together, and Ruth joins us. We usually stay close to Sari's kampong or pretend we have to do some shopping. Just walking around town is not allowed. I guess the Japs think there's a plot brewing when some people get together!

August 25, 1942

The Japanese are really in control and occupy a huge area. In the Indies they started bombing Tarakan in East Borneo because there's a lot of oil near that place. That was in December already. They took it in January. In February they bombed Surabaya which has a large harbor and it is, I believe, the main military harbor. Now they have most of the Indies, and have renamed Java. It is called Djawa now, and I feel as if there's nothing left of the old Java as we knew it.

The natives are greatly impressed by Japanese power and the loss of prestige of the Europeans. But most natives have adopted a passive, waiting attitude. Few are actually helping the Japanese even though the Japs freed Sukarno and the other Merdeka leaders. In July Sukarno came to Bandung from South Sumatra which really bugs Aunt Beatrice! Especially when the Japs promised the "rebels" as she called them, independence in return for their collaboration! But as yet political parties have not been allowed.

Still there is hope. The Japanese air force may have been strong but the American morale after Pearl Harbor has returned to its former healthy state and the American military power has started to mushroom. The civil defense drills stopped in March when the Japs arrived. But they started them again, *because they expect attacks from the Allies. Earlier this month the Americans landed on Guadalcanal and chased out the Japanese forces. The Americans, a weak lot at first, are now in the attack mode.*

This does not stop the Japs from conquering other places and making their presence felt. Some guerrilla groups led by Dutch military officers were arrested. Their leaders will probably be beheaded or shot. There are plenty of rumors about the Kempeitai, the Japanese Secret Police who don't bother with justice or trials. In June there was a flood of arrests on Java by the Kempeitai.

August 28, 1942

In May more European men were arrested, but I'm not sure if that was the Kempeitai. These arrests involved civilian men. Those who could still keep their jobs had to wear a white arm band with a red ball. The Dutch called these workers "ball boys." But now all white men are in camps, as well as those Indos who had claimed Dutch citizenship. We were able to send a parcel to Papa, and a few postcards in Malay, but no letters. It's better than nothing. I hope they reached him.

Everything has become more expensive and they blame the Arabs and Chinese. The Japanese had started arresting Chinese on Java, but Grocer Wong is still here, looking more worried and sad than ever. Even though he's probably wondering when his turn will come, he's still doing business, and his customers include Japanese soldiers and officers. After all they need food like everyone else. Because of the shortage of money many people are trying to sell clothes and household articles.

September 2, 1942

There were some celebrations for Queen Wilhelmina's birthday a few days ago. I hope no one gets killed for this. Mama says our savings are running out. We had to exchange our money for Japanese invasion currency, as they call it. The Netherlands Indies money is worthless. The Red Cross work has been stopped in Bandung, because the last of the European personnel were arrested. In Surabaya the Red Cross was invaded by the Kempeitai. That means that all Red Cross work on Java has stopped.

September 20, 1942

They are interning all white men except Germans. After the war started in Holland all Germans in the Indies had been interned, and later freed because Japan had formed an alliance with Germany. German sailors appeared in Java's harbors. The Japs are also still doing their best to make friends with the natives. They allowed Mi'raj to be celebrated, the Ascension of the Prophet Mohammed.

When I heard that the Japs are taking over the plantations, I had to think of Aunt Hanna. I still feel sad and bitter about her. Uncle Philip is a POW. In July it was decreed that the prisoners of war have to be treated "firmly but humanely." The basic principle is "No work, no food", "Kalau makan, musti kerdja."

I wonder if Papa knows anything about what goes on in the world, and if so, what he thought about it. I really miss him!

Writing about Papa sent Jasmine's mind into turmoil. She closed the diary. It all flooded back, the soldier who had beaten Papa, then had loomed over her. She had scratched his face and beat him. It was incredible! Papa! He just lay there, after he had whispered, "Forgive them. . ." She had tried to forget, to forgive. Sometimes forgiveness was easy, but now she hated all of them.

By the time she went to bed the bad feelings faded a little. What did it help to feel angry? That night in her dream she was in a dusky land and the last rays of the sinking sun formed a golden gate. A man wearing a long white robe, with watchful eyes, opened his arms to her and she felt peaceful.

It was late October, the middle of the *kentering,* and Papa had been gone for months. Jasmine remembered his warnings not to go into the *kampong* but talking to Sari had been necessary.

One day she found her friend all dressed up in her Sunday best. Sari said relatives were coming over for *Lebaran,* and they were going to exchange presents, and have a *selametan.* Sari grinned. "It's not going to be much of a *selametan.* No money, and without new clothes you can't celebrate *Lebaran* properly."

It was true that natives were beginning to suffer from lack of clothing. The Japs were trying to fix the problem and

Jasmine hoped something would be done soon. In spite of the clothing problem, Jasmine left the *kampong* in a better mood, but when she came home, she found Mama close to crying. Ellen and Yvonne tried to comfort her. Ellen said, "The military prisoners are going to be moved overseas, maybe to Japan."

Uncle Philip! Jasmine was glad Papa had not been in the army, but she was sad about Uncle Philip. She wondered if they'd ever see him again. At least Aunt Hanna was safe in heaven.

They were soon told that all women and children who were not Eurasian or native were to go to camps also. Of course not all of them could go at once. They did it town by town and they had to find places that could serve as camps, mostly sections of a city or town. They called them 'protected districts', *tempat perlindungan.*

Mama was calm. She had probably expected this. Jasmine wondered if Mama had forgotten about Holland which was still occupied by the Germans, and Jasmine was relieved that they were not able to go there. But what about after the war? Perhaps the *Merdeka* people would get their independence, and where would that leave the Dutch?

The news about the Allies was more optimistic now. There was a battle at El Alamein in Egypt, and in early November the British conquered it. That was far from here, but a Dutch submarine attacked a Japanese convoy. That was good news but no one was sure if that convoy was carrying Dutch military prisoners, maybe Uncle Philip.

One evening, after supper, Jasmine and Yvonne sat side by side on the sofa, looking at *Pilgrim's Progress*, which Yvonne had unearthed. She had been enchanted by the idea that they were going to be like pilgrims. Jasmine did not like the pictures. She remembered the poster at Aunt Hanna's. It might appeal to Yvonne, but Jasmine hoped that nothing as dreary as those lonely hills was going to happen to them. She intended to have as much fun as possible. Camp could not possibly be as bad as hell.

That night Jasmine dreamed that she was walking along a dike in the *sawah* with Mopsy. The water surged up like a *bandjir* and the stretch of dike she had just walked over was flooded. There was a monster that looked like Mr. Boon. He rode a tank, a gun in one hand and a photo album in the other. The tank thundered past her. The photo album dropped from the monster's hand, and fell open. Strange aunts, uncles and cousins rolled out of it. The album closed on Jasmine, and she was squeezed between the pages. The tank rode over Mopsy. The aunts and uncles shouted, "Come with us, or you'll be shot!"

Jasmine yelled, "I won't go!" The tank rolled to the bridge, but the bridge was out because of the *bandjir*. Mr. Boon chased the aunts and uncles, who flew screaming back to Holland.

"Jasmine." Hands tugged at her.

"I won't go!"

"Camp won't be so bad. We'll get used to it."

"No, Holland."

The soft hands kept pulling. Jasmine floated in the sky, with the stars and the moon. Then she fell, a sickening fall.

"Jasmine. . . "

She woke with a deep sense of helplessness against forces too powerful. It was always best to stay good friends with God.

The next day Mama said they were going to bring Mopsy to the Boon's.

Jasmine was shocked. "Why?"

"Because we cannot take him to camp. I'm not sure when it's our turn to go, and I want a good home for him."

"Not to the Boon's!" Jasmine cried out.

"Mrs. Boon is a kind person." Jasmine was surprised at Mama's gentle tone. "We have no choice. They're the only ones of the people we know who don't have to go into a camp. They'll take good care of him."

There was nothing more to say, and Jasmine lapsed into a dejected silence. She had known deep down that she would have to say good-bye to Mopsy. But after Papa had left, it was Mopsy who had given her the sense that the war would soon be over. Mopsy was a piece of their old life.

That evening when she took Mopsy for a walk, she was filled with an aching remorse. She had been so careless about him the past years. Mrs. Van Waal had said, "What you don't look after, you'll lose." Now she was losing Mopsy. She sat down on a rock beside the road, hugging the dog tightly, her head on his. She took him to bed, and Mama did not object.

At the Boon's it seemed as if Mopsy knew how she felt, for he sat quietly beside her. Jasmine's throat was too choked for tears.

Mrs. Boon said cheerfully, "Come, I'll give Mopsy something to eat."

Slowly Jasmine let go of the white, fluffy head, and whispered, "Bye, Mopsy." He wagged his tail, and whined a little.

"Come, Jasmine," Mama said gently, tugging at her arm.

After teatime Jasmine walked through the yard. A bird flew under grey clouds, throwing out a long complaint. She thought of Walter, of the kite, first beautiful and alive, then dead and ugly. Marto's work. *Merdeka* would prevail. She sat down on the grass, and cried. She tried to pray, but no words would come.

It was dark when she finally got up.

Gradually a foreign feeling crept among the familiar ones, crowding out all others. Resignation. She stared into the evening. A train rolled through the land, a lighted snake crawling towards other places, like Bandung, Magelang, Batavia, places now taken over by the enemy. Yet, there was a voice in the rolling of the train, promising marvelous things in the future. There was a lot of happiness waiting somewhere, once this misery of war was over. That thought was like a golden sun breaking through a grey sky, light streaming from a wide-open gate.

Chapter Thirty

The Pilgrims

December, 1942

*I*t was not until the middle of December that the Dutch women of Tenang had to get ready to go to their camp. The news made Jasmine angry, because she could have kept Mopsy longer. But the pain about Mopsy had blurred, and Jasmine tried to imagine what camp would be like. Some said it was hell, others that they would be protected. To her, camp was like being closer to Papa. And in a way the prospect of living together with others was exciting.

"It's like going to the *pondok*," she said to Mama, who was frantically delving into a pile of clothes on the sofa.

Mama said, "Camp may seem like a holiday in the *pondok*, but it's not."

"How long will they keep us there?" Yvonne asked.

"I have no idea," Mama said.

"Where's the camp, and how are we going to get there?" Jasmine asked.

"The Japanese have not discussed their plans with me. All I know is that we'll leave before Christmas."

"We won't have a Christmas tree?" Some of Jasmine's excitement faded.

"I doubt it," Mama said, "but that's the least of our worries."

Jasmine thought of Mopsy again and suddenly the sense of aching loss was back. She walked out of the room, trying to hold back tears. She did not want to cry. All of a sudden she wished Sari could come with them, but natives did not go into camps. Jasmine was desolate that she would never see Sari again. If they ever got out of this camp, everything would be different.

The next afternoon Jasmine went to tell Sari about the camp.

Sari looked depressed, and didn't comment.

"What's the matter?" Jasmine asked.

"There was trouble at the *dessa* of my Aunt Itjam and Uncle Koesomo, Sukandar's parents. They killed some people and the *Kempeitai* arrested Alimin. Talitha is still here with her baby. She's afraid of what will happen to her husband."

"Why was Alimin arrested?" Jasmine thought that was strange. Alimin was a native.

Sari looked at Jasmine with a troubled face. "The *Kempeitai* thought he had been with one of the Dutch guerrilla groups that are still fighting in the jungle."

"What made them think that?" Jasmine asked.

"Eight Japanese soldiers with an interpreter came to the *dessa* and began searching the houses. They found some weapons but no one could tell how they got there, so they thought Dutch guerrillas had been there. They asked the *lurah* a lot of questions. The *lurah* said none of them were in contact with the guerrillas, but they weren't convinced, so the Japs shot the *lurah* and his son and arrested Alimin and several other men."

In spite of her own troubles, Jasmine felt terrible about what had happened to Sari's relatives. The Japanese commander Lieutenant-general Hitoshi Imamura had been replaced by a tougher general last month. Tough for the Dutch, but perhaps for the natives too. Everything was more confusing than ever. She had thought the natives were going to be their own worst enemies. Yvonne had said that the Dutch would be like wandering pilgrims. Now it looked like the natives would be too.

After a short silence, Sari said, "Sukandar came back from the Mission."

Jasmine felt a twinge of her old misgivings, even though she and Sukandar were on better terms lately.

"He's changed," continued Sari.

"In what way?" asked Jasmine.

"He's quieter, more thoughtful, especially after the death of Lea. He went to your house and talked to your Aunt Beatrice. She asked him to forgive her."

Jasmine said, "I know, I was there."

The Pilgrims

Sari suddenly grabbed Jasmine's arm. "Come with me."

They crossed the road to a house where they found Talitha leaning against the doorjamb. She looked sad and depressed. Sari went to her and hugged her. Jasmine stood aside, feeling uncomfortable, but when they sat down on the top step, she joined them. Odors of cooking hung in the air. A *tong-tong* beat a dull sound through the silence.

A child began to cry from inside the house. Talitha got up and went in. A few minutes later she came out, her son in her arms. Sastro, Doctor Jansen's chauffeur, followed. Jasmine wondered why he was here. Probably to find another job. He looked serious, not at all like the fun-loving man Jasmine remembered.

They talked for a while about Alimin and when he might return, but Jasmine's attention drifted. She thought of all the people they had left at the Mission, hoping they'd be all right.

Talitha leaned against a post, nursing her baby. She was a beautiful woman, in spite of her sad face. Jasmine felt sorry for her. Who knew what the *Kempeitai* would do to her husband. There had been a lot of stories about them. Someone's hands had been chopped off because they thought he had stolen something.

It had started to rain. Steady streams of water rattled on the roof, and they were surrounded by a curtain of water. Someone came running towards them. It was Sukandar. He jumped up onto the porch, and pulled his hand through his wet hair. He really had changed. There was a haunted look in his eyes. Jasmine felt uncomfortable, but looked at him with respect.

Talitha got up. With a fluid motion of her hand she pulled her hair back into a knot. "Let's go in."

They followed her. They found Aminoto on one of the benches, huddled in his shoulder cloth against the chill. Talitha put the baby in his cradle. The kerosene lamp hissed; a woven bamboo basket with rice hung steaming above a pan with boiling water. Talitha moved slowly, as she made another fire between some bricks beside the steaming pan. She placed a black iron frying pan on it, in which she poured some coconut oil and started to fry fish.

Aminoto went to get a cup of tea then turned to Sukandar. "Talitha told me you went back to your parents and to the Mission. How are things over there now?"

Sukandar, squatting on the tightly packed earth, started to talk in a monotone. He had gone to his parents who were happy to see him. He was glad there was now peace in their hearts about the choice he had made. Then he went to the Mission to find out how things stood there. Everything was still a mess, and most of the people had left and other families had come to live in the houses. Nusomo was still there, which had surprised him, but he suspected that the families who were there needed his skills as a teacher. He had stayed with Nusomo, until someone recognized him as one of the men who had helped the 'nDoro. He barely saved himself from being taken and probably killed.

The Pilgrims

Sukandar's toneless voice stopped. He got up and went to stand on the threshold.

They all waited. No one spoke, and Jasmine felt the familiar choking sensation in her throat. The square seemed so peaceful, and it confused her. Was there not a war? People killed? It was all deception, this peacefulness.

Sukandar started talking again. "Djoyoboyo. His prophecy has come to pass. The time for the *Orang Tjebol*, the Little People, has come, and Java is on the verge of suffering as it has never suffered before."

Aminoto joined him in the doorway, saying, "But after the *Orang Tjebol* have ruled for a while there will be freedom for the people again, *Merdeka*. The islands will again belong to us."

Sukandar said, "I wish everything had stayed the way it was. We are all going to suffer. If we thought the Dutch were bad, we were mistaken. The Japanese have succeeded in turning the people against each other. The Japanese do not believe in justice. When the Dutch discovered a crime, they searched for the guilty party, but the Japanese don't bother. They grab whomever they can, and punish them to make an example to others."

Jasmine realized that only Sari knew that he had come to see Aunt Beatrice.

Aminoto said sharply, "I know you've turned your back on *Merdeka*, but you can't possibly condone everything the Dutch did here!"

Sukandar burst out passionately, "*Merdeka*? What is *Merdeka* except freedom for *all* people. With the Japanese here *Merdeka* is meaningless. The misery is going to spread to the smallest *dessa*, and they will rob our country more thoroughly than the Dutch have ever done."

No one said anything. Jasmine looked at Sari who was staring at her cousin.

Talitha said, "Perhaps we can learn from all these things. It says in the Koran, 'There are moments when your difficulties are useful and necessary.'"

Aminoto looked at her. "I thought you had rejected the Koran."

Talitha produced a faint smile. "I still remember some things in it. But the Bible is better."

Aminoto opened his mouth to say something, but Sukandar interrupted. "Let's not argue about that. All I know is that there is a God who does not approve of hatred. All of us should pray for love and freedom for all people, no matter what creed they profess."

The rain had stopped. Some children played under a *waringin*, and curious women stared at Sukandar, when he raised his voice. The women came closer as if they wanted to speak to him, but he did not seem to notice. He stared across the square and said, tentatively, "Jesus must be the real prophet, the only True One."

Jasmine gaped at him. She had heard him ask Aunt Beatrice for forgiveness, but she hadn't realized that he believed that about Jesus. Although still shy with him, she could not

The Pilgrims

help asking, "What about Mohammed? Isn't he the prophet of the Muslims?"

After a few moments of silence, Sukandar answered, "Mohammed was just a man; Jesus must be the Son of God."

Jasmine hoped fervently that he meant it.

Sari still stared at her cousin, open-mouthed.

Sukandar smiled, a melancholy smile. "I did go to the Dutch school and I remember the stories."

Aminoto looked angry. "What's the matter with you? You know you were born to be a leader, and we expected great things from you. And you've thrown it all away because of the Infidel religion! Be careful what you do. You may just have called a curse on yourself!"

Ignoring Aminoto's angry outburst, Sukandar looked at his uncle, still with that melancholy smile. "I thought you didn't believe in curses! Yes, I was born at the crack of dawn, but does that mean I am destined to become a leader like Sukarno?" He paused, then spoke more firmly. "Yes, a Child of the Dawn, a *child*, that's what I was, and I thought like a child. But as soon as you become a man, you're supposed to put away childish things."

Aminoto looked at him, his lips tight. He was just going to say something, when Sukandar interrupted, "I never could understand Aunt Sugi and her faith. To me her beliefs were totally incomprehensible. Now I know different."

"What brought about the change? I suppose my wife has talked you into things she shouldn't have." Aminoto seemed calmer, although he still looked sullen.

"Many things happened, but the final thing that changed my heart was that the *'nDoro* of the Mission asked my forgiveness, because of the bad opinion she had of me."

Sukandar's face had lost its haunting look. There was almost a joy in it. He continued, "I told her I had forgiven her, then I said that she had to forgive me too, because I had always hated her, and for no reason. I told her that I knew she was a good woman and had done a lot of good for my people and for Lea. So I asked her, "Could you forgive me?" Sukandar smiled faintly. "She did." Then, reflectively, "Forgiveness comes from the one true God."

Shortly after these astounding revelations, Jasmine went home and found Mama in a frenzy of sorting and packing. She had already sorted some things, but when the news of the definite date had been announced for them to go into a camp, she attacked the task with vigor. She sent the children to get their suitcases and clothes. Jasmine looked at the things Mama tried to sort out from the pile. "Are we taking all this?"

"Goodness, no!" Mama said. "We have to carry most things ourselves. A few small pieces of furniture and our mattresses will get picked up."

They had to roll up the mattresses and tie them with ropes, and put their name on them and on the furniture.

Moving and packing had become part of their life it seemed. Everywhere in the dining room were piles of clothes, dishes and cutlery, pans, books. How were they going to choose the most essential?

The Pilgrims

Mama had a dress in her hand, studied it with a frown then stuffed it in a suitcase.

Yvonne came in with a book. "Can we take this?"

"What is it?"

"*Pilgrim's Progress.*" She handed Mama the book.

"Too heavy," Mama said. "Why this one?"

"It's neat!"

Mama sighed. "There's so much already. I just hope I won't forget anything important."

Yvonne's face sagged.

"Oh, all right." Mama took the book and put it one of the suitcases.

Jasmine put her arms around Mama's neck and kissed her on the cheek. "You're the best mother in the world!" A little embarrassed, Jasmine grinned at Yvonne.

Ellen came in. "Can I take some books?"

"You too!" Mama laughed a little, and sighed. "Okay, a few. Not the heaviest please."

Jasmine wondered if Mama would remember to take her diary. She was going to bring her own, and some pencils, but was not sure how she could manage it without them being seen. They had heard that the Japs didn't allow writing materials in camps.

A few days later a *dokar* took them to the Breda house, where they were to stay one night. After the Bredas had left to live in Magelang, the house had stayed empty. And now two families had to fit in each room. The Carter mattresses were close together on the floor of the front room in the farthest corner, away from the window. They were squeezed tightly beside the mattresses of others. Suitcases stood helter skelter in between them.

The women were trying to put order in the chaos. Yelling children were making up new games, finding new hiding places and friends. Jasmine saw many kids she had never seen before. People had moved in from some of the smaller towns, because they were afraid to live in such isolated places.

In the wide hall wooden benches stood along the walls. Jasmine sat down on the first one. She felt sad, but not really about being here, nor about Papa. She had got along without him for half a year so far. It was as if she herself had changed. The future was uncertain, and it felt as if she were floating in a dark vacuum.

The bench was rough, but there was comfort in its roughness. Her hands moved along the edges, as if they wanted to become one with the wood. The bareness of the house seemed to symbolize all the things she had lost. The empty shell of a house was like them, robbed of dignity.

Suddenly she felt the humiliation sharply. The three hundred-year rule of the Dutch was over. Four ships had been replaced by many huge battleships, submarines and cruisers, not to mention the fighter planes, the Zeros.

She hated the Japanese for so upsetting their lives. Of course they had created new hope for the *Merdeka* people. Yet the Japs had not come to help the natives, but to rule over them. And according to Sukandar the natives were worse off

The Pilgrims

than before. Jasmine hoped the Japs were going to be badly beaten some day.

She shifted restlessly, and stretched her legs. What did it matter? They had to make the best of things. Some day they would see Papa again.

She got up and walked to their room. Yvonne sat on the edge of the mattress, and on her lap lay *Pilgrim's Progress*. She leaned over it attentively. The room was dim, the shutters partly closed, because Mama, Ellen and some other people were having an afternoon nap.

Jasmine sat down beside her sister.

Yvonne looked at Jasmine, and whispered, "We're going to be like pilgrims." She read a short section in whispers, then stopped. The girls were silent for a while, as Jasmine was struggling with the story's meaning. "Why did you want to read it now?" she whispered.

"I want to get used to the idea of what we are," Yvonne said solemnly.

"Why are you so convinced we're like pilgrims?"

"Well, first of all, pilgrims wander. Also, they never take much with them, only what they can carry."

Jasmine began to relish the idea of taking part in a pilgrim journey.

Another few minutes of silence followed, only broken by the soft rhythmic breathing of the bodies stretched on the various mattresses. Yvonne leafed through the book, and the girls studied the drawings. The pilgrim bent low beneath a heavy pack. He seemed to stagger, fall. Then there was the place where the cross stood, and where he could dump the pack. Jasmine could feel his relief, but there were more struggles after that. The world was grim at the moment.

"Come on, let's go out." Jasmine jumped up, knocking the book closed.

Yvonne put the book down, her interest in the Pilgrim had faded for the moment.

They skipped towards the piles of unpacked things on the lawn, belonging to the homeless internees. Their modern day pilgrimage had begun in great disorder.

December twenty-two, Jasmine wrote in her diary the following morning. *Christmas in a few days.*

An hour later they left for the station in a *dokar*. At the side of the road, near the shed where they had watched the *Wayang Kulit,* Jasmine saw Sari and Sukandar. They were standing very still. Jasmine did not dare wave at them, but tears pricked her eyes. She might never see them again. Suddenly she realized how much Sari had meant to her.

She turned away and saw Marto on the other side of the road, holding up a *merah-putih* flag. Marto did not seem worried about the Japs seeing the flag, for she grinned widely, then stuck out her tongue.

Jasmine shrugged. To her surprise she felt no anger. Poor Marto would discover soon enough that the Japanese cared only about themselves. She remembered Papa's words: *Try to love all people.* At the same time she thought, a little cynically, that at least she would never have to see Marto's tongue again.

The Pilgrims

They reached the station, got out of the *dokar* and went into the waiting train. The train ride was like all others, except that the cars were more crowded.

When they arrived in the town Ambarawa, they left the train and were ordered to pick up their baggage and start walking.

Jasmine tried to remember their last Christmas with Papa, and a comforting thought came to her. Papa had said that the Allies would triumph. Why he was so sure, she didn't know. The last rumors about the Allies proved that they were still far from victorious. But the Allies would win, and there would be peace on earth, good will to men.

Hope for mankind.

A Child in a stable.

A Baby Pilgrim in a lowly place.

In a camp.

Everything would be all right again.

Some day.

Word List

A

Ach ja	Dutch expression of resignation
Afrikaantjes	marigolds
Allah	akbar Allah is great
Alang alang	long grass
Ampun	forgiveness
Angin	wind
Anglo	charcoal brazier
Api	fire

B

Babu	maid
Bagoes	beautiful
Baik	good
Baleh-baleh	bamboo cot
Bandjir	flood
Bapak kami yang ada di sorga	Our Father who art in heaven
Blanda	white person

Boleh	can, may, allowed
Budi Utomo	Sublime Endeavor
Bung	brother

D

Dalang	narrator in Wayang performance
Dessa	native village
Djago	rooster
Djagung	corn
Djongos	male house servant
Dokar	two-wheeled horse buggy

G

Gladakker	mongrel dog
Grobak	cart drawn by water buffaloes
Gulah djawa	brown sugar
Guling	long round pillow
Gunung api api	fire mountain (volcano)
Gunung	mountain

I

Inlander	one way for the Dutch to refer to a native
Inggih	yes in *Javaans*
Insh	Allah as Allah wills

J

Javaans	minority language on Java

Word List

K

Kabar	news
Kabar angin	wind news
Kabaya	buttoned over blouse
Kalau	if
Kampong	group of native houses in cities or towns
Karbauwen	water buffaloes
Kentering	doldrums
Kembang	*sepatoe* hibiscus
Kerdja	work
Klambu	mosquito netting
Kokkie	native cook (female)
Kompenie	a name natives used to refer to the Colonial Government
Kraton	palace
Kulit	leather
Kumpulan	meeting
Kwe kwe	soft soybean cake.

L

Larong	flying white ant
Lebaran	Muslim feast day after the month of fasting
Lekas	fast, quick, at once
Lurah	native head of a district

M

Magrib	sunset, evening
Makan	to eat
Malam baik	good evening
Mandoer	overseer
Mantries	caretakers
Mas	gold
Mata glap	temporarily insane
Melati	jasmine
Merdeka	free, independent, freedom
Merah-putih	red-white
Mevrouw	Mrs. (Dutch)
Musti	have to

N

'nDoro	lady (*Javaans*)
Nonya	married lady
Nonnie	girl

O

Oliebollen	sweet dumplings (Dutch)
Oma	Grandmother (Dutch)
Orang Tjebol	little people

P

Pak, bapak	father
Pandita	teacher, preacher
Pangerang	prince, lord

Word List

Pelisie	police
Perlindungan	protection
Pitjih	skull-cap, small cap
Pondok	hut, small house
Pundi?	where are you going? (*Javaans*)

R

Ramayana	Hindu legend
Ramadan	ninth (fast) month of Muslim year
Rampokkers	robbers, plunderers

S

Salat magrib	time of evening prayer
Salat	prayer
Sambal	spicy paste, made of Spanish peppers
Sarekat Islam	Islamic Union
Saudara, Saudara	brothers
Sawah	wet rice field
Sayoer	prepared vegetables
Selametan	religious thanksgiving meal
Slamat djalan	good-bye
Slendang	sling in which a woman carries her child
Sinterklaas	Dutch Santa Claus
Sirih	betel (used in chewing tobacco)
Stroop	sweet, fruit drink

Strootje	cigarette
Sudah	already, often used as an expression of resignation

T

Tangsi	barracks
Tani	farmer, peasant
Tempat	place
Tempat perlindungan	protected district
Tida apa	it doesn't matter
Tokeh	gecko
Toko	shop, store
Tong-tong	hollow vessels to make a loud sound
Trima kassi	thank you
Tuan	sir, lord

V

Volksraad	People's Council (Dutch)

W

Waringin	large fig tree with aerial roots (banyan)
Wayang Kulit	shadow play
Wayang	puppet
Warong	eating place, stall

CPSIA information can be obtained at www.ICGtesting.com
Printed in the USA
LVOW07s2335021113

359698LV00001B/4/P